SPARTACUS III

THE PHARAOH'S BLADE

BY

ROBERT SOUTHWORTH

Robert Southworth

Copyright Robert Southworth 2015.
All rights reserved. This book may not be reproduced in whole or in part without the written permission from the author.

The Spartacus Chronicles

DEDICATED TO LINDA.

YOU ARE MY INSPIRATION.

INTRODUCTION

In the year 1484 BC a young boy walked with his head slightly bowed. Beside him, a mature attractive female could not help but smile at his nervousness. She reached out a hand and stroked his cheek as she had done so many times in the past. It was an act almost motherly but the child flinched, uncertain of allowing such intimacy.

'You need to have no fear of me, Thutmose,' she whispered.

The boy did not answer he merely eyed the woman before him. Thutmose could recall the days when he would have gladly shown affection and basked in her comforting. Those days seemed so long ago now.

His father had died and relationships had changed and not for the better. The woman was not merely a stepmother but also the ruler of these lands. If he was to take his rightful place and be crowned, then it would only happen if the woman before him allowed it to be so.

He could not take his eyes from her. Suddenly a grunt from behind shattered the silence. It was a guttural grunt, quickly followed by the sound of something heavy landing upon the floor. Thutmose turned to observe their only bodyguard lying upon the ground, crimson liquid staining the earth where he had fallen. Confusion clouded his mind; this was a walk he had taken many times before and its safety had never been in question. From the shadows, a dark clad figure stepped forward, his hand holding a blade dripping with blood.

'Thutmose, run!' the woman cried.

Without thinking, he raced away, desperate to put distance between the assassin and himself. He had gone little more than twenty paces, then surprisingly even to himself he stopped, and turned, observing his stepmother.

The killer had moved closer to his prey, the dedication to completing the task etched upon his face. The female struck out at the man's face but the assassin swatted the attempt away and smashed her to the floor. Thutmose felt anger flow through every sinew within his body.

'Hatshepsut, for the good of these lands, you must die.' The man snarled.

'Then be quick and spare me your speeches,' she said scowling.

'Very well—'

The remainder of what the man was about to say was lost as a terrible screech broke the air, making both assassin and Hatshepsut raise their head to the skies. Above them, a great falcon sounded its displeasure at some unknown annoyance. It seemed to draw the attention for an eternity but eventually the man focused upon the unpleasant task before him. Raising the blade above his head, he made an attempt to take the life of the woman before him. He had not seen another figure approach from behind or heard the footsteps as they charged towards him. Realisation of the danger he was in only became apparent when the figure landed upon his back and a blade plunged deep into the side of his throat. The assassin raged, trying to throw his attacker from him, but Thutmose would not be shaken from his hold. Once again, his blade found flesh, and suddenly he was falling as his enemy died even before crashing to the earth.

Three figures lay upon the ground. One would never rise again, but two were just as still as the dead man. They held one another's gaze until their eyes watered with the pain.

Finally, Thutmose spoke. 'I thought that you would kill me and place one of your own children upon the throne.'

'Thutmose, I loved your father. I would not dishonour the man by going against his wishes. Besides, is it not possible that the love shared between father and son be extended to me also?' Hatshepsut had tears of a different nature within her eyes.

'I was sure…'

'That when I took power, I would do so to deny you what is rightfully yours? Thutmose, I took power to prevent others seeking what they have no right to possess. When the time is right, you shall have what your father wished and after today, I have no doubt that the gods desire it, too.'

'The gods?'

'Seker sent his messenger to distract the man from his task; this gave you time to act. Thankfully, the falcon god did his work well and we shall live another day. With Seker's patronage, Thutmose, I believe greatness will wash over you. The actions you have performed today shows you have the heart of a warrior; our lands will prosper when you rule.' Once more, she reached out a hand to stroke his cheek. It had been too long since they had shared genuine affection.

Thutmose moved closer and embraced her tightly.

***

The years passed and the boy became a man, and he found himself in the centre of a huge courtyard. It seemed that all of Egypt had gathered in one place. They wanted to pay homage to the young man who would now take his throne next to Hatshepsut and rule as co-regent. He gazed around at all the faces and genuinely he could see only happiness. A fact, he had realised, was in no small way thanks to Hatshepsut; she had calmed many rebellious souls in the past few years. He stared at the still beautiful woman despite her years and received a smile and a wink in return.

Hatshepsut raised her arm and the courtyard fell silent, all eager to hear the words that their beloved ruler was about to say. 'When my husband died, I thought I would never love again, but I was wrong. I have grown to cherish my people and this land with all the passion that I held for my lost love. I have been privileged to have children that I am extremely proud and also be stepmother to others that I am equally proud. Today we gather to celebrate the coming of age of Thutmose, where he will take his rightful place by my side and rule. One day, he will lead alone; until that day I hope to advise a man who will be revered far beyond the borders of our lands.'

Thutmose never replied to Hatshepsut's words for public speaking still did not come easily to him and he avoided it whenever possible. So the young man bowed to Hatshepsut and then raised his hand in salute to his people.

'It was as a boy that Thutmose showed that he was a warrior at heart, for this, I am eternally grateful. To mark this occasion and to show my gratitude, I have commissioned a special gift to be presented to Thutmose.'

She raised her hands and the crowd parted to allow a procession to begin the journey down towards the centre of the courtyard.

Thutmose had never seen anything like it. All the religions from the various sects were marching as one. Usually these men argued about which god should have precedence over the other, eager to gain power for their priesthood. Finally, the procession stopped just before Thutmose. A wooden box was immediately brought forward. It was placed in the hands of the priest who worshipped Seker. In turn he stepped to his front, opened the box and then bowed with the gift set above his head.

'This gift, Thutmose, is no ordinary weapon. All the religious houses of the land have blessed it. The dagger itself was made by the finest weapon smith, and I believe that Seker guided his hand personally when it was crafted.'

Thutmose reached inside the box and removed the dagger. For quite some time his eyes would not leave the vision of the weapon. The blade was ordinary, but the guard was skilfully crafted to look like the wings of a falcon, the handle its body and lastly the pommel was the screeching head of the same bird. Its eyes were set with the deepest darkest red gems he had ever seen and in his hand, it felt as though it were just an extension of his body. He finally raised his head meeting the looks of those around him; slowly he raised the dagger above his head.

A tremendous war cry erupted from the young man whom many would not have believed possible. However, their shock evaporated as they too added their cries to that of Thutmose.

***

The years and battles raced by, Hatshepsut died but her gentle guidance had given Thutmose the calm intellect needed to compliment his warrior spirit. Egypt was more powerful than it had ever been; Thutmose had reigned for over fifty years. In excess of three hundred cities had fallen to their armies and yet at this time when joy should prevail, the land filled with sorrow.

Thutmose was dying, with the help of Seker. He had achieved more than any could have wished for but now the old pharaoh was tired and deserving of his place among the gods. Thutmose called one last meeting for only his most loyal subjects, and as they gathered in the same courtyard that the young man had been crowned, they knew the end was near. Thutmose called his friends close.

'You have followed my orders without question all these years, my friends. I am glad so many of you have survived to see the end of the bloodshed. I have one further request and though many of you will not agree with my wishes, I hope that your love for your pharaoh will see those wishes carried out.' Thutmose paused. 'The Seker dagger must be taken from this place, taken and hidden where the powerful men will not be able to find it.'

'But, my lord, surely will not the dagger protect these lands?' asked Itep.

'Itep, my friend, my children are not warriors and to give the dagger to someone else within the kingdom could make this land vulnerable to internal war. Then in the future, other kingdoms may find the draw of the legendary dagger too much to resist and attempt to take it by force. My mind is set in the matter, though it pains me to have come to this decision. The reason you have been brought here is that I require one last service. For the dagger to be kept from all that seek it, there must be dedicated men who would keep it safe. The dagger must leave our lands and be taken far away where the knowledge of such a blade does not exist. The men willing to do this task must leave their homes taking their families with them. It will be their descendants who will be charged with guarding the dagger many years hereafter.' Thutmose watched, waiting for the reply from those before him. All stepped forward, their loyalty even after so many years, touched the man deeply. 'Very well, go to your homes. Coin will be plentiful you will not suffer because of your loyalty to me. Be ready to leave by the rise of the sun. Do not inform any within these lands where you go or what you carry.'

A familiar small wooden box was brought forward. Thutmose had not seen the box for many years and just for a moment, he was back in the great courtyard when it thronged with people and the excitement of a new regent filled the air. A minuscule tear rolled down his cheek as he returned the dagger to the box. He gave one last stroke of the beautiful and powerful falcon, which adorned the blade and then the lid closed.

The next morning Thutmose watched from his balcony as the small train of wagons disappeared into the distance. When finally, they left his view, he raised his eyes to the sky and felt the cool breeze upon his tired face.

'Well, Hatshepsut, how did I do?'

He walked back to the interior of his rooms, where he took time to rest. The great warrior breathed a deep sigh, closed his eyes and was gone.

CHAPTER ONE

Many years had passed since the death of the mighty pharaoh. Far from where he was laid to rest, two ships limped away from a mysterious land. The ships had been three when they'd approached the land and many more men had accompanied them on their search for vengeance. All had sought the destruction of one man who had been responsible for the death of so many loved ones. The gods granted them their vengeance, but at a terrible cost as many friends lay bleeding in the glutinous mud that seemed common place in those lands.

Victory did not bring about a cheer or take the pain of grief from weighing so heavily on their hearts. However, the man they hunted had met a fate that he had deserved but the struggle to bring about that fate had been long and arduous. Exhausted both physically and mentally the men within those ships had been forced to sail before the winters of 68 BC descended and returning to loved ones in distant lands became impossible.

A young man was restless; his beloved was with child when he left her side. He knew that if all had gone well, then the child would already be in this world. Plinius had never been a patient man and his desperation to see mother and child was making him irritable with most on board. He wished that Aegis had been there to whisper words of wisdom and comfort to soothe his impatient spirit. That was impossible because Aegis had perished like so many others at the hands of Flabinus.

Both Cassian and Spartacus had tried in vain to calm the youthful warrior with the men becoming frustrated and almost surrendered to the temptation to throw Plinius over the side and let the waves take him.

The gladiator, Spartacus, stormed away from the discussion looking out to sea rather than to his young friend. A silhouette on the horizon caught his eye, the large ominous black shape divided and then came two. Before long, five dark shapes spread out on the horizon. Even a land lover like Spartacus could tell that his little convoy would be no match for those that closed on their position so readily.

'Cassian, what do you make of those?' Spartacus asked trying to remain calm and not make a tired crew anxious at what loomed ahead.

Cassian moved to Spartacus' shoulder and followed his gaze. 'That could be trouble. Can we evade them?' Cassian's question was emitted to the mists with little thought that it may be answered.

'There is no possibility of escape. The gods have bestowed far better wind to their sails.' Vectrix joined the conversation.

'Then we wait to see what fate the day brings. Spartacus, if you would try to keep Plinius close, we must take away the opportunity for aggression to begin by accident,' Cassian ordered.

Spartacus nodded and moved to find the young warrior. He doubted even Plinius would be so reckless as to initiate aggression when it was clear that his friends were totally out matched. However, just to be certain, he would try to distract him. This would not be an easy task as both crews were now aware of the possible threat, which appeared ever closer.

As Spartacus sought out Plinius, Cassian gave the order that both ships should make no attempt to move away from the approaching ships. The anxiety hung thick in the air; the crew watched as the small fleet that approached suddenly split. One singular ship seemed to continue its original course with its comrades falling behind, almost becoming motionless on the steady surface of the water. As the lone vessel neared, it seemed to take on the form of a living shadow. The sails were the deepest shade of ebony matched only by the very timbers, which so effectively cut through the aquatic barrier.

When the craft was no more than a hundred paces away, Cassian and his crew could see figures, moving like black bugs, traversing its decking. The sight was so foreboding that Cassian compared the figures to fleas riding the demonic hound, Cerberus' back, its three heads viciously guarding the gates to the underworld, snapping its saliva-filled jaws at any uninvited guest. Now the vessel was within spitting distance of Cassian's own craft. The anxiety could be tasted upon the salty breeze as men braced themselves for an unprovoked act of aggression.

The black vessel loomed tall over Cassian's now seemingly fragile vessels. Like a dark cloud, it threw them all into shadow and threatened to unleash an unstoppable torrent, which consign them all to oblivion. Then a figure appeared on the upper rail of the black ship and called out Cassian's name in full. Cassian shocked to hear his name must have delayed his answer too long, for the unknown figure let his voice ring out once more.

This time Cassian moved so he could be seen, he spoke confidently. 'You have me at a disadvantage. Who calls out my name and brings five ships to ensure that I answer?'

'I cannot give the name or reason, only that I require you and your vessels to take the same path,' the figure replied.

'I am sure you will understand that for the safety of my men, I am reluctant to take such a journey when your intentions are unclear.' Cassian endeavoured to keep his tone neutral, devoid of emotion.

'Your hesitation is admirable, however, look around you. If I required your deaths, it would have been only too easy. That at least should go some way to putting your mind at rest.'

Cassian was getting bored with the enforced pleasant conversation. He knew as he glanced around the faces of his men, that he had no option but to accept the terms made by the stranger and his superior fleet. The men around him looked to him to guide them on the safest route possible, unfortunately, the path they must travel was not of his choosing and its destination obscured by mist.

He clenched his fists, the whiteness of the knuckle betraying his frustration.

***

The storm eventually blew itself out; the clouds parted and a burning sun baked those upon the deck of the small flotilla. Though Cassian ordered some rainwater to be gathered while the rains still fell, the strong winds mixed the salt from the sea with that of the precious falling liquid. The situation was becoming desperate and Cassian knew he must swallow his pride and send word to the stranger. He straightened his back and took in a large gulp of air; he closed his eyes and tried desperately to calm the anger within. As his eyes opened, Vectrix was standing to his front.

'The lead black ship has changed its course. Look for yourself, Cassian, it heads towards land.'

Cassian moved passed Vectrix and rushed to the rail; the Gaul had spoken the truth.

'Which port do they intend to enter, Vectrix?'

'I have sailed these waters many times, Cassian. Our destination can only be Gades.'

'Then Gades is where we will learn answers.' Cassian felt relief. He knew Crassus had few friends in Hispania and if these were his men, then they would try to stay clear of the lands loyal to Pompey. 'Give the order, Vectrix, we are to change course and follow our dark sailed comrades, and hope the gods light our way.'

***

The port of Gades hummed with activity; trading vessels of all shapes and sizes busied themselves in the art of procuring wealth. Only two ships of the black fleet entered the port; the remaining three held their position just a little way out to sea. However, both of Cassian's vessels moved into the harbour, the men on both ships keen to feel the solidity of ground and to taste liquid upon their lips.

Vectrix and Lathyrus on their respective vessels bellowed orders, and the crew reacted with the utmost speed and efficiency. When Cassian finally placed his feet upon the heavy wooden planks of the dock, he dispatched men immediately to gather supplies. Before long, his most trusted advisors joined the studious Cassian. Spartacus, Lathyrus, Vectrix, Melachus plus the youthful Plinius and Tictus, gathered around him, eager to hear his plans.

Tictus was the first to speak. 'I do not understand; if they mean to imprison us why allow us to come ashore? They guard the port.' He pointed to the three ships, in the distance. 'But we could easily slip away in these crowds.'

'We have no idea how many of those black dogs are in this place, Tictus. I would not dismiss foul play just yet.' It was the recognisable growl of Spartacus, that answered

Tictus and Cassian could tell the warrior in Spartacus was becoming impatient at the mists of secrecy.

Lathyrus interrupted Cassian's thoughts. 'Whoever they are, they are well financed. Those vessels are fresh and designed for both speed and destruction. Though we encountered little trouble upon the seas, I know well-drilled crews when I see them, these are no farmers plucked from their lands against their will.'

'So we have men of resource requiring our presence but at least at the moment not our deaths.' Cassian could not help a little shake of the head in bemusement at the situation.

'It seems we will soon learn more of our mysterious friends.' Spartacus nodded towards three men who were picking their way up to the dock. As Spartacus spoke his hand slowly moved towards the hilt of his sword that nestled tightly against his thigh.

Cassian recognised the first of the three men; it was the stranger who had so successfully instilled a loathing within him.

The three men came to halt only paces away and once again, it was the stranger who spoke. 'Cassian, I would ask that you and those that you trust, accompany me. I can confirm only that my intentions are honourable and both you and the men who serve you, will not be harmed.'

Spartacus stepped forward. 'Firstly, I do not serve any man. Secondly, know this, if your intentions are foul and a trap is in your mind, no matter the outcome, I will seek you out and the carrion birds will feast on your flesh.'

'I did not intend insult.' The stranger's tone was designed to calm. However, the stranger did not falter before the warrior's stare, and it was clear he felt no fear.

For a moment, no words were uttered and Cassian could feel that danger was near and he moved to pour water on aggression's fire. 'I see you have brought two men and that signals that you offer no violence at this time. Only a fool would be so confident in his own prowess with a blade. Lead the way and we will follow.'

The stranger nodded and turned briskly and marched away. His two comrades matched his strides.

Cassian turned to those close. 'Keep your anger caged, at least until we know what kind of enemy we face.' His words were aimed at young Plinius, but the young warrior seemed uninterested in the proceedings.

CHAPTER TWO

The port resembled many others within the empire, the lowly brushed shoulders with those of real wealth. Small children dressed in little more than rags cried for food as finely dressed merchants casually ignored their fate while speeding to make more wealth or spend it in one of the many brothels. Every level of society could be seen within a hundred paces, including criminals who tried to walk within the shadow. Those wishing to keep their hard earned wealth avoided the shadows, or took precautions in the way of hired blades to protect them from harm.

Every port was awash with those willing to take rather than earn, and Gades was no different. Some thieves would use deception and would merely use sleight of hand to obtain another man's purse. Others were more pragmatic, preferring club or blade to relieve the owner of coin.

One such group of thieves eyed the dark clad figure that so carelessly displayed his bag of coin for all to see. Firstly, they planned to separate the man from his friends and then his coin. It was a simple plan; four men would create a diversion, giving time and space for a second group of four to force the main target to give up his wealth. If the prey put up a fight, then a blade to its ribs would subdue his spirits.

Cassian and his men were blissfully unaware of the stranger's pending danger. However, they were perfectly placed to witness the robber's attack. First, a small wagon was manoeuvred between the robber's victim and his comrades. It was turned upright spilling pomegranates to the alleyway floor creating chaos. Then the second group of robbers moved in to collect their prize. Cassian and Spartacus watched as the lead cutthroat raced in, eager for coin. The stranger did not draw a weapon but simply moved to the side. He avoided the blade and caught the arm which had wielded it. The robber's eyes bulged with shock at the speed of his victim. That shock intensified as he felt the powerful blow, which struck his elbow. Bone shattered and flesh ripped apart as bone forced its way into the daylight. Another powerful blow hit the unfortunate robber in the throat; he died quickly gasping for air that would not come. His body was thrown into the path of another onrushing thief, sending both corpse and attacker sprawling to the floor. The remaining two miscreants seeing the fate of their comrades approached with more care, weapons drawn, planning not just robbery but murder. Nonetheless, the stranger remained perfectly still, his blade still remained sheathed. One attacker screamed and swept his blade forward; his target being so inviting and unmoving, but in a moment, he was gone. His sword arm too was caught, but it was not held firm like before. The helpless attacker spun around, his blade suddenly striking his own comrade under the chin. It was a poorly maintained weapon, but a common blade driven with such speed can reach a terrible conclusion. Blade met chin, driving upwards through the jawbone, brain and skull. With a loud crack, it erupted through the top of his comrade's head, brain matter clinging disturbingly to the blade. The owner of the blade, saddened at his own error was short-lived as a powerful hand grasped his chin and jerked his head violently around. A crack signalled the man's death, and like some mournful dance, both bodies trembling their death throes, fell and thudded to the floor in perfect timing. The remaining four criminals seeing the fate of their friends, did not seek revenge but raced into the crowd, craving only escape. The stranger bent down and wiped a single drop of blood from his person onto the tunic of one of the fallen. Then without ceremony, he simply rose and continued his journey.

Spartacus watched the man walking away and inwardly marked the stranger as dangerous.

***

'Even if they intend us no harm, I might just gut the bastards for treating us like shit.' Spartacus growled. He turned to look for support from his fellow companions.

'Calm yourself, Spartacus,' Cassian said, attempting to soothe his friend.

'How can you say that, Cassian?' replied Spartacus. His face reddened, clearly reaching his limit of patience. 'They force us to follow them, separate us from men and vessels.'

'The legendary warrior has a temper, I see.' An unknown voice echoed in the shell of a room.

The group turned as one to stare at an approaching figure, most remained rooted to the spot but all watched for an impending attack.

Cassian, however, moved forward, his look of shock turning to a beaming smile. 'Adrianicus! By the gods, you are supposed to be dead!'

'Cassian, old friend, it is good to see you after all these years.'

'But how?'

'An arrangement with Pompey, it ensures I can carry out certain duties. Forgive me for the way in which you were brought here. However, when you have heard my reasons, I am sure you will understand the necessity.'

'Then you had best explain,' Spartacus blurted out before Cassian had the chance to respond, the warrior's anger had not been quelled.

'My sources tell me that Cassian considers you a friend, Spartacus, I hope that we too can forge such an alliance.'

'I have enough friends, what I want is answers.'

Adrianicus laughed. He was the second man that day to show no fear of the legendary warrior. 'If not friends, then let's hope not enemies.' He paused. 'We both tend to kill those that stand against us.' The threat was dressed in a silken smile but landed as heavily as any axe.

Spartacus tamed his anger, resisting the urge to rip the man's throat out. 'Only the gods know what the future brings, but death comes to us all. Only some are harder to kill than most.'

Cassian took the slight pause in conversation to try to diffuse the situation. 'Adrianicus! For the sake of my sanity. Tell us why we have been brought to Gades?'

'Of course, Cassian, but it will take time and I have a room prepared so we can talk in comfort. Besides, we should at least hold a goblet to celebrate the reunion of old friends.' With that Adrianicus motioned for them to follow then he turned and walked ahead.

Spartacus moved in close to Cassian and whispered, 'Arrogant shit, isn't he?'

'Yes, but he also is a very dangerous man, Spartacus, with both his mind and a blade.'

'Can we trust him?' asked Lathyrus who joined the twosome after witnessing the conversation.

'Of course not,' Cassian said laughing, 'but we can trust that he is loyal to Pompey and has been for some time, though I do not know why.'

The men gave each other a perplexed look and followed Adrianicus.

***

The prepared room was functional at best; there had been no attempt at putting on a show. The seating was no more than crates and crude benches and the food displayed was simple but filling, obtained from the local market. Adrianicus was already seated; on his right was the stranger who had so expertly dispatched the robbers on the streets of Gades.

'This is Sikarbaal. He regrets that your first meeting could not have been more cordial.' Adrianicus enthusiastically motioned for them to come forward. 'Come sit, take some refreshment.'

'I must impress on you the need for answers, Adrianicus.' Cassian's patience too was also wearing thin.

'The time has come, Cassian. You will know all the information at my disposal. However, part of that information I am sure will bring you all a great deal of joy.' He paused revelling in the confusion spreading across the faces of the men opposite. 'While you were busy carrying out a great service to Rome, Pompey sought to safeguard your families. Now the time has come for Pompey to attend pressing senatorial duties and his focus must be elsewhere. He knew he would not be able to keep your families safe for much longer, and therefore, he instructed me to grant them secure passage.'

'Where are they?' Plinius was suddenly attentive and for the first time interested in the proceedings.

'Plinius, isn't it? I hear you are a great talent with the blade, perhaps you will do me the honour of sparring with me?'

'Of course,' replied Plinius. 'But where are my family?'

'Well, they are here in Gades. Pompey believed that those best suited to their protection are the group that cares most for their safety.'

Cassian and the others excitedly started to ask questions but Adrianicus held up his hand, to halt those questions. 'The moment we have finished you shall be taken to them. However, I have a considerable amount to discuss with you and I shall need your undivided attention.

'Cassian, many years ago when we were just boys your father used to tell us tales of great heroes. One such tale involved a pharaoh of Egypt, who with the help of a blade bestowed on him by the gods, never tasted defeat in battle. Do you remember?'

'Of course, Thutmose and the dagger of Seker but what have those stories got to do with us?'

'The dagger is not a myth, Cassian, it is real.'

'So Pompey wants the dagger?' Spartacus asked still unable to keep his annoyance from his voice.

'Pompey has no need of trinkets, Spartacus, he has never tasted defeat. However, there is one man who yearns for military successes and the support of the senate to allow him the chance to gain those successes.'

'But the dagger is lost,' interrupted Cassian.

'We believe we know of its location, but rather more importantly, we believe that Crassus also knows.'

'So, if Pompey does not need the dagger, why all this secrecy?' pressed Spartacus.

'Because Crassus knows the value of a symbol, with the dagger in his hand, the senate will grant him all the troops he wishes.'

'Men willing to die for a symbol,' scoffed Spartacus.

'The legions have conquered half the known world with an eagle on a staff. The slave army which caused Rome so much trouble cried freedom to rally the hearts and minds of men.'

'Freedom is not a symbol.' Spartacus was beginning to become angry once more.

'Spartacus, we are both men that have tasted war. I, like you, believe it is the quality of the leader and the troops he leads which determines a battle. However, a symbol whether it is held aloft on a banner or held within the heart of men can mobilize the masses. Perhaps even more importantly it can convince public opinion that the cause is true.'

'So Crassus wants the blade. What is he prepared to do to possess it?'

'You know Crassus; he will spend his wealth and remove all obstacles. However, it is not Crassus that concerns Pompey, it is the location of the dagger.' Adrianicus paused ensuring he had their full attention. 'We believe that the dagger is located in the city state of Commagene and that King Antiochus now guards the famed blade. Commagene falls within the borders of the Armenia, however, that empire is falling apart, beset by internal conflict. Commagene has stood proud in the chaos, mainly due to its troops which have guarded its borders with ferocity and skill.'

'So what has changed to put the dagger in harm's way?' asked Cassian.

'Two summers ago, a great plague raged through the lands. The plague has now gone but with it took many souls. Unfortunately, it cut the forces of Commagene in half and now the defence of the kingdom seems impossible. This would not have been a problem if Mithridates of Pontus had not decided to expand his empire in the region. It is our belief that Crassus has been trying to manipulate Mithridates, it is also our belief that Crassus has completely misjudged the situation, he cannot control the Pontus king.'

'But what of the rest of the Armenian empire, surely they will raise troops?' asked Cassian.

'You would think that would be the logical answer, but the region is anything but logical. Armenia is in a state of turmoil, various factions are trying to remove their leader Tigranes from his seat of power and one of those factions includes his own son. We believe that Tigranes has joined forces with Mithridates in a plot to convince the people of Armenia that the Pontus invasion is really a rescue mission to prevent Roman and Parthian influence growing in the region. Once Mithridates completes the invasion, Tigranes will be in his debt and we understand the ambitions of the Pontus leader lie far beyond that of Commagene. Pompey thinks Mithridates will either strike at Roman territories or the lands of Parthia.'

Cassian nodded his head as though suddenly all was clear to him. 'This means that a member of the senate, who has suddenly gained support for a military campaign, by obtaining the famed dagger of Seker, will be able to pick his target. If Crassus has convinced Mithridates that Parthia should be his next target, then Crassus will use his influence to also lead a campaign against Parthian lands.'

'Exactly, but Pompey believes that Mithridates is just as likely to attack Roman lands. Besides Rome does not want war with Parthia, it would be a drawn out affair, one which we have no means certain of winning,' replied Adrianicus.

'I am sorry but what has this to do with us?' asked Spartacus.

'Rome cannot commit troops, it would only enforce the lies that Tigranes and Mithridates have spread through the region. To this end Pompey has hired mercenaries that served him well in previous campaigns. However, they will be severely outnumbered and Pompey believes that your talents, Spartacus, would serve the state of Commagene well.'

'Why would I do the bidding of Pompey or any Roman for that matter?'

'Pompey has been in secretive talks with the Parthians, they will also be supplying troops. However, that is not the only service they are willing to provide. Pompey has secured for the men in this room lands to settle within the Parthian empire. Spartacus, Cassian, you want to be free of Crassus within those lands he has no influence? Pompey will wave your debt to him, Cassian, if you carry out this task. In short we offer you the chance to start a new life beyond the reach of those who wish you harm.'

'So all we have to do is defeat an entire army with a few thousand men, in a land where we will have no idea who are our friends or enemy. Tell me, Adrianicus, where will you be when the fighting starts?' asked Spartacus.

'Spartacus, I know you feel no trust towards me, but on this journey we shall travel together. Let us hope by its completion I would have earned that trust. Now you have families waiting and I require an answer for there is little time to delay.'

Many questions were asked but by the time the speaking stopped, only one man chose to take a different path to those that would travel to Commagene.

'I am sorry, Cassian, but I am no warrior.'

'You have done more than I've asked of you, Vectrix, take a vessel and any men that wish to return home,' replied Cassian.

'You will not leave this place until we have long departed,' interrupted Adrianicus.

'I am not yours to command,' replied Vectrix angrily.

'Adrianicus, Vectrix is a man of honour and will not betray you or his friends.' Cassian held his old friend's stare until the man suddenly relaxed.

'Very well, but please do not discuss our intentions with the men. Those wishing to return home may do so, and the men who wish to follow Cassian can remain joyfully ignorant of our true intent.'

'When do we leave, Adrianicus?' asked Cassian.

'Two days,' Adrianicus replied reluctantly, now unsure whether to discuss any plans with Vectrix in close proximity.

'Then Vectrix and the rest of the men will spend this night with us. That includes the men at your command also.'

'But the risk?'

'Vectrix is part of our family and as such will spend one night in comfort. As for the men we will take on this fool's mission, they need time in each other's company.'

'Why?' Adrianicus asked, his confusion all too evident.

'You are asking these men to overcome a great deal, including an enemy far superior in number. These men must be willing to bleed for each other.' It was Spartacus who answered and after a short pause, added, 'Before trust and friendship can be earned, men must grow used to one another in their shadow.'

CHAPTER THREE

Adrianicus rose and if he'd felt any ill will towards Cassian for going against his wishes, he certainly did not let that annoyance show upon his face. 'I think you and your families have waited long enough to be reunited. Come, let us put the thoughts of war to the back of our minds. Tonight will be spent in relative comfort and hopefully a little joy.'

Adrianicus did not wait for a reply but moved towards the door, the others quickly rose and followed. Lathyrus delayed just long enough to sweep up a succulent looking roasted fowl, though he wanted nothing more than to lay his head in a place of comfort, it would be foolish to leave such a tasty morsel behind.

'Is it far?' Plinius asked, his excitement at the chance to see Chia almost overwhelming the young warrior.

'No.' Adrianicus smiled. 'Pompey has a number of villas throughout this region. It is fortunate that the one in Gades is situated near to the dock and is perhaps one of the more lavish properties. Cassian, once I have made you comfortable at the villa I shall have word sent to your men that they should join us.'

'Thank you, Adrianicus,' replied Cassian.

It was not long before the group were passing through a heavily guarded doorway when Spartacus noted that Adrianicus had placed far more protection around this building than the warehouse. He wondered if Adrianicus had shown genuine care for their families, or it was part of the game to gain trust. They moved forward beyond the courtyard and entered the villa through yet another impressive doorway.

'I have not informed your families of your arrival, it is always difficult to ensure a schedule when the gods may have turned the seas against us. Still, I expect that your sudden arrival will be heartily enjoyed.'

'Thank you for your kindness, Adrianicus and for the protection of our families,' replied Cassian.

'For an old friend, it is nothing. I will send word to your men and arrange a feast to celebrate both the joining of families and the start of a great adventure. I shall leave you for the present, you will need time with those you love.'

Adrianicus had not been untruthful as to the quality of the villa. It was both spacious and luxurious. Pompey had spared no expense in the furnishing. As the group moved through the villa they could not help but be impressed by the entire building. Suddenly, a child's laughter erupted and from a doorway just to their front, a boy hurtled into the corridor.

'Titus, my son!' Cassian held a hand to his mouth, tears welled within his eyes.

The boy turned on hearing his name and for a moment stood motionless, as if the figure before him was a stranger. Then a smile developed rapidly and the boy came running.

'Father!' he screamed.

Cassian caught the boy and the embrace was long and unrestricted. Cassian could not help the tears falling freely and he did not care for one moment who observed them fall. The commotion within the hall had not gone unnoticed and soon more than one set of footsteps could be heard approaching at pace. A boy younger than the first was the next to appear and he stood mesmerized by the man holding his older brother. He seemed unable to bridge the small gap that separated father and son, despite Cassian beckoning him closer.

Flora then entered the rapidly shrinking corridor, her face erupting into sheer delight at the sight of Cassian. She held in her arms a young girl who Spartacus recognised as the child he had plucked from the slaughter carried out by Flabinus and his men. A slaughter, which seemed to have happened so long ago, but the mere thought of it sent ice down the warrior's spine.

'Cassian, I have dreamed of your return for so long.' She blushed. '*We* have dreamed.' She corrected herself struggling to hide the crimson flush to her cheeks.

'The joy of this day has been eagerly awaited by us all,' Cassian replied and once again beckoned the smaller child. The boy however, held his ground and clung to Flora's gown.

'Sectus, go to your father. He has travelled far just to see you smile.' As Flora spoke she gave a gentle push and the boy hesitantly moved forward. He picked up pace and then suddenly was half running, half tripping towards Cassian.

The boy was prevented from falling by Cassian who held both boys close. He looked to Flora. 'I have you to thank for my boys' happiness.'

Flora moved forward and kissed Cassian in greeting, but most in that corridor recognised that the moment of intimacy delayed just a fraction than was needed.

'No thanks are required, Cassian. They have been a great comfort and will grow to be fine men.' She leaned forward and kissed him again and he did not shy away from the affection.

'I am delighted to see you, too, mother.' Tictus stepped forward as he spoke. He did not expect the pure emotion that would erupt from his stepmother.

'Tictus!' she cried. Rushing to the young warrior, she proceeded to embrace him, as if letting him go would mean to lose him forever.

'Do not cry, mother.' Tictus tried to calm Flora.

'I thought you — I thought...' She stopped, fearing to say the words.

'I have fine warriors to ensure my safety.' He paused then added, 'And even finer friends.'

Spartacus uncharacteristically placed a calming hand on Flora's shoulder. 'He speaks the truth, Tictus is a friend to us all and we would lay down our lives for him. Besides, he is capable in his own protection.'

'Flora.' The interruption was reluctantly made by Plinius.

'Plinius, forgive me.' She wiped tears from her face. 'Chia is with Cynna in the garden.'

On hearing Flora's response both Plinius and Spartacus asked for the garden's location and then hurried away. Flora noticed that both Lathyrus and Vectrix seemed a little out of place, and so she approached both with warmth and greetings.

The sun still shone brightly in the sky and as Spartacus and Plinius entered the gardens they both were momentarily blinded by the sudden brightness. Steadily they grew accustomed to the intrusive light and eagerly glanced about for what they craved. At the end of the gardens no more than fifty paces away, two women and a number of children played. The elder of the two women suddenly looked up and a smiled, she leant forward and whispered something in the younger woman's ear.

'Do not tease me. Cynna. I fear my heart will break.'

'I do not tease, Chia,' she replied in a gentle tone. 'The gods have answered both our prayers.'

Chia turned, and to Plinius' delight he could see that she held a small child in her arms.

An invisible force held him tight. After the many days away his entire being had cried out to be with the woman he loved and now that the moment was at hand.

'Spartacus,' Plinius whispered, though he did not know why.

'It's a warrior thing, Plinius. We are so used to the filth we face each day that when true beauty stands before us, we freeze as if in terror. Go to your family, young warrior, savour each moment. The beauty in this world is all too fleeting.'

Both warriors moved slowly forward until they stood face to face with their respective partners. Plinius, Chia and the child were all suddenly one, as the young warrior's arms wrapped them all together.

Cynna on the other held her ground, her happiness showing the brilliance of her eyes.

'You are looking old,' she jested.

'Have to find yourself a young buck to keep you warm, then,' replied Spartacus.

'And what makes you think I haven't already?'

Spartacus suddenly looked more serious. 'This.' He placed a hand above his heart. '...and this.' His second hand moved to the blade at his thigh.

She stepped in closer and kissed him. 'You forgot one...' Her hand quickly moved up the inside of his thigh, coming to rest on his manhood. Spartacus coughed, embarrassed by the intimacy, as they were not yet alone.

The two warriors and their families did not seek out others within Pompey's villa but enjoyed the time within the opulent gardens.

***

Cassian woke early the next morning. He entered the banquet hall to find that Vectrix and the other men that would be leaving them were already feasting on a substantial meal. Cassian joined the men who had so valiantly served at his shoulder and faced many dangers. Part of him was glad that these men were not part of the mission that he and his warrior comrades were about to undertake. Nonetheless, a more selfish part of him wished that these battle-hardened men would once again be at his side. The group seemed in good spirits and it was not long before all had eaten their fill. The time had come to depart for the dock and Cassian decided that he would take a last journey with his comrades.

Spartacus rushed from the villa as the group were exiting the villa courtyard. A few of the men teased the warrior about the reason he had risen so late in the day. Spartacus took the banter in good humour and all began their journey to the vessel that would take some of them at least back to the loving embrace of their families.

The craft had been laden with all the supplies that it could carry, and soon the men were boarded and ready to depart.

Vectrix idled slightly so he could have one last conversation with Cassian. 'It has been an honour to serve with you, Cassian.'

'The honour was all mine. I doubt that we would have been successful in the hunt for Flabinus without your aid. The vessel belongs to you, Vectrix. I hope that it brings you great wealth in the future.'

'I feel that I must say something, Cassian. Please forgive my words because they are not meant to insult but are as a warning.' Vectrix seemed unsure whether to utter his next words.

'What is it, Vectrix?' Cassian replied trying to put Vectrix at ease.

'It is Adrianicus. I do not trust this man. I know he is an old friend, Cassian, but I cannot help distrusting his intent.'

'Finally, someone who agrees with me,' added Spartacus.

Cassian held up his hand in protest. 'I know trusting Adrianicus may bring dangers to us and our families, nonetheless, if one day we wish to live in peace and far from the influences of Rome and those that seek power, then I feel we must take that risk.'

'Be careful, my friend. For all your sakes keep this man under close watch, for I believe him more a snake than a man.'

Eventually Vectrix relented in his warnings and the last farewells were spoken. Spartacus and Cassian watched the small vessel disappear over the horizon. Both men could still hear the warnings within their mind.

Chapter Four

Vectrix smiled; although the sun had not fully gone down, the darkness was beginning to claim the day. Despite the lateness of the day, Vectrix would not slow his pace. He was not completely sure of the reason himself; but he knew that every sinew within his body wanted to place a great distance between his vessel and port of Gades. The face of Adrianicus kept visiting his mind and though the Roman was a friend of Cassian's, Vectrix felt a deep loathing and distrust of the man.

Vectrix looked to his own sail and delighted in the brisk wind which buffeted the heavy cloth.

'Vectrix, you should rest, you have not closed your eyes since we left the port.'

'Perhaps you are right, Medus,' replied Vectrix. His eyes now fixed on the gathering mists to the rear of his craft.

'Go, I will keep the men at their tasks.'

'Thank you, Medus,' Vectrix responded and then added, 'If you should ever want a life on the waters, there will be a place for you on this vessel.'

'Argh … it is a fine offer but I am a farmer and besides I have a wife waiting for me.'

'She would not be happy with you away on the waves?'

'She would be less happy with me visiting all those ports filled with women.'

'A temper, has she?' Vectrix smiled.

'A ball in each hand and shows no reluctance to squeezing each one.' Medus laughed loudly.

Vectrix joined in his comrade's laughter. 'Very well, Medus. I shall take some rest, call me if you see anything.'

***

Vectrix tried to gain a comfortable position and with one last look towards the darkness he settled to slumber, his body and mind suddenly feeling weary. It was not long before sleep took the anxiety and replaced the images of treachery to that of a place he had once called home. The mists of the past swirled within his mind; images came to prominence and then drifted away. Eventually, one image emerged and lingered and in the background the vista gained solidity until it resembled a place he knew as a young man. Men, women and children danced around a huge fire, song and laughter filled the air. A constant image of a beautiful woman smiled lovingly and brushed a strand of deep auburn hair away from her face. Any person not privy to those dreams would have observed a sleeping man reaching, trying desperately to hold an invisible figure. Vectrix, however, was ignorant of the real world lost completely in a past no longer obtainable. The Gaul would have happily stayed in that world, the ghosts of the past soothing his heart and mind.

Slowly at first the smiles began to ebb away, the laughter became screams. The fire, which had brought warmth to the dancers, now raged. The tongues of the fire spat fourth, taking hold of both person and building. It consumed all within its path, consigning all to damnation. Then the female appeared once more, gone was the smile, her face now only revealed fear and sadness. The flames took her, too, her features turning from beauty to ash with only Vectrix to bear witness. A tear rolled down the old sailor's face but he refused to open his eyes to the real world.

'Vectrix! Wake quickly!'

The Gaul felt a firm hand on his shoulder and the attempt to shake him back into the realm of men. Finally he relented and allowed his eyes to open; it seemed strange that he could still smell burning flesh.

'What is it?'

'We are under attack,' replied Medus.

Vectrix jumped to his feet and raced to the rear of the vessel. On his way he noticed part of the craft rail was charred black. He watched the mists and darkness but could determine no enemies intent on violence. Then in the distance, two streams of fire erupted and just for a moment, the outlines of two ships could be clearly observed. As the balls of fire rose into the sky, the images of the vessels from which they came disappeared once more into the darkness. Vectrix knew that those vessels, which lurked in the distance, would mean destruction for his craft and men.

'Why are they attacking us?' asked Medus.

'We have too many secrets. Medus, if you can swim slip over the side, we can escape as all who remain here will die.' He paused. 'Try to get home to that woman of yours,' he said in a more calmer tone.

In the distance, two more balls of fire arched into the night sky. All aboard watched with fear as they eventually started to fall and breathed with relief as both fell short of the vessel. Vectrix knew it would not be long before his craft would fall prey to the bombardment.

'Over the side! Those of you who can swim do so, those that cannot, I suggest you learn.' As Vectrix's words ended a great crash threw his world into chaos. Men screamed, some from pain others from blind panic. Vectrix regained his footing and realised he had been thrown at least seven paces from where he had been standing. He looked to the sail and the gods seemed to confirm his destruction by stopping the winds and forcing the sail to hand motionless.

'Swim, you bastards, get away from the ship!'

Time seemed to slow as Vectrix watched those that were able to leap into the dark water below. He considered joining them in their attempt to seek survival in the murky depths. Almost immediately, though, he shook the thought from his mind and instead reached to the deck to retrieve a wine skin. The vessel was now listing badly so he braced himself against the rail and drank deeply from the skin. Cassian had made sure that the wine was of a good quality and quietly Vectrix thanked his friend for a decent last drink. The acrid taste of the wine forced the taste of the smoke from his throat and stood watching the darkness for the vessels which had sealed his doom. More time passed and more wine flowed but the situation would not allow Vectrix to lose his sobriety. Finally, a dark vessel manoeuvred alongside the desperate sinking craft and a figure appeared at its rail.

'The men that have entered the waters know nothing of your secrets, Sikarbaal,' Vectrix shouted defiantly.

'We will not hunt them,' Sikarbaal said and paused then added, 'I take no pleasure in this task.'

'Pleasure or regret makes no difference, you still carry out the task. Be warned, Sikarbaal, try this treachery with Spartacus and all that black armour will not prevent him from ripping out your devious heart.'

Sikarbaal looked to Vectrix but did not reply and then reluctantly nodded his head. The sound of bowstrings mixed with that of burning timbers filled the air. A thud was heard and Vectrix gazed down at the two shafts that now pierced his chest. The old sailor slipped to the deck of the craft and as if in some mournful response, in turn slipped beneath the waters.

Sikarbaal looked on as Vectrix left the world of men. He had been in the employ of Adrianicus for many years and in that time committed many dishonourable tasks. He had come to the conclusion that with each of those acts he had lost a part of himself. Vectrix had seemed a fine man with friends that had held him in high regard. Sikarbaal had never known true friendship and he was unlikely to, as long as he served Adrianicus. He shook his head at his own shame and inwardly made a promise that this task to Commagene would be his last and the last time he would be walking in Adrianicus' shadow. He indeed knew that leaving the service would be as dangerous as any mission he had undertaken. He knew many of the Roman's secrets and that could mean Adrianicus would rather he lie bleeding in the dirt than be roaming free with the knowledge he possessed.

'Do we kill the survivors?' One of his men posed the question expecting Sikarbaal to pronounce a death sentence.

'No, they are no threat to our mission. Besides, if they make it to the shore then they deserve the chance to witness another sunrise.' He paused. 'Back to Gades, we have preparations to make.'

***

Cassian had spent most of the day ensuring Lathyrus had all he required to guarantee his craft would handle the voyage to Commagene. He had sent Spartacus to purchase weaponry because much of what they already possessed had succumbed to the ravages of battle. The warrior had returned with two wagons overflowing with his endeavours.

'Not one piece of black. I have no wish to look like those bastards.' Spartacus smiled smugly.

'We are on the same side, Spartacus,' replied Cassian.

'That does not mean I have to like the dogs. Honestly, Cassian, you must wonder about the intentions of your old friend?'

'The man I once knew was a good man. Nonetheless, I am not a fool, Spartacus. I know that time and experiences can change a person. I also know that we embark on a mission that is not of our choosing or design. I have gambled that the result will be of benefit to our loved ones. Be assured that I will not allow Adrianicus to place those same people in danger.'

Spartacus always knew that Cassian would place his friends before the mission that lay ahead, but it still sounded good to hear the Roman say it out loud.

'Speaking of the mission, how many men does Adrianicus say we will have at our command?' asked Spartacus.

'He hopes that our number will be around eight thousand, added to that you will have the forces of Commagene and then what the Parthians dispatch to aid our quest. There is also the possibility that many more will join our ranks.'

'They are more likely to join the ranks of Mithridates, especially if Tigranes decides to fight. We could be facing two armies, Cassian.'

'Adrianicus believes Tigranes has no stomach for a fight, he is an old and weary man, Spartacus.'

'An old man clinging to power and an old beast can sink its teeth into flesh as easily as a young one.'

'I know, Spartacus.' Cassian was struggling with the gladiator's negativity. 'We can only hope to deliver a crushing defeat on Mithridates' troops, maybe then Tigranes will be fearful of leaving his seat of power.'

'This campaign seems filled with hopes and possibilities, Cassian. War is never certain but this task is ridiculous in the extreme.' Spartacus shook his head as he uttered the words.

Cassian placed a hand upon his shoulder. 'Then I will need your help to make sense of the shadows, old friend.'

'My help?' Spartacus laughed. 'I am a warrior, Cassian, I see the enemy and I kill the bastard, that is all.'

'Spartacus you took a slave army and nearly defeated the mighty Roman Empire.'

'We lost, Cassian.'

'You achieved far more than any Roman general could have hoped to achieve. These men that we journey to fight are not of the legions and they do not have Crassus or Pompey at their lead.'

'I achieve more than any Roman general? I would not let Adrianicus hear you say those words. He will run screaming to Pompey.'

'Adrianicus and Pompey can both kiss my arse. My allegiance is to my friends and loved ones for I have already lost too many because of the arrogance and greed of Roman senators.'

'Finally, you are starting to make sense.' Spartacus smiled and landed a jovial punch upon his friend's shoulder.

***

Another day passed before the convoy was once again ready to take to the sea. Surprisingly, Adrianicus decided that he would join Cassian for the first part of the journey.

Spartacus busied himself with tasks that would keep him a healthy distance away from the Roman. Plinius, on the other hand, seemed to welcome the man responsible for his reunion with Chia and his son. The young warrior over the last few passing days would even take to sparring with Adrianicus, an activity that he would usually partake with Spartacus. The sparring was taken at a gentle pace and in good humour. However, on the third day both men seemed to wish to be a little more forceful as if they wanted to know more of the other's true skills.

The pace was such that Plinius slipped and as he struggled to regain his footing, his weapon struck Adrianicus on the right cheek leaving a deep red mark. Plinius held up his hand to apologise but the apology was met with fury. Plinius was forced to defend against the savagery of Adrianicus' attack. Blow after blow was aimed at the young warrior, the intention to cause injury. Plinius defended valiantly but finally a blow caught him hard on the upper arm causing him to yelp with pain and drop his own weapon. Adrianicus moved and raised his weapon, his face contorted with rage. The next would be devastating to Plinius but as Adrianicus swept the weapon down his world suddenly turned upside down. He had been thrown by an unknown force but within a moment he was rising to his feet, the thirst of his anger still not quenched. Nonetheless, he was stopped abruptly as a blade was suddenly pointed directly at his throat.

'Give me a reason and I will gut you like a fish,' spat Spartacus.

Adrianicus looked to the menacing warrior and then to Plinius. A smile replaced the look of anger. 'Forgive me, Plinius, your blow released the beast in me. I hope you are not badly injured?'

Plinius did not answer. Chia had rushed to him and was tending his wound.

'Perhaps, Spartacus, we can continue this another time when both parties are armed.' Adrianicus' smile narrowed slightly, his eyes burned into Spartacus.

'It will take but a moment to fetch you a blade,' replied Spartacus holding the man's stare.

'We are on the same side, let this be the end of the matter,' interrupted Cassian.

'Well said, Cassian,' said Adrianicus, his beaming smile returning.

Cassian rounded on him his anger clear for all to see. 'I think it best if you continued this journey aboard another vessel.' Cassian had declared for all to see where his allegiances lay.

'Agreed, I have much to do,' replied Adrianicus. The crimson blush of both annoyance and embarrassment showed clearly on his face.

Spartacus waited for Adrianicus to walk away and then approached Plinius. 'Is the arm broken?'

'No,' replied Plinius and then added, 'thank you.'

'Thank you? Do not give me thanks. A word of advice, Plinius. Take your mind from Chia's tits and place it on the task in hand. The next time a man tries to remove your head do not stand there like a love sick boy.'

'Spartacus! How dare—' began Chia.

'Be quiet, woman. This is not a game. A good man dies as easily as a bad one. If you love Plinius, allow him to focus on his duties.'

'Watch your mouth.' Plinius stood, anger etched upon his face.

'Finally, the warrior has returned.' Spartacus did not give the opportunity to reply but simply turned and walked away.

CHAPTER FIVE

The convoy continued on its long journey. Occasionally other vessels would join their voyage and the following day disappeared as quietly as they had entered. Cassian guessed that they'd became part of the convey because of the extra protection travelling as a component in a much larger fleet afforded them, nonetheless, like all the craft that were present, they required supplies. They would break off to enter the nearest port, perhaps hoping to rejoin the fleet at a later date.

Cassian's thoughts were interrupted as he heard laughter; it was clear that the departure of Adrianicus had allowed the mood of the crew to lighten. Cassian had taken a step back and allowed Spartacus to work the men hard. The gladiator had all the men working at their blade skills, he was tough and relentless in his training but each man knew that his efforts were to keep them alive. Many of the other passengers and crew watched the training bouts as they busied themselves with their own tasks.

Spartacus' wife Cynna watched the training as she prepared a meal when Chia approached and then seated herself without a word and proceeded to help prepare the meal. The silence lasted some time; it was an awkward silence the weight of words not yet spoken becoming oppressive.

Finally, Cynna spoke. 'Plinius still seems angry at Spartacus.' Her tone was pleasant, matched by the warmth of her smile.

'Is it any wonder?' replied Chia.

'I imagine it depends on whether you should be angry at a man who cares enough to keep you alive.' As Cynna spoke, she looked up from her work and for the first time held Chia's gaze.

'Plinius is a fine warrior, few can match his skill with a blade,' Chia answered struggling to hold onto her anger.

'That is true. Plinius is a fine warrior.'

'Say what you mean, Cynna.'

Chia was becoming flustered, she had expected a disagreement with Cynna but the woman's constant affability made an argument impossible.

'Spartacus once told me that a warrior can be skilled with various talents. Nonetheless, they count for nought if the mind that controls them is not focussed upon the task in hand. A determined warrior armed only with a rock can be a deadly enemy. You fight with your head, then with your blade and rarely with your heart,' Cynna said.

'Spartacus cares a great deal for Plinius?'

'Spartacus cares for all his friends,' replied Cynna and then added, 'but I believe he sees a lost son in Plinius. Not that an entire legion of Rome could prise that information from his lips. My husband would rather Plinius remain angry at him and stay alive, than to have held his tongue and see his friend fall.'

Chia sat silently for some time and then suddenly she was gone.

Cynna smiled and as she worked began to sing. Her smile deepened as she observed moments later Chia and Plinius moving towards the area of the vessel where Spartacus was training. Chia kissed Plinius and gave him a gentle push and then she returned to Cynna and without a word busied herself with her previous task.

Plinius reached out and grasped a wooden training sword. He tested its weight with a couple of slashes and illusory blocks against an imaginary foe.

'May I train with you, Spartacus?'

'Your arm is not yet healed,' Spartacus replied.

'It is sore, that is all, a reminder to prevent future foolishness. Besides, I once observed a man beat three men without the use of his regular sword arm.'

'Sounds like an arrogant bastard.'

'Yes,' joked Plinius but added, 'but he is also a better friend than I deserve.'

Words were no longer needed between the warriors. The two trained hard moving with a speed and skill that amazed all that sailed on the craft.

Chia watched and as she did so, a small tear rolled down her cheek. 'Will they forget the quarrel and be as they once were?' she asked Cynna.

'By the end of this night I expect both will be drunk. They will be loud and as brothers. They will break wind and brag on the quality of their wives tits,' Cynna replied shaking her head in mock dismay.

'Really?'

'Chia, both Spartacus and Plinius are fine warriors and honourable men. Nonetheless, they are still just men and we must make allowances.'

Both women laughed at their husbands' expense.

***

Spartacus slowly opened his eyes; the morning light and warmth washed over his body. He had left the arms of Cynna when the night was still young. Thoughts of what lay ahead troubled his mind and he knew the first part of their journey was nearing its completion. Time had been spent restlessly pacing the deck, his mind trying to make sense of the madness of the mission. Eventually, he found a quiet section of the craft and settled down. He forced the fears from his mind; risking his life held no terror but his family were rarely in danger. Now they accompanied him on the path to danger and it unsettled the warrior greatly.

'Wine?' The familiar booming voice of Lathyrus disturbed his reluctant awakening.

Spartacus raised his head slightly as his eyes focussed on the wine skin being held to his front. 'Thank you,' he replied taking the morning offering.

'I think this morning will be of interest to you lovers of the land.'

'What?' Spartacus asked, the lack of sleep still bearing down on his senses.

'Look for yourself,' the big man replied as he pointed beyond the vessel's rail.

Spartacus forced himself to the standing position and then allowed his eyes to follow the direction that Lathyrus had indicated. The warrior could not stop his jaw dropping in amazement as before him countless vessels queued in eagerness to make land. The chosen port seemed inadequate for the task, more suited to small fishing boats than a military expedition.

'What is this place?'

'I have never sailed these waters and even if I had, I would not have picked such a lowly cesspit. What fun could a man looking for entertainment find in such a place?'

'Seems Cassian has brought us to the gates of Hades.'

'I expect Hades would have a better class of whore.' Lathyrus barked with laughter.

Spartacus smiled, though in truth he felt little joy. 'We best wake Cassian.'

'I will fetch him,' replied Lathyrus.

Spartacus continued to watch the hectic port. The vessels obviously carried troops and all they required for a campaign. Around the port he could see tents being erected and the telltale wisps of smoke as campfires were being lit. The thought of another battle made Spartacus feel exhausted, he seemed to have been fighting all his life. The men preparing their camps would be feeling the same, but for the moment they busied themselves with a soldier's chores. Nonetheless, blood and pain would follow and for some, their fears would become a reality.

When Spartacus had been a slave, the risking of his life had been a simple affair, especially when you have nothing to lose, apart from a life of servitude to those to whom you have nothing but hatred. He grew to love the cheer of the crowd and to a certain extent enjoyed the killing of his opponents in the blood-soaked arena. Then Batiatus threatened his family and so he killed not for glory but for their safety and freedom. His enemies were no longer the skilled gladiators of the empire but the trained soldiers of the legions. Freedom was snatched from his grasp and the slave army smashed to bloody ruin. He should have died that day but the gods had not finished their terrible game. Since he was a boy all he had known was blood, pain and the loss of those he loved. His hand tightened on the craft's rail, anger coursed through his entire body.

'How many fighting men do you estimate?' Cassian approached Spartacus.

'Uh,' was all Spartacus could manage as he fought to control the anger.

'How many?' Cassian repeated, not noticing his friend's mood because his gaze was concentrated on the port.

'Too far away to be accurate. Besides, we do not know how many are aboard those vessels. A few thousand at least, I doubt it will be enough.'

'Let us hope more will join our banner,' replied Cassian.

'Fight for a foreign army against their king, I would not hold your breath, Cassian.'

'Then at least let us hope that those sent against us are poorly led.' Cassian was becoming frustrated with Spartacus' negativity yet again. Both men fell to silence; inwardly they gave prayer to the gods.

***

Many days' ride from Spartacus and the port, another army was preparing for a bloody campaign. It did not concern itself with numbers for its ranks swelled with each passing moment.

Watching its progress three men sat on their mounts taking advantage of a slight incline in the terrain. Two of the men were Roman and although they doubted the quality of many of the troops before them, both knew the size of the army would be more than enough to complete the task. This would not be a mission where the skills of the legions would be required.

The taller of the two smiled and broke the silence. 'Commagene will not stand against such a force.'

'Do we have information on what stands against us, Rubius?'

'Both the agents of Crassus and Mithridates confirm that we will face no more than ten thousand men and they will be no army but merely a collection of mercenaries.'

'I am surprised that Crassus places so much emphasis on this fabled blade,' added the third man.

'Crassus only seeks the blade to gain favour with both senate and the citizens of Rome, Democolese. He places far more trust in the prowess of the legions and of course his own impressive abilities,' replied Rubius.

'He has spent a small fortune to gain that favour.'

'The cost is a small tear in the vast ocean that is his wealth. Crassus is a man of considerable resources.' Rubius finished talking, his attention switching from the thousands of men preparing for war, to that of a single group of riders. At the lead of those riders a rider was resplendent in gold armour which shone in the morning sun. 'It seems Mithridates has dressed for the occasion.'

'My king merely wishes to inspire the men.'

'I imagine the treasure they will gain from this task would be enough inspiration.' It was the shorter of the two Romans, Victus, who now spoke.

Democolese felt that the Roman had insulted the honour of his men but before he could respond Mithridates arrived.

'Ah, Rubius, preparations go well I see?' Mithridates inquired.

'The army nears the point of readiness.' Rubius bowed his head in honour of the king.

'There really is no need for you and your men to accompany the army. Or does Crassus expect us to steal away his prize?'

'The senator merely wishes to hear first hand of your inevitable victory. Besides, Crassus is a fastidious man and likes to know where his wealth has been spent.'

'We should all be careful of the things we cherish. Tell me, Rubius, does Crassus care so little for his bastard son that he is prepared to see him die in a foreign land?'

Mithridates revelled in the shock portrayed by Rubius. 'Crassus is not the only man with agents, Rubius.'

'Crassus believes that all men must make their own way in this world, blood counts for nought.'

'By the gods! What a ridiculous idea! Blood is all that matters. Kings are born, Rubius, and those that were born in shit, will die in shit!'

'Indeed, my king.' Rubius recovered his calmness. 'Nonetheless, in Rome we have no kings and so must muddle along the best we can.' Sarcasm can be a dangerous trait, but Mithridates simply laughed off the reply.

'King or senator it matters little, Rubius, if plans fail. I understand that Pompey intends to stop our endeavours?'

'A feeble attempt to assemble a mercenary army. A few thousand men will not prove a problem. Pompey has failed as will his men.'

'Good and what of our other plan?'

'Victus will cross into Armenian lands this very night.'

Mithridates looked at the squat Roman; he seemed to be making a mental judgement. Then a moment later the studious look turned into a beaming smile. 'Very well, let the hunt begin. I look forward to you bringing glory to my name, Rubius.'

The king nodded and rode away, accompanied by the cheering of the troops.

Chapter Six

The following day five hundred men led by Victus crossed into the lands of Armenia. To the untrained eye these were men serving in the legions of Rome. The armour and weaponry matched and all marched in step beneath one single standard. The five hundred men had travelled for less than half a day when they spied the small village.

The local inhabitants were not unduly concerned, soldiers often passed through the village and it offered a chance to enhance their income. Furthermore, there was no war with Rome and the village was of no strategic importance. The children of the village darted in and out of the ranks of men, laughing and pulling faces at the fighting men who never broke their focus. At the front of the column, Victus rode a white horse which only aided his attempt at self importance. An elderly woman sensing an opportunity took a skin of wine and strode to the man she perceived would be most likely to have spare coin. She uttered words that Victus did not understand and then held the wine aloft. Victus smiled and took the wine and quickly allowed it to wash the dryness of the day from his throat. He had been in these lands a short time and already he had developed a loathing for its climate. Victus threw a couple of coins with the former Emperor's head emblazoned upon them to the woman. The old woman attempted to catch her reward but was too slow and they landed in the dirt. She hurriedly bent in case any other tried to claim what was rightfully her prize. She smiled as the cold metal finally rested in her palm. She was still showing her delight as she rose to stand when the blade struck, flesh from shoulder to hip torn apart.

As the woman's blood drenched the dirt around her now unmoving form, the remainder of the village descended into madness. Screams mixed with the scraping of blade from scabbard.

'Kill them all!' Victus ordered calmly, though his eyes portrayed his excitement. His men obeyed his order with terrible efficiency. The men of the village tried in vain to either defend their loved ones or shepherd their families to safety. Heavy footsteps closed on all those seeking to escape the bloodshed; their calls for mercy cut short by the slash of a gladius. Men, women and children shared the same fate, torn from the world of man by relentless butchery.

At the far end of the village, one man stood against the Romans and had already sent two men sprawling never to rise. This had given him time to guide his wife and child beyond the perimeter of the village. Nonetheless, they would require more time to be clear of danger. With a heavy heart he kissed those that he loved and sent them sobbing upon their way. The villager had fought many battles and had hoped to live out his days in peace. Resigned to his fate he turned his bloodied sword in hand and waited for death. It would not be long before the first attacker rushed towards him; it was a foolish approach with little thought to the quality of the defender. A blade was ripped upwards taking the attacker through the chin, face and skull. The defender without ceremony withdrew his weapon and prepared to meet further attackers that now approached with more caution. For some time he defended the blows from two enemies but eventually a blade struck at his thigh. The man slashed down with his blade and took the hand from his opponent. The cut to the thigh slowed his movement; on seeing this, the Roman charged with his heavy shield and both attacker and defender were sent sprawling to the floor. The villager punched with all his might smashing the throat of his assailant, causing him to choke and gasp for breath.

The villager now free from his enemy's grasping hands tried to rise, but as he did so a blade ripped into his back. The man knew his time was at an end; he looked to the horizon and spied his family disappearing from view. He smiled and closed his eyes before four more blades tore through his flesh.

Eventually the screams of the village had fallen silent. Only the crackle of fire on timbers could be heard as the homes of the slaughtered were put to the torch. Victus sat on his mount and surveyed his work with delight. To his front a soldier bent to collect the coins next to the old woman's body.

'Leave them.' Victus paused. 'The wine quenched my thirst, it is only fair that she receive proper payment.'

The soldier was confused by his officer's words but had learned not to question an order, no matter how foolish. Eventually, all the soldiers returned to their original formation and waited for further orders.

Victus swelled with self-importance. 'Men, you have done well today, but our task is not yet complete. I wish we had more time to celebrate our success but we must depart with all haste.'

'What about our dead?' asked one of the senior soldiers.

'Our mission slows for no man, they remain where they fell.' Victus urged his mount forward as he finished speaking. Victus knew that if the plan was to work then all that stumbled across the forlorn village must know who was responsible.

As Victus and his men moved from the village their victims lay bleeding on the ground. The deceased were guilty of no crime but merely expendable innocents in the games of the powerful.

***

Adrianicus led the army away from the port, an action that caused only disappointment in the many whores who had delighted in the chance to earn a great deal of coin.

Spartacus and Cassian remained fifty paces beyond the Roman. 'You do realise that most of our troops cannot communicate with one another,' Spartacus stated.

'That is a concern,' replied Cassian, 'but our numbers are greater than we ever expected. Furthermore, they looked like they have seen many battles. Experienced troops will be needed on this mission.'

Spartacus could not argue Cassian's point. The various troops from around the known world did seem to be warriors forged on battlefields. Deep down the former gladiator knew that these men would make an effective fighting force, although he was loathed to admit to that fact.

'These men may have worth, Cassian, but I see no cavalry or archers.'

'You did not have those when you led the slave army.'

'I had slingers, besides you forget one important thing.'

'What is that?'

'The slaves that fought alongside me are no longer in this world.'

'The Parthians will provide both archer and horsemen.' The voice came from behind Spartacus and Cassian. 'And the quality of both will be a test for any Mithridates sends against us.'

'If they make an appearance, Sikarbaal,' replied Spartacus.

'They will join us. The Parthians are in essence honourable in their dealings. They kill each other with frequency but it is seen as bad form not to honour a deal once it has been struck.'

'Then they had best arrive in all haste. It takes time to mould men into an effective fighting force and any delay may spell disaster.'

'I have heard many tales of your great exploits leading the slave army, Spartacus. If there is a man in the known world that the gods would allow to achieve such greatness again, it would be you. I doubted Adrianicus when he said this task was achievable, but with you at our lead that doubt is turning to hope.'

Spartacus was shocked by the compliment, especially from an individual that had previously been an annoyance to the former gladiator. Spartacus made to reply but words failed him and so he simply nodded his gratitude at the praise.

Cassian smiled at his friend's discomfort but chose silence rather than taking the chance to tease the warrior.

The remainder of the day was spent marching. These were toughened warriors from around the known world and no stranger to hardship. Nonetheless, with the heat generated from the relentless sun coupled with the necessity to wear full armour in a foreign land, even these men felt the energy sap from their rapidly tiring bodies. Dust rose from the beaten track to sting the eyes but no warrior would waste precious water to wash away the invasive dirt. When at last the sun began to dip beyond the horizon, the sky turned to vibrant amber and the beasts fell to silence. Men looked to their officers and hoped for pity, yearning to hear the order for camp to be made. Finally that precious command was given and greeted along the column with sighs of relief.

Cynna and Chia left their wagons and approached Spartacus and it was the wife of the gladiator that broached the subject of leaving the camp. 'We want to gather wood for the fire and perhaps find some wild berries.'

'Tend to the children. It is too dangerous to roam these lands.'

'The children are well cared for and we have been in those wagons for too long. Our legs grow stiff with the cramped conditions, besides we need to be useful, Spartacus.' Though her words were asking for permission, her face was set and prepared for an argument.

Spartacus knew that Cynna was in no mood to be swatted away like a troublesome fly.

'Stay close to the column. Do not stray beyond our scouts.'

'Still worried about my safety after all these years?' Cynna's face softened into a loving smile.

'I am concerned for whoever may attack you. No man deserves that fate,' replied Spartacus finally managing a grin.

Cynna stuck her tongue out at the warrior and received a playful slap to the behind as punishment.

Spartacus watched the two women making their way through the camp.

Before the women could disappear from view Spartacus signalled for two of the black clad warriors to come closer. 'Those two women, you will ensure their safety.' He paused and then added, 'At a discreet distance.'

'We do not follow your orders. I will see what Sika—'

The man's reply was cut violently short. A blade was at his throat in the blink of an eye. The man was forced to look directly into the eyes of Spartacus.

'You will do as I say or you will not draw another breath. Do you understand?'

'Yes,' replied the warrior. His tone now held no malice only fear.

'Then you had best run along.'

'Spartacus!' The voice came from behind the great warrior and he was forced to turn from his observation of the two black clad warriors scampering away. Sikarbaal and another man were advancing in his direction making Spartacus wonder if Sikarbaal had seen the altercation with some of his men.

Sikarbaal smiled and that smile contained genuine warmth. 'Spartacus this is Cleomenes,' he said with enthusiasm.

Spartacus was surprised to see Sikarbaal in a state of excitement and also felt awkward that the mentioning of Sikarbaal's companion's name should actually mean something.

That awkward moment vanished when the unknown warrior burst into laughter. 'I see my name has not yet earned the same status as yours, Spartacus. Maybe on this mission I may remove the normality of my name.'

'Forgive me you have me at a loss,' Spartacus replied unsure of how to respond.

'Spartacus this is Cleomenes,' Sikarbaal interrupted, but seeing the still blank expression upon Spartacus' face added, 'direct descendant of the mighty Leonidas of Sparta.'

'You're a Spartan?'

'The gods have bestowed that honour upon me. Alas, they have showed little favour to my people in many years.'

'Nonetheless, a Spartan warrior is worth many on the battlefield,' replied Spartacus.

'We have more than one, Spartacus.' Sikarbaal was almost hopping with joy. 'We have five hundred to add to our ranks.'

Spartacus too felt the excitement being experienced by Sikarbaal. The centuries may not have been kind to the state of Sparta, but its troops were still respected and feared by much of the known world.

'Calm yourself, Sikarbaal we are just men.' Cleomenes said. 'It is a long time since Spartan troops made the enemy tremble at the mere sight of us joining the battle.'

'Then together, Cleomenes, we shall restore that fear,' Spartacus said and could not believe that the words had left his mouth. Nonetheless, he could remember his own father telling him as a boy of the great exploits of Leonidas and other warriors of Sparta. He held out an arm for Cleomenes to grasp in friendship.

'That we will and send our enemies on that sorrow-filled journey to the next world. Even Charon will curse our names for sending him so many to carry across the Styx.'

'Spartacus, where are the two guards I posted here?' asked Sikarbaal.

'They were here to guard me? I sent them to watch over the women as they gather wood for the fires,' replied Spartacus.

'Good ... good. I shall carry on with my duties. I am sure you and Cleomenes have lots to discuss.' Sikarbaal turned and walked away without waiting for a reply.

CHAPTER SEVEN

Two men picked their way through the small undergrowth and restrictive tree cover, as they did their eyes never left the two women two paces to their front.

'You saw the speed of the man. We haven't a chance of killing Spartacus and getting clear of the army,' the shorter of the two men whispered.

'We were not ordered to kill the man. Our orders were to stop him from leading this poor excuse of a fighting force.'

For a moment the taller of the men turned to stare at his friend. 'What are you saying? Do not talk in bloody riddles, we face real danger here and need a plan.'

'You have seen him, quick and strong. If that was not bad enough the man is alert at all times. As a warrior it would be difficult to find a weakness but as a man his vulnerability is plain for all to see. Whenever that woman is close, Spartacus is more blushing boy than warrior. Kill the woman and you destroy the man.'

The other man looked to his front at the laughing Cynna. 'It will be some time before they are missed and it has been a long time since I felt a woman beneath me.' He smiled as the mind provided illustration to his cravings.

'Don't be a damn fool. Your cock can wait for its pleasure. We need to be clear of the scouts before their bodies are found.'

***

Back at the column, Sikarbaal had quickened his pace. He spied Plinius applying a keen edge to a particularly lethal looking blade.

'Plinius, forgive me but your women, which way did they go?'

'Towards those trees.' Plinius pointed. 'Why?' Plinius had risen to his feet sensing that Chia may be in trouble. 'What is going on?'

'Follow me,' were the only words Sikarbaal uttered in reply as he set off at pace.

Plinius was at his side. In moments as was Tictus, who had seen his friend moving at speed. He would not be found wanting when those he cared about faced danger.

Moments later the three burst into the trees which slowed their progress. However, it gave them the opportunity to listen for an indication to Chia and Cynna's location. Suddenly, the unmistakeable sound of a body smashing through the undergrowth could be heard approaching their position.

Chia emerged to their front with a frantic look upon her face.

'Chia!' Plinius cried rushing forwards.

'Cynna!' She breathed heavily. 'You must help Cynna.'

Her legs gave way and Plinius only just managed to reach her falling body before she crashed to the leaf strewn dirt.

'What happened?' Sikarbaal asked trying not to look at Chia's breast as it protruded through the torn tunic. He had noticed Chia around the camp, her beauty had captivated him but on realising she was Plinius' woman he had made a point to stay clear.

'Two men attacked us, but Cynna knocked one senseless with a rock. We broke free and ran but the other man was gaining on us so Cynna made me hide and she drew the man's attention. I waited for the opportunity to break from my hiding place. Please you must help her.'

'Take her back to camp, Plinius, we will find Cynna.' Sikarbaal was a natural leader and so his order was delivered with confidence. Plinius did not question the order because although he wished to see Cynna safe his priority was ensuring Chia's safety.

Sikarbaal took off further into the trees. They were moving with speed but with enough caution to enable any detection from the enemy. They had not been travelling long when Tictus spotted a figure upon the ground. They approached steadily and as silently as the woodland floor would allow. Sikarbaal recognise the figure almost immediately as one of the men he had posted to guard Spartacus. The fallen man was showing signs of waking despite a nasty wound to the side of his head.

'Stay with him, Tictus. Be careful he's a slippery bastard.'

'Oh, that will not be a problem,' replied Tictus. The young man threw out a fist catching the waking man in the jaw. The blow sent the man once more back into darkness.

Sikarbaal moved forward knowing that Cynna may already be dead and the person responsible could well be beyond any justice that he could bestow. He pressed on. From time to time he would stop his progress to listen. The rustle of the branches in the pitiful breeze and a beast moving through the undergrowth were all that came freely to his ears. Then some kind of hawk screeched some unknown displeasure high above. The suddenness of the sound made Sikarbaal reach for his blade until he realised the source. He was about to relax when in the distance he heard another scream. He picked up the pace disregarding previous caution.

'Whore!' The man screamed his hatred.

'Fuck you!' Cynna replied defiantly.

A fist answered her disobedience knocking her savagely to the floor. 'When I have finished with you, Spartacus will not know which end is head and which is tail.'

'You best be quick. If Spartacus catches you, the world will see you for the snivelling coward you are. When you face a real man you will piss and cry your way to the next world.'

The attacker moved forward his anger beginning to rule his actions; his right hand clenched a dagger. He so wanted to hurt this woman and end her arrogance. The attack faltered as his momentum was halted as Cynna's knee made contact with the man's groin. He took a moment trying hard to fight back the agony that coursed through his body. Then slowly he took a deep breath and straightened his back.

'You fucking bitch.' His voice trembled. He made to move forward again but this time it was the coldness of a blade at his throat that stopped him.

'If I was you, I would drop the dagger.'

'Sikarbaal I—' The words were cut short as he was spun around to face his former superior. A fist smashed into the bridge of his nose causing him to yell with pain.

Sikarbaal looked passed the injured man to Cynna. 'Are you harmed?'

'Never better.' She smiled then walked forward and kicked her attacker once more between the legs.

Her victim crumpled to the floor but his chance at nursing his injuries was short lived as a laughing Sikarbaal pulled him to his feet. 'I am sure Spartacus will want to meet you.'

***

The morning sun greeted the waking troops. The previous day's event had kept many of those soldiers talking late into the night. The excitement soon returned when each man was told to take position on the slopes of a small hillside. The gods had seen fit to create a natural arena with the hillside sweeping around a flat piece of ground. As the men filtered onto the hillside they could see two men both of which had thick ropes tied tightly about their hands.

Adrianicus approached Cassian shaking his head in dismay. 'Why does Spartacus not just kill these men and be done with it?'

'He would not be dissuaded,' replied Cassian.

'Then try again.'

'You should learn an important fact about Spartacus. If his mind is set and a path chosen only death will prevent him from continuing on that journey.'

'But this is madness.' Adrianicus could see no point to Spartacus' plan.

'I agree. Adrianicus, you and I are mere mortals. Spartacus is a legend in his own lifetime. That status has been bestowed upon him by the gods for it is clear to me that he has not craved power or glory. If we are to survive this task Pompey has placed before us, we must use all our resources and be of no doubt that Spartacus is our best hope.' Cassian finished speaking just as the crowd erupted in cheers.

A figure devoid of a weapon, armour or even clothing had entered the arena. Cynna and Chia had also taken their place in the crowd but could not see the figure so they pushed and weaved their way into a better position. They finally reached the front, Chia stopping dead in her tracks.

'Oh, my.' She gasped quickly before raising a hand to her mouth to hide the shock.

Cynna smiled. 'Spartacus is a good man, Chia, but as you can see he has other qualities.'

Spartacus had entered the arena naked, his bronzed body showing signs of battle. The men admired the scars and the women admired his prowess. The crowd began to quieten all waiting for Spartacus to speak.

'Many of you have fought at my side, others know of my deeds. I, like many, stood against the tyranny of Rome.' Some of the crowd cheered, others shifted uneasily from foot to foot. 'My entire life has been filled with blood and pain. Loved ones and friends have been taken from me by those that seek power. Today I say no more. I stand before you in defiance of those wishing to take what I hold dear in my heart. These two men wished to kill the woman that I love. They did not have the bravery or honour to stand before me and challenge me with a blade. There may be others within this crowd who may wish to harm those close to me.

'I give clear warning, no empire, nation or state will protect a man that succeeds in such a task. If your intentions are corrupt you have one opportunity and that opportunity is now. You may leave this very day and face no reprisals, but be warned if you stay and are determined to commit treachery, your punishment will become clear.' Spartacus paused and nodded to Tictus and Plinius. Both men stepped forward and cut the bonds of the prisoners, then after retiring a safe distance, threw a blade to each.

'We should go,' Cynna whispered to Chia.

'I have seen men die before, Cynna and both of these men are deserving of nothing but death.'

'Chia, these men will not just die. Spartacus is sending a message and it will be brutal and unrelenting. This time would be better spent with our children.'

'I want to stay,' replied the determined Chia.

'Very well.' Cynna moved back through the crowd as her husband began to speak once more.

'Kill me and win your freedom, but if you fall do not expect mercy.'

The prisoners had little choice, escape was impossible. Besides, two armed men against an opponent without a weapon was at least an opportunity for freedom.

The men bent and collected the blades lying in the dust. They were no stranger to battle and so each felt that surge of confidence as their hands closed around the hilt of a weapon. Both prepared to attack, crouching low, each trying to determine the best way to slaughter the naked man before them.

The taller of the two men was first to make his move, he darted forward quickly but the swipe with his blade was clumsy. Spartacus slipped by the blade and then with tremendous speed drove a thumb into his attacker's eye socket. The crowd gave a united wince knowing the agony that blow would have caused and then cheered Spartacus' skill. The second prisoner took the opportunity to slash at Spartacus; the blow opened a small cut on the gladiator's forearm. Cassian tensed, fearing that Spartacus had misjudged the situation. His friend, however, acted as though the wound did not exist. He turned with amazing speed and disarmed the attacker in one movement. The prisoner dived from harm's way knowing he could not defeat Spartacus without a blade. He reached for the blade but a powerful foot came crashing down breaking bone at the point of impact. Spartacus was in no mood for mercy; he reached down and pulled the man to his feet. Another powerful blow broke the prisoner's ribs, blood shot from the unfortunate man's mouth. His fate would be delayed, for his comrade had overcome the pain and fear of losing an eye and now advanced once more on Spartacus. Like a fool, the taller prisoner screamed as he attacked which only acted as a warning. The weapon thrust was caught in mid manoeuvre, the gladiator holding the wrist of the prisoner. A hand again shot forward, the resulting scream left the crowd in no doubt that the prisoner had been relieved of his remaining eye. Spartacus moved away leaving distance between himself and his enemy.

'Do you see what happens to those that threaten my family?' he asked the crowd, turning full circle so all would see the intent on his face. 'Fight by my side and be as a brother. Honour begets honour, in treachery lies only death.' He rushed forward and brought a powerful elbow down on the collarbone of the prisoner who nursed his ribs. The recipient collapsed to the ground unable to gather the strength to remain standing. Spartacus collected a fallen weapon, the blade of which still shone unblemished by the spilling blood. The now blind prisoner stumbled around, arms outstretched pleading for mercy.

Spartacus flicked the blade and removed the blind man's hands. Ignoring the screams again he spoke. 'There will be only death.'

He removed the blind man's head with one stroke, the crowd cheered. Without delay Spartacus crossed to the other prisoner, grasped him by the hair and promptly delivered a killing blow.

The crowds erupted and then slowly at first a name was heard. The intensity of the chanting grew and suddenly the name Spartacus was being shouted from every section of the arena.

'You just cannot bet against the man. All warriors just love him,' Cassian shouted to Adrianicus above the cheering.

'Let us hope that his cause remains ours,' replied Adrianicus.

'Be true with Spartacus and you will have a great man at your side. Trickery will not endear him towards you, Adrianicus.'

'You place too much stock in this man, Cassian.'

'I pay him the respect he has earned. You would do well to follow my example.'

Adrianicus' false smile returned. 'Of course, I would have it no other way.'

CHAPTER EIGHT

Victus emerged from a small hut, the smile on his lips accompanied with a flushed redness to his cheeks. He gave a satisfied backward look across his shoulder into the interior of the building. 'A fine woman. These lands have promise.'

The unmistakeable whimpering of a female could be heard within the meagre home.

A young soldier smiled. 'Are we taking her with us?'

'Whatever for? Burn her, burn everything.'

Screams rose from another village. The terrified sounds hung like a morose fog just beyond the reach of man. Only the flames from both building and corpse rose to meet them. With a voracious appetite the fire consumed the woes of the innocent.

Victus struggled to climb aboard his mount; his earlier exertions had sapped the energy from his knees. Once seated he scanned the village. 'Men, our raids are at an end. Tonight we will make camp and enjoy a fine feast in honour of all we have achieved.'

The men cheered his words and Victus allowed their adoration to soak into each and every one of his sinews. Then he saluted them and the order went up for all to prepare to leave. The column of men reformed and set off at a brisk pace. Victus took one last look at the forlorn village and smiled.

It did not take long for the destroyers of the innocent to find the pre-arranged place to camp. Victus was in fine form laughing and joking with many of the men. He made sure all had a good meal and plenty of wine. Finally when he was certain he could slip away unnoticed, he moved towards the shadows. The guards were not a problem; after all they were looking for dangers from beyond the perimeter. They would never have guessed that a man would be attempting to leave the safety of the camp.

Victus eventually broke through the trees into a small clearing. His eyes searched the outskirts of the open land until at last they came to rest on a single figure.

'Forgive me. I came as quickly as stealth would permit.'

'I trust you encountered little resistance?'

'The villages succumbed easily enough with the loss of just a few men,' replied Victus trying hard not to show his pleasure.

'The news of your success has already begun to filter through the countryside and local populace.'

'Just following orders, Rubius.'

'Following orders? You were instructed to burn villages and make example of a number of individuals, only.' Rubius' tone had changed from pleasant to one which now seemed aggravated.

'I thought it prudent to generate both fear and hatred,' replied Victus defensively.

'I do not wish you to think, if the results are nothing but bloody slaughter.'

'They were villagers and of no importance.' Victus could not understand why Rubius was so upset.

'If this ruse is discovered and the people of these lands find out the real culprits of the crime then you have guaranteed our destruction. A burned village can be paid for with coin but the slaughter of women and children, demands a higher cost.' It was not the real reason why Rubius was so angered by Victus but he did not want his second in command to think him weak.

'Forgive me, Rubius. I acted with the best of intentions.'

'I have prepared your next task.' Rubius handed over a scroll. 'You will safeguard a river crossing. May I suggest you follow these orders.' The words were spoken calmly enough; nonetheless, the threat was clearly there.

Victus nodded his obedience, turned and walked away without uttering a single word. He trampled through the undergrowth fighting back the anger burning within. He approached one of his own guards, who was clearly sleeping at his post.

'What the fuck are you doing?' Victus kicked the man from his resting position.

'I...' His words were cut short.

Victus struck the man as he tried to stand and then kicked out. The guard screamed out his agony as his nose exploded in blood and mucus. The scream must have alerted those men sober enough to care as shouts and footsteps could be heard in the distance. Victus pulled the sentry to his feet the volcanic anger within still not abating. He punched the man again and again until the unfortunate recipient slipped into unconsciousness. Men arrived from the camp, confusion etched upon all their faces.

'This man slept when he should be alert to any dangers that you all face. I will not have such dereliction to duty.' Victus let go of the man's tunic allowing him to slip to the floor. Victus looked to his men. 'I will not tolerate it.' He raised his heavily studded sandal and brought it smashing down on the man's unprotected skull. The foot was raised and smashed down no less than five times. The result was a bloodied pulp that had once been a man's head. Those who witnessed the act looked on in horror but not one man raised a voice in protest.

Victus looked at their faces and with his anger finally under control he smiled. 'I will need to bathe.' He paused. 'And then I suggest more wine.'

***

The column had been travelling for half a day with Spartacus taking the lead. Only the scouts were in advance of the veteran gladiator.

Cassian had to hurry to draw alongside. 'You seem deep in thought, old friend?'

Spartacus did not reply and Cassian was made to announce his arrival by placing a gentle hand on the warrior's shoulder. 'Sorry, Cassian.' Spartacus seemed to lurch from the deep realms of his mind. 'I think it would be best if you asked Adrianicus to join us.'

'There's a problem?'

'We seem to have some new friends.' He nodded in a direction. 'Just beyond that ridge. I have seen riders trailing our progress.'

'Friend or foe?' asked Cassian.

'Too far to be certain, but then in these lands who can be certain of anything, no matter the distance?'

'I will fetch, Adrianicus.' Cassian made to move out at speed but Spartacus caught him gently by the arm.

'We do not know how closely they watch our ranks. I would have them believe we are an organised force. Do not rush and let all our unit leaders know without causing a panic.' Spartacus spoke with confidence, which comforted Cassian who, despite his prowess with a blade, still did not consider himself a warrior.

Cassian moved away his attempt at looking casual, causing Spartacus to erupt in laughter.

'What?'

'I doubt you will make a living in the theatre, Cassian.' Spartacus continued to laugh.

'Bollocks,' Cassian replied as he strode away.

It did not take long before Adrianicus was at Spartacus' shoulder. 'It could be the Parthians,' he suggested.

'Or Armenian, then again it might be troops loyal to Pontus.' Spartacus spat on the ground. 'This is a fool's mission.'

Adrianicus was annoyed by the gladiator's comments but refrained from replying. He turned and called for a mount.

'What do you think you are doing?' asked Spartacus.

'We need to know to whom these riders owe their allegiance.'

'By getting a sword in your gut?'

'If that is the case, try not to mourn my death too deeply.' Adrianicus gave a cheeky smile then urged his mount towards the unknown force beyond the ridge.

'Bloody idiot,' Spartacus called after the man. Although in truth he could not help feeling admiration for Adrianicus' bravery. Spartacus knew that if the riders did prove to be hostile then the Roman would be a dead man with no hope of survival.

Spartacus continued to watch Adrianicus until he disappeared over the ridge and out of view. He half expected to hear the sound of blade against blade and the mournful cry of a dying man. No sound came and after a brief pause Spartacus raised his hand and the troops marching to his rear came to a halt.

Cassian approached. 'What's the plan?'

Spartacus looked to the skies, his face a mask of concentration. He sighed. 'Prepare camp. Triple the scouts and the men are to remain fully armed at all times.'

'Is that all?'

'On each side of the camp I want fifty men battle ready. Make sure they are relieved regularly so all receive rest and nourishment. Best get Plinius and Cleomenes to help you organise the men.'

It was some time before the camp was fully established. The scouts had reported that the mysterious troops from beyond the ridge had completely vanished along with Adrianicus. A search party was formed but no sign of the Roman could be found. Not even a drop of blood to suggest he had encountered aggression of any sort.

Spartacus was forced to call a meeting of those he saw as natural leaders within the camp. As they gathered, many looked to Cassian for a decision of what to do next. Cassian however, looked to Spartacus. The gladiator suddenly felt isolation of leadership. It had been some time since he had commanded men and recently he had been content to enforce the decisions made by Cassian.

Spartacus cleared his throat and for a few moments looked at each of the men gathered about him. 'First, I must ask a question.' He turned to face a figure dressed in black. 'Sikarbaal, have you any information relating to the disappearance of Adrianicus? Why would he be so foolish to ride towards a force of unknown warriors?'

'If his actions were planned in advance then he did not make me aware of those plans.'

Spartacus eyed Adrianicus' man, looking for signs of deception.

Sikarbaal must have guessed the reason for the scrutiny and felt compelled to speak further. 'I have served Adrianicus for many years. In that time I have lied, stole and killed to fulfil his wishes. Nonetheless, I give my word for what it is worth. I have no explanation for his actions.'

'If that is true we have to accept that Adrianicus may be lost,' said Cassian.

'Or playing some sort of game,' replied Plinius. It was clear that the young warrior's adoration for Adrianicus was at an end.

'The fate of Adrianicus is beyond our control. We must decide on our next course of action,' added Spartacus.

'We carry on with our mission. Commagene still requires good men and Spartans are not farmers.' Cleomenes tapped his blade to emphasise the point.

'But who are we fighting? Who, if anyone, can we trust?' Spartacus paused, not wanting to sound desperate. He opened his mouth to speak again but a noise from the far end of the camp stopped the words. Spartacus jumped to his feet and raced in the direction of the disturbance. A scout on horseback was moving at great speed towards the gladiator. The rider launched himself from his mount covering the final few steps by foot. The man gasped struggling to fill his lungs with air.

'What news?' Spartacus asked his face showing his concern.

The scout took another breath. 'Riders,' he said then paused taking another breath, 'riders coming this way.'

'How many?'

'Thousands,' the scout replied, his fear evident.

'Well report, you bastard. Do they form for an attack?' Spartacus was rapidly losing his temper at the lack of information leaving the scout's mouth.

The scout's face seemed to change as though somewhere within his mind a new thought had emerged. 'No,' he said timidly, 'they are just ambling towards us in column.'

'What do you want us to do, Spartacus?' Cassian asked as he moved to Spartacus' shoulder.

The answer was not immediate. The old gladiator looked into the distance and then to the skies. 'Nothing.' His reply was brief.

'Spartacus?' Cassian failed to understand the answer.

'If they meant to attack they would already be bearing down upon us.'

'You think they are friends to our cause?'

'I did not say that. I simply believe that at this moment they have no intention of destruction. We must ensure our sentries are not too nervous. Pass the word that no aggressive acts are to take place without orders. Gather our officers and prepare a tent to give welcome to our guests.'

'It will be done,' replied Cassian.

Spartacus called for a mount. He would take a closer look at the threat.

***

Cassian had arranged the tent in the very centre of the camp. He was just adding the final additions to its presentation when a shout of warning emanated from the far side of the camp. He looked towards the disturbance but his concentration was disrupted by a deep growl of a voice.

'I hope Spartacus knows what he is doing. Spartans do not like to sit around on their arses and wait to be slaughtered.'

Cassian looked at the man; he had not been introduced to the Spartan leader but could not help being annoyed at the man's questioning of his friend's judgment. 'Look to your own failings. Spartacus will not falter,' he snapped.

Cleomenes held up his hands in mock defence. 'Quell your anger. I meant no disrespect.'

Cassian realised that he had been too quick to lose his temper. 'Forgive me, I am no soldier and ill suited to its trials.' He walked into the tent to join Sikarbaal, Cleomenes followed.

'Nonsense, you may not know me, Cassian, but I am all too aware of your exploits. Besides, any man that Spartacus calls friend must first have earned that honour.'

Any response from Cassian was cut short because Spartacus stepped into the tent. 'Our guest will be here soon. Adrianicus rides at their front.'

'Then it seems we have more allies to swell our ranks. I shall inform the guard.' Sikarbaal made to act on his words.

'Hold your ground, Sikarbaal. Adrianicus may well be at their lead but as yet, we do not know why. We must all remain alert until we are certain of the facts.'

Sikarbaal returned to his original position. Spartacus seemed compelled to explain his decision. 'Adrianicus may find himself forced to carry out the bidding of an enemy. Or a more sinister reason may be behind his reason to lead that column.' Spartacus did not elaborate but all within the tent knew he suggested that Adrianicus might have turned traitor. An awkward silence fell on those present, a silence that did not lift until a guard entered.

'Three men approach the camp, Spartacus.' The guard did not wait to be asked his news, he had learned that the former gladiator had no patience for the usual soldiering protocol.

Spartacus glanced around at the men around him. 'Shall we see what the gods have delivered?' He did not wait for an answer but immediately exited the tent. Those within followed and believed they would walk to the exterior of the camp, but Spartacus only went a few steps before stopping.

'Are we waiting here?' asked Cassian.

'Apparently I am commander of this army. So they come to me,' replied Spartacus.

***

The three riders travelled alone, the troops they commanded held their ground just beyond the camp's perimeter.

The warriors that Spartacus commanded however, watched with a nervous interest. They knew one rider but the other two were strangers and both rode without fear despite being so far from their own men. Spartacus also watched the riders approach, his focus mainly on Adrianicus. He wondered if the Roman had betrayed the army.

The riders came to a halt to Spartacus' front and for a moment, a heavy silence settled on the camp.

'We thought you were lost, Adrianicus,' Spartacus stated.

'Forgive me, but a matter of great importance arose which required my immediate attention,' Adrianicus replied.

'It seems our enemies have been slaughtering the inhabitants of villages. Those that survived claimed the attackers wore the uniform of Romans. I needed to ensure that my allies were not responsible for those atrocities.' The reply did not come from Adrianicus but from the youngest of the riders. Although, he was young he spoke with a confidence not usually attached to one who looked so raw.'

'Your people?'

'I am Tigranes of Tigranes the Elder who rules as far as the eye can see and beyond. I am used to my subjects bowing in my presence but I suppose we can dispense with the usual formalities.'

'I am honoured to play your host.' Spartacus paused. 'However, I am a free man and the time has passed that I bend a knee to any man.'

'I see the rumours of Spartacus are correct. Quick with tongue and blade and a back that will not yield.' The third man entered the conversation.

'And you are?'

'Just a humble Parthian obeying his masters.'

'These are important men, Spartacus,' interrupted Adrianicus.

'Look around you, each man within this camp has worth.'

'Then let us drink to those men. We have much to discuss and I fear little time to do it.' Tigranes dismounted as he spoke.

Spartacus nodded his agreement and inwardly admired the young Tigranes. So many men of his standing were content to bathe in pomp and ceremony but the young ruler seemed to prefer action and plain speaking. The gladiator looked to the perimeter and smiled. His army would welcome the column of riders. They would provide mobility to his force and the bows would bring death to his enemies.

He may not have numbers on his side but soon he would test the warriors of Pontus.

Chapter Nine

The wine was poured and all stood in anticipation for someone to speak. Adrianicus cleared his throat. 'Mithridates does not travel with his army. Nonetheless, the numbers of our enemy are impressive. We will need to be creative to ensure victory.'

'How many do we face?' asked Cassian.

'At least three to one in their favour and their ranks threaten to swell to an even greater number.'

'Then we need to bring them to battle at the earliest opportunity.' As Spartacus spoke he focussed his attention on a map to his front. 'This river, how many days march is it?'

Tigranes stepped forward. 'Three at most and we shall arrive before the enemy, even if they march through the night.'

Spartacus nodded his gratitude but continued to study the map. His finger traced the meandering line to the point where a small crossing was shown on the papyrus. 'This could be troublesome. We need to remove the opportunity for our enemy to outflank us.'

The Parthian now decided to speak. 'It is news of that bridge that my scouts report. The force responsible for putting the villages to the torch has left the main enemy camp. As we speak they are heading towards that small crossing.'

'I thought you took Adrianicus because you were not sure who attacked the villagers?'

'The reports arrived after Adrianicus became our guest. They clearly see the crossing to be important to their plans.'

'Thank you.' Spartacus paused suddenly aware that he did not know the man's name.

Tigranes obviously guessed why Spartacus had faltered. 'This is Balen commander of our allied Parthian troops, evidence of Parthia's support for our cause.'

'Only if we are victorious. If defeat is our fate then we do not exist.' The Parthian smiled ruefully.

'Then we had best gain victory for all our sakes,' replied Spartacus.

'So we stop them at the bridge?' asked Adrianicus.

'The bridge would slow their advance and diminish the advantage of numbers,' added Cassian.

'That would be my usual course of action, but their numbers are growing. We need a quick victory. I plan to take the fight to them but the bridge will provide a fallback position if not all goes well. We can even destroy the bridge and force our enemy into days of marching using valuable resources and energy,' Spartacus announced.

'Even longer if that smaller crossing is destroyed.' Tigranes paused. 'I have confidence in your plan with the exception of the smaller crossing.'

'We cannot allow it to stand.'

'You misunderstand my intention. The bridge should be destroyed but the enemy force being sent to capture it must first face retribution for their actions. My people demand that I take action for their loss.'

Spartacus studied Tigranes and recognised a determination to see his orders carried out. 'Balen, how many of the enemy move on the smaller crossing?'

'Initial reports put their number between four and five hundred men. All of which are infantry,' the Parthian replied confident of his facts.

Spartacus took his time and studied the map at great length. Finally, he looked up at the men around him. 'We will destroy the bridge and the enemy. Balen have you a few spare mounts?'

'We are Parthian, Spartacus, we prefer the company of horse flesh to that of our women.'

'That leaves all the more for me.' Lathyrus barked with laughter. The tension in the room broke and it did not take long until song was raised with a little aid of fine wine, compliments of Tigranes. Lathyrus as usual told his tales of adventure and of the beautiful women that he had bedded. The importance of those around him did not diminish his bravado and the old sailor brought more than one blush to the young ruler's cheeks. Eventually all stumbled back to their own tents. Children laughed and lovers playfully scolded their arrival, the day that had offered confusion and fear had succumbed to night and at least a little joy.

***

Spartacus and those that would accompany him on the mission set out at first light. The gladiator's head still swam from the effects of too much wine the previous night. Nonetheless, they moved with speed and covered the ground with a relentless determination.

Within a few days, they had crossed the great river via the small bridge and sent scouts in search of the enemy. Spartacus ordered fifty men to prepare the bridge for destruction; he ordered a quick meal and then the main force moved down the small track which was away from the crossing.

They had been travelling for some time before Cassian spoke. 'Do you think it wise to leave so many men at the bridge? The enemy will be nearly twice our number.'

Before Spartacus could reply to Cassian's question Balen gave a short bark of a laugh and then asked a question of his own. 'Tell me, Cassian, why do you think my people have never bent a knee to your mighty empire?'

'I am not a military man.'

'And neither are you a foolish man. Look at my men, cast your gaze to the weapons that we favour.'

Cassian looked at the curved bow, the likes of which he had not seen before. 'Are all Parthians armed with such a bow?'

'Not all but many. The finest bows the gods have bestowed on men and the finest horseflesh to carry us like a storm towards our enemy. The Roman legions are formidable, but they are also slow and lack the fluid movement that my empire has to offer.'

'He means the legions would be slaughtered long before they could bring their power to bear,' added Spartacus.

'Your masters seek power. Why do they not simply invade Roman territory if they command such fine armies?' Cassian asked feeling a little defensive.

'Because of the same reasons, we would lose all our advantage. Defending their own lands means the legions would select where any battle would be fought. They would build their defences and our strengths would count for nothing. Gone would be our chance to strike at the enemy and retreat to a safe distance. Pompey understands, that is why he will not attack Parthia,' Balen said.

'Crassus would, he is blinded by wealth and the opportunity for military glory.'

'You know Crassus?'

'He has been trying to kill us for some time,' replied Cassian.

'But failed.' Balen laughed and slapped Cassian on the shoulder.

'Our number has been greatly reduced and we have lost many loved ones,' Cassian replied solemnly.

'I feel hatred for the man without ever meeting him. We have such men in our empire. They are a curse to any land that they occupy. He needs a blade in his gut and I would be happy to carry out such an act.'

Spartacus smiled at the Parthian's words. 'You could be killed in the stampede, many seek that honour.'

A scout moving at pace ended any further conversation. On his arrival he began to give Balen his report but the Parthian held up a hand to stop the scout from continuing. 'Your report should be made to Spartacus.'

The gladiator nodded his gratitude to Balen. It was a small gesture but left all the men present aware that there was only one leader.

The scout to his credit did not resist the change in command. 'The enemy are camped not far from here. Marching at their usual speed they will reach the bridge in less than two days.'

'This is not ideal, we will retreat,' announced Spartacus.

'Retreat?' Balen raised his eyebrows to emphasise his shock.

'We want to kill the enemy, Balen, but we also want to preserve our own numbers. To do that, we must choose where we fight carefully. There is a place on the trail behind us, which will provide the means to achieve our aims. The place I have in mind will offer protection and the ideal position to use those bows. If your men are as good as you say, the enemy will not have time to scratch their arses.'

Balen laughed. 'Lead the way, Spartacus.' The orders were given and the small column about-faced and moved back along the track.

***

Victus stretched and called for wine. He spat on the ground; his mood at being sent on the mission to capture the bridge had darkened. The mood made far worse by a night's sleep out in the open air. He'd shouted orders and even felled one of his men with a powerful punch for not responding with enough haste to an order. The orders continued to flow until at last every man was ready to move out.

The continuous riding had made his thighs raw and all he craved was to sink his weary body into water and forget the hardships of a long march. The small force lurched forward, only the sound of sandal on track broke the normality of the day. The men chose to march in silence, knowing Victus would like nothing more than to make an example of one of them. With each step the sun rose higher into the sky and as it did, so did the ferocity in which it burned. Armour was never the most comfortable but in these conditions it seemed to double in weight and any tender flesh would feel its rage. When the sun was at its highest Victus called for the men to rest. The act was not for their sakes for he had little empathy for the common soldier. He ordered water brought for his horse and as it drank, he climbed a small rise in the ground to observe the surrounding area. He scanned the horizon and it was not long before his gaze came to rest on a small homestead.

A woman bathed a child, unaware that she was under observation. Victus could also feel the refreshing liquid washing over his body, his tongue slid over his sun parched and cracked lips.

'You...' Victus could not remember the warrior's name. He shrugged; the man's name, after all, was unimportant. 'Do you know how to read a map?'

'Yes.' The reply came from a senior warrior who would have liked nothing more than to gut the arrogant bastard.

'Good.' Victus threw a scroll at the man. 'Take the men. I shall join you at the bridge.'

'You are leaving?'

'Scouting mission,' Victus lied.

'Is it wise to go alone?' The warrior did not want any blame should this fool get himself killed.

Victus was about to scold the man but then reconsidered. 'Give me your two best men.'

The veteran called out the names of two men.

It was not long before Victus and his bodyguard were moving away from the column.

The veteran warrior watched Victus and looked towards the small homestead. 'Scouting, eh? Lying bastard. I hope she cuts your cock off.'

***

The day wore on with the heat becoming increasingly more oppressive. The dust rose from the track as heavy sandals stamped their discontent. The veteran soldier stopped for a moment and walked to the rear of the column hoping to see Victus. He had been placed unceremoniously in command but he would willingly put his loathing for his officer aside to rejoin the ranks. He disliked giving commands, or rather, he disliked the responsibility. He removed his helmet and wiped some of the sweat from his brow. The first scream made him jump and then glanced frantically in the direction of the noise.

Any order he would have given was cut short as an arrow thudded into his cheek. The force of the impact threw him to the ground. Agony raced through his entire face and he added his own screams to those that now erupted from the small force. He tried to stand but another arrow struck him in the back. His world seemed to slow and he had time to think how strange it was that the second blow seemed to add no further pain.

He dropped to his knees, to see his men panic-stricken. As his eyes blurred all he could witness was the destruction of his comrades. He had grown used to the cries of pain but now another scream spilt the air. He knew this from an attacker keen to add yet more agony to their foe. Then the thundering of charging horses filled his ears as the enemy closed for the kill. The veteran allowed himself to slip to a fall; he knew that escape and survival were impossible. The wails of his men drifted away, as his mind forced itself to think on times passed. His hand moved slowly to wipe the blood from his eyes only to reveal the enemy standing above him. If he had met this man on the battlefield, he would have been filled with fear but this was no battle, merely a slaughter. The veteran looked at the man with no fear. For a moment they held a gaze. The enemy's eyes were not filled with anger but simply with resignation at a task which was to be completed. A blade was raised and then pushed down hard and the unwanted responsibility was taken from the veteran.

Chapter Ten

A child sat crying next to the body of its mother. Three men moved away from the scene of sorrow. Two of the men walked, the other sat upon a white horse. Although the men were different in almost every way inwardly, they all craved similar experiences to what had just occurred, they cared not for the fallen woman or a child that faced starvation. It was those thoughts that would keep them contented until they rejoined the column. Time had no meaning and the distance would be covered quickly and without complaint.

The three men were oblivious to their own aches and pain but more importantly to the warning signs which spelled possible danger. If they had focussed on their task, they may have noticed carrion birds circling in the sky above. The birds eyed a tasty meal; to them the slaughter was just an opportunity. Misery and death were of no importance, in that way they resembled Victus and his comrades. It was not until Victus rounded a severe bend that he saw the first body. The unfortunate soldier lay face down in the dirt; a large shaft had smashed through the helmet into the relatively soft skull.

'You!' Victus motioned to one of his men. 'Scout up ahead.'

The warrior looked physically shaken by the request but years of obedience would not be denied. He forced his legs forward; slowly he picked his way up the track.

Victus watched nervously as the man disappeared around another bend. Both he and the other bodyguard listened for the cry of a man in pain or the clash of a blade. No sound came and they waited for what seemed an age, suspended in a world of fear. Eventually a man stumbled into view, so unsteady on his feet was the distant figure, that Victus thought him to be injured. The figure then lurched forward and vomited. Victus looked on disbelieving that one man's guts could dispel so much liquid. Victus urged his mount forward without much conviction and it took time for the horse to understand its rider's intention.

Upon drawing closer to the man Victus forced himself to speak, it was no more than a whisper because he still feared that an enemy was close. 'Where are the men?' he asked, although deep within he already knew the answer.

'Dead — all dead,' replied the warrior fighting back more bile that rose in his throat.

Victus was suddenly very aware of a new fear trickling down his spine. His entire force had been slaughtered and he did not have so much as a scratch to show for the disaster. He doubted Rubius would look favourably on his absence from the column as they met their end. Victus felt a new danger, even though the enemy had obviously moved away. His mind raced, trying to find an answer to his precarious position.

He motioned for the guard down the track to remain at his location and then placed a hand on the other man's shoulder. 'Come, we must gather evidence on the enemy,' he whispered. 'It will aid our main force and perhaps gain vengeance for our comrades.'

The soldier had no wish to return to the scene of the slaughter but nodded his compliance. Victus and the warrior picked their way back up the track.

Victus suddenly stopped, sadness etched upon his face. 'They were fine troops, my heart aches for the loss of such men. Tell me, what was this man's name?'

The soldier looked at the dead man but his face was covered in a mixture of blood and dirt. He bent and using the corpse's own tunic attempted to wipe the blood away and revealed the man beneath. He did not hear the weapon slide from its scabbard, too intent on his task. Recognition of the fallen man was never made, a hand clamped over the warrior's mouth and a blade sought out his flesh.

Victus retrieved his blade wiping it clean on his victim. He plucked an arrow shaft from the body of one of his men and then walked from the scene of the slaughter. As he did, he noticed that no enemy bodies lay amongst his men. Did the enemy take their dead or were the enemy so skilled, that his men failed to register one kill? Within his mind, he started to concoct a report that would satisfy Rubius. Eventually, he reached the remaining bodyguard who looked perturbed that Victus was alone.

'Where's...?' He tried to ask a question but Victus interrupted.

'He will be along shortly, his stomach could not take the terrible sight and it is voicing its concern. Tell me do you recognise this type of arrow?' Victus tossed the shaft to the man.

'No, it's definitely not of my homeland or Greek,' replied the guard.

'What about the markings on the shaft?' Victus moved closer to point out the strange symbols.

The soldier dropped his head to look closer his eyes narrowing trying to make sense of the diagrams. A previously hidden dagger thrust upwards taking its victim through the bottom of the jaw. Bone and tissue smashed aside; the brain registered the blow by allowing those same eyes to bulge. The soldier managed to push away from Victus and take a couple of awkward almost infantile steps and then crashed to the ground.

Victus looked at the soldier's last few death movements without emotion and then bent and retrieved the arrow. His plan was nearly complete. Knowing Rubius would look for any reason to demote him to the ranks his story must not appear suspicious. He sighed and then approached a gnarled tree, which stood adjacent to the track. Raising the arrow shaft, he placed its base against the tree. He took a deep breath and with all his might pressed himself forward. He screamed his agony as the shaft buried itself into his flesh. For a moment he thought he would faint, the world racing about him preventing clarity of thought. He closed his eyes, took in large gulps of air and slowly he regained control.

It was some time before he summoned the courage to move and when he did those movements were slow and pronounced. Climbing his mount intensified the burning agony from his wound but eventually rider and horse stepped away from the slaughter. Victus looked at his wound; he would rather have inflicted the pain closer to the main army but knew the wound must not look fresh. Victus thought Rubius was a bastard but conceded he was a clever bastard and not easily deceived. Victus gritted his teeth and forced his mount on, cursing Rubius with each step.

***

Adrianicus was suddenly aware of cheering and Tigranes appeared at his shoulder.

'It seems Spartacus was successful and the men already idolise him,' the young ruler announced.

'Yes he has done well,' he replied.

Tigranes was no fool and noticed the less than enthusiastic tone. He eyed Adrianicus for some time before he spoke. 'You do not share the men's faith in Spartacus?'

'He is a mighty warrior,' replied Adrianicus.

'But?'

'Spartacus is a man of the heart. It controls his actions.'

'I thought you assured me that Cassian could keep our warrior friend under control.'

'I fear that Cassian has fallen under Spartacus' spell. Even my trusted Sikarbaal seems to hold him in too high regard. They say his woman Cynna is a witch.'

'Who says? Do not weave your web of lies with me, Adrianicus. If you believe Spartacus will become a danger then make plans to eradicate that threat. Nonetheless, at this time Spartacus is an asset and be sure that it is not your bruised ego that aims bile at the man.'

'My only wish is to safeguard Pompey's wishes. Personnel glory is of no concern,' replied Adrianicus.

'Then you are a better man than any I have met in this world. All men hunger for the love and loyalty from those they command. To be honoured by those that serve you because of the man you are and not the position that you hold, is true honour indeed.'

'Not I, the shadows are my kingdom. The whore, beggar, and assassin my soldiers; I have no need of love from such creatures.'

Tigranes looked at Adrianicus and knew the intelligent resourceful Roman was being untruthful, even to himself. Further conversation would have to wait because Spartacus and his returning troops neared.

Tigranes raised his hand in acknowledgement of the victorious men. 'All went as planned, I trust?'

'It could not have gone better,' replied Balen. 'The bridge is destroyed and our enemy has been dealt a great blow.'

'Vengeance has been delivered, then?' Tigranes asked, keen to hear the fate of those guilty of slaughter.

'Not one of them walks in this world. My empire would revel in the destruction of a force and the fear of the legions will become a distant memory,' Balen added.

'Those men were not of the legions, Balen,' Spartacus interrupted, 'mere hired blades dressed to look like Rome's legions to spread hatred in these lands.'

'The legions would have fared better?' asked Tigranes.

'Our casualties would have been more substantial. However, the outcome would have been the same and victory achieved,' Spartacus replied.

'How can you possibly know that?' Adrianicus could not help but question Spartacus' assumptions.

'Because, Adrianicus, in this instance the details which matter in war favoured our side. The terrain and element of surprise were enough to ensure victory.'

Adrianicus looked away annoyed at being put firmly in his place by Spartacus.

The gladiator eyed Adrianicus for a moment and then addressed Tigranes. 'You and the main army have travelled a great distance while I was dealing with the smaller crossing, how long before we encounter the bridge?'

'The quality of our progress is down to Adrianicus and his organisation.' Tigranes paused, obviously trying to build a bridge of his own. 'We will camp for the night and reach our destination within half a day's march. The troops of Commagene will be with us the following day.'

'Many thanks, Adrianicus.' Spartacus only received a nod in recognition of his gratitude. 'Now if you would excuse me, I wish to visit my family.'

Tigranes accepted his request and as Spartacus departed the cheers rose from the men once more.

***

As Spartacus and Cassian moved through the camp, Plinius and Tictus, who had just returned from a scouting mission, joined them. They talked briefly but all were anxious to be with their families.

Chia was stood talking to Sikarbaal who carried firewood.

Plinius approached Chia from behind and grabbed her in a loving embrace. 'Sikarbaal, are you moving in on my woman as I risk life and limb?' Plinius jested.

'Not at all, just ensuring your families are safe,' Sikarbaal replied.

Chia turned and kissed Plinius.

Spartacus took this as the moment to leave and he and Cassian went in search of their own family.

Sikarbaal lingered a while and watched Plinius' hands roam freely over the body of Chia. The notion he had stayed too long caused him to blush and he rushed away.

Spartacus and Cassian heard the laughter of children and as they rounded some large tents, the view came as a shock. Lathyrus chased the children and acted the fool causing them to laugh and scream with delight. Cynna and Flora were soon at Spartacus' side and watched the old sailor entertain the children.

'He would have made a fine father,' Cynna suggested as she watched such a large man be so gentle with the little ones.

'Lathyrus was a father, two boys, I believe,' replied Cassian.

'What happened?' It was Flora who asked the question despite fearing the answer.

'He has never spoken freely of their fate. Nonetheless, when he has filled his belly with enough wine and sleep takes him sometimes I hear him sob for their loss. My father would not discuss it, but did say that only the strongest can carry such a weight of sadness. It was of Lathyrus that he spoke,' replied Cassian.

'I never knew,' Spartacus said and for the first time realised that he and Lathyrus shared a common bond.

'He hides his pain, plays the fool to disguise the hurt. I believe he spirits the feelings away for fear they will consume him with the sheer agony of the sadness,' said Cassian.

'Well for the time being at least he is content and so are the children.' As Spartacus spoke, he swept Cynna into his arms. He did not speak any further as he carried Cynna to the tent and disappeared from view.

'Cassian, would you mind coming with me. I have a serious matter that I must discuss.' Flora's tone was serious and Cassian was left in no doubt that the issue would not wait.

'Of course,' he replied. He followed her to his tent confused at what the issue could be. As he entered the tent he spied a wine skin and grasped at it. He walked past Flora and then raised the wine to his lips and drank deeply of the liquid. He closed his eyes trying to focus because he always felt awkward and a little foolish in Flora's presence. He turned and dropped the wine skin with shock. Before him, Flora stood disrobed, her body looking as sumptuous as he always believed it would be.

'I am sorry, Cassian, but as you are too gentle in your ways, I thought it best that I take matters into my own hands.'

'Flora, you do not owe me any debt.' Cassian had protected her since her husband's death and Cassian feared she offered herself out of a sense of duty.

'Cassian, for an intelligent man you can be very foolish. I do this because I want to be in your bed.' She paused for a moment and suddenly looked less confident. 'Or do you not find me attractive?'

Cassian did not speak but rushed to her and embraced her with all his heart.

Outside the tent, Tictus had guessed what occurred within. 'I will just prepare some food then, shall I?' The question was for his ears only as he knew that nobody was listening. Feeling a little unappreciated he went in search of food and, more importantly, wine.

Chapter Eleven

The bridge was an impressive sight, spanning the river like a giant's hand aiding weary travellers. Camp was made and true to Tigranes' words the Commagene troops were arriving the following day.

Tigranes had decided to throw a huge feast in honour of the gods in the hope they would grant victory. Spartacus was not the kind of man who relied heavily on the whim of the gods but he knew how other men needed to believe that the deities were on their side. He thanked Tigranes for the gesture and tried his best to help raise the morale of the men. The former gladiator preferred to be alone before a battle but he knew as leader, the responsibilities outweighed personnel needs. Nonetheless, when the backslapping and cheering died down and men took to drinking and singing songs, Spartacus made his way to the bridge and gazed into the night.

'So the battle will take place here?'

Spartacus turned to see Cynna striding towards him. 'Out there,' he replied.

'It is a shame. It is such a beautiful place.'

'I doubt it will look so beautiful tomorrow.'

'So why fight? We could just leave this place to its fate.' Her voice trembled slightly.

'I fight so one day we may live in peace without fear of the shadows.' He pulled her close trying to ease her fears.

'I know, my love, but why does it always have to be you?'

'I guess the gods favour me.' He smiled. 'Besides, I gave my word and the others will only go and get themselves bloody slaughtered if we leave.'

'You are a good man, Spartacus,' she whispered gazing into his eyes.

'I am a bloody fool,' he replied.

'Well, that as well.' She smirked and then more seriously added, 'So when the battle takes place, kill the bastards and then let us find a place to call home.'

Spartacus nodded and held her tight, he stared across the bridge to where men would bleed and scream their agony.

***

Despite the bridge being such an impressive beast, preparations were still made to bring it crashing into the waters below. There were no guarantees in battle and so Spartacus must prepare for defeat as meticulously as victory.

Scouts raced across the mighty structure at regular intervals bringing any news on the enemy. Spartacus and Cassian spent most of their time examining the terrain on which the battle would take place. It was a concern to both; the ground was filled with small undulations and loose rocks. Experience told Spartacus that advancing armies could easily lose cohesion on such a surface.

The gladiator decided to discuss his plan with Cassian at length. 'I have an idea but it is a risk.'

'I am no soldier, Spartacus, but I am fairly certain that all decisions in battle are a risk,' replied Cassian.

'We will need wagons and a trench dug.' Spartacus paused looking into the distance. 'There. See the natural rise and then the fall in the ground?'

'I see it,' Cassian replied. He had guessed what Spartacus proposed. 'How many men will be required?'

'Not many, it is all about the timing.' The gladiator stared at Cassian as if wondering whether to utter his next part of the plan. 'I will need you to lead the main force.'

'The men will want you at the head of the army, Spartacus.'

'I will be of more use out there.' He once again pointed to the same patch of ground.

'You know I have no desire to lead men in battle, Spartacus. Not after ... after Aegis.' Cassian struggled to say his old friend's name.

'Many good men died that day. Aegis may well have been the best of them but his death was not down to you.'

'You did not see his face when he turned from me that day? I had betrayed him, Spartacus.'

'You were trying to keep him alive, he knew that.'

'I failed. It is because of me—' Cassian did not finish his sentence because Spartacus interrupted.

'Men die. We give orders and following those orders lead them to their deaths. Good men, friends and family perish by our decisions. Each one that passes to the next world takes a little of us with them, but we do what we must. I have no other man that I can trust with this task. Adrianicus and Sikarbaal are as likely to plunge a dagger into my flesh as they are to strike at the enemy. Plinius and Tictus are just children and Lathyrus would get drunk and miss the bloody battle. I need you, Cassian, there is no other.'

The two held a gaze for some time one, hoping the other would change his mind.

'Very well, Spartacus.'

***

Rubius was running through the camp, the news he had received had been disturbing. He burst into the large tent, which was allocated to the army's healers. Before him, Victus was outstretched receiving treatment. His second in command was pale as though some unknown mystical creature had turned the forlorn figure to marble.

'Will he live?' The question was for the nearby healer though Rubius' eyes never left the ailing Victus.

'He has lost a lot of blood. The shaft has caused a lot of damage. We will need to take the arm.' The healer's words seemed to drag Victus back into the world of men.

'No,' he mumbled and then with more force, 'you can't.' Victus groaned.

'Calm yourself, Victus. Tell me where the men are.'

Between sobs, Victus tried to relay to Rubius the fate of his command. 'We never reached the bridge.' He paused as pain coursed through his body. 'Arrows, so many arrows. We had lost half our number before we saw the enemy.'

'Rubius.' The healer wanted to stop the questions and be allowed to continue his work.

'This is important,' Rubius snapped. 'Please, Victus, tell me all you know.'

'My men were mostly dead or dying only a handful were left standing. I formed them up and ordered the charge; we were all going to die anyway. I thought it best to take some of the bastards to the other world with us. The arrow took me before I reached the enemy and sent me sprawling to the ground. That is the last I remember of the battle, I woke some time later in a small ravine.'

'The bridge?'

'I am sorry, Rubius. I have failed.'

'Rest easy, Victus. I have need of your services.' Rubius turned and nodded to the healer that he may continue his duties.

He strode from the tent his feelings were mixed. The truth of the matter was that he disliked Victus but in a foreign land with enemies close, the loathsome creature was the closest thing to a friend that he possessed.

Democolese approached Rubius. 'How is he?' he asked.

'The wound is severe, he will lose the arm,' replied Rubius.

'And the bridge?' Democolese showed more concern over the question.

'I will send scouts but we can assume that it no longer stands.' Rubius spat the words out as if the loss of the bridge were poison to his gut.

'That means our enemy intends to hold the main crossing and hope our numbers count for nothing with such a small frontage to attack.'

'It's a good tactic.'

'I would do the same. It will be a bloody day.' Democolese wondered on the quality of the enemy because secretly he doubted the metal of his own men.

'Then we had best get moving, it would be unwise to allow our enemy the chance to prepare.'

***

The call went up as the enemy were spotted in the distance. The arrival had been expected as the scouts had trailed the enemy for some time, but the dust rising on the horizon had caused a stir amongst the men. Spartacus, Cassian and Cleomenes stood at the very far end of the substantial wooden bridge.

'They will not come this day.' Cleomenes spat on the ground as he spoke and then lifted a wine skin and drank deeply.

'How can you be sure?' asked Cassian.

'The bridge entrance is too small to risk a frontal attack in poor light. A new day will bring the slaughter.' Cleomenes smiled at the chance to earn yet more glory for his people.

'Cleomenes, I have a task for you and your Spartans. However, I will doubt that you will offer gratitude.'

The Spartan leader eyed Spartacus suspiciously. 'Well, out with it, Thracian,' barked Cleomenes.

'Tomorrow will bring battle. I intend to take that battle to our enemies. If the gods grant us good fortune then we shall catch them by surprise. If my plan fails then we will need a strong defensive position at the bridge to allow our troops safe passage.'

'You want us to remain behind and not enter the fight? Spartans are warriors, Spartacus, it is what we do.' Cleomenes looked aghast at the mere suggestion.

'No, Cleomenes. The men of Sparta achieve victories. If we fail tomorrow then only by retreating in the proper manner can we hope to fight another day.'

The Spartan looked at Spartacus and then ruefully out beyond the crossing. 'My men will guard the bridge,' he finally replied. 'If you would excuse me, I will need to tell the men.' Cleomenes did not wait for a reply but strode off in the direction of where his men prepared for battle.

'That is one disgruntled Spartan.'

'It cannot be helped, Cassian, I would have men at my back that I can trust.'

'And what of Adrianicus?'

'He shall be at my side. If the gods do not favour us then I would appreciate the chance to take that bastard with us.'

Cassian laughed. 'He is on our side, Spartacus.'

'That may be but he is still a devious bastard.'

'Spartacus,' a voice hailed from their rear.

The two men turned to see Balen approaching and at his side, Tictus. The young warrior looked positively glowing with excitement making Spartacus and Cassian wonder what the young man had on his mind.

'Your men, are they ready, Balen?' asked Spartacus.

'My men are always ready, Spartacus, but it is of another matter I wish to speak. Young Tictus has expressed a desire to join my riders in the battle tomorrow. After seeing his skill with a bow I believe he would excel along my men.'

Spartacus looked at Tictus who beamed with happiness as he clutched a Parthian bow.

Tictus noticed the gladiator admiring the weapon. 'A gift from Balen. I will need to practice if I am to match his men.'

'Then you had best get to it and not shame your friends,' replied Spartacus.

'Yes of course.' Tictus raced off without another word causing Balen to laugh at the young man's excitement.

Balen then turned to leave but Cassian laid a hand on his shoulder.

'Balen I have a request of my own. I would appreciate if you would keep the boy alive. He and his mother are special to me and I would find it a great burden to deliver news of sorrow to a woman who has already carried too much grief in her life.'

'I will watch over him as if he was my own flesh,' replied Balen.

'Gratitude.'

'No gratitude is required. Are we not all brothers before the enemy?'

Final preparations would take time and so moments spent with family were brief. Spartacus and his friends however, were determined to spend at least a little time in the presence of loved ones.

'You are going out into the darkness with so many enemies, so very close.' Cynna spoke to Spartacus in whispers, the anxiety etched upon her face.

'The darkness can be a comforting friend as well.' His reply was gentle in tone designed to soothe her sadness.

'When will you return?'

'Not this night, a task must be completed,' he replied.

'Come to me at the battle's end.' She hesitated and then with a breaking voice said, 'And stay alive, my love.'

'That is my intention, my love, besides I have this big ox to watch my back.'

Lathyrus had just appeared at Cynna's shoulder. 'I shall reach into the next world and pull him back if necessary, he will return to you.'

Cynna leaned forward and placed a kiss on Lathyrus' cheek. 'You come back, too.'

'Much more affection like that and I may kill this old bastard myself and take you as my bride.' Lathyrus barked out his laughter.

In moments, all of Spartacus' friends were near, their women all close to tears. Cassian and Tictus wished the others good fortune; it seemed strange that they would not be entering the darkness with their comrades.

Flora fussed over Melachus, conscious that he had no real family near.

'It does not seem right, not to be at your side, Spartacus,' Cassian said finally giving voice to his feelings.

'We can exchange places if you wish,' Plinius replied smiling nervously.

'Our roles are set and each of us perfectly suited to those tasks.' Spartacus looked directly at Cassian hoping the Roman would gain confidence from his support.

'I wish I could wield a sword,' announced Chia.

'Then how would we mere men gain glory?' Plinius raised his hand as he spoke and wiped a single tear from her cheek. His thumb stroked the delicate flesh of her face and he mouthed the words of his love.

Farewells were said and most were left behind. Cassian, however, walked to the bridge with Spartacus.

'You have command, Cassian. Have the Parthians ride out first and chase any enemy cavalry away. Their bows can then turn their attention to the flanks of the infantry. Pick your moment to launch the main assault. They will not expect it and it should sow confusion. Keep Cleomenes on the bridge, the enemy must not be allowed to overrun that position.'

'It will be done,' replied Cassian.

As they neared the bridge Cleomenes watched for any movement in the darkness.

'Our scouts have pushed theirs back to a safe distance, you are clear to leave.'

'Gratitude, Cleomenes.' Spartacus turned to see Adrianicus at the head of a large number of his black armoured troops. 'Looks like we are ready to move out.' Spartacus motioned for the men to follow him into the night. The warriors silently crossed the wooden structure and entered the darkness. Cassian watched until the last man dissolved into the shadows.

'Good fortune, my friend,' he whispered.

Chapter Twelve

Cassian had risen early; the responsibility of taking command of the army had led to a troubled sleep. For some time he walked the camp until eventually he found himself near the crossing once again. He crouched down low and looked at his hands, they trembled slightly. He did not know why but he stretched out a hand and grasped at the dirt.

'Talk to me, Aegis.' He pictured his long dead friend within his mind's eye. 'The days have been poorer without you, dear friend.' Cassian knew that the dry soil would not speak but he needed the wisdom of his old healer now.

'You will find no answer or lost friends in the dirt,' sounded a voice.

The interruption to his thoughts made Cassian look upwards but the early sun obscured the face of the speaker. Just for a moment, he thought that Aegis had returned in his hour of need but then quickly shook such an idea from his head.

'And where will I find the answers?' Cassian asked of his unknown and uninvited guest.

'Within here.' The figure pointed to his heart. 'Answers and lost friends dwell together.' Without another word, the figure turned and walked away.

Cassian observed the figure walk away, he shook his hand free from dirt and realised that the hand was now devoid of a tremble. He took a long deep breath and strode towards the bridge.

Cleomenes had also risen early, his eyes fixed firmly on the enemy in the distance. He turned, hearing Cassian's approach.

'Greetings.'

Cleomenes smiled and offered wine.

Cassian accepted the gift and was glad to see the Spartan was less annoyed at his duties defending the bridge. Or at least had come to terms with what must be done. 'Is there any movement?' Cassian asked.

'Oh yes, but we have time. It is best to see an enemy's intention. Also we can ensure our men are well fed because only the gods know how long this battle will last.'

'Of course.' Cassian paused. 'Cleomenes, I am no military man, what do you make of our troops?' The question raised in the hope of reassurance.

'They are not Spartans,' replied Cleomenes and then he laughed. Then with more thought he added, 'The Parthians are lethal with their bows and I have never seen troops so skilled on horseback. How they fight with a blade I cannot say, but I feel we have men that we can rely upon. The men for Commagene are well drilled and arrived from a long march in good order and they train constantly honing their skill with a weapon. Our black armoured friends seem to be a mix of former men of the Roman ranks and bandits, which means they are more difficult to judge but I would not freely turn my back on them. The rest are fighting to eat and they will probably feed the carrion birds by the end of this day.'

A party approached from the camp. Tigranes and a man Cassian recognised as the leader of the Commagene troops were in deep conversation. The two men were accompanied, at a suitable distance by what were unmistakeably bodyguards. The two men stopped twenty paces short of Cassian. It was clear that the conversation was not for his ears and it bothered Cassian that allies were being secretive on the eve of battle.

Tigranes looked concerned but finally nodded and the party moved forward.

'What is wrong?' Cassian asked firmly, he was in no mood to play political games.

'Nothing.' The young ruler's response was anything but convincing.

'Tigranes, my friends are out there amongst the enemy, if you have news I will hear of it.' There was no mistaking the fact that Cassian had just given Tigranes an order.

One of his bodyguards dropped a hand to his blade and moved towards Cassian. His progress was halted as Cleomenes stepped forward. 'One more step, bastard and I will spill your guts.' The Spartan growled.

Tigranes held up a hand and a thankful guard retreated. The young ruler blushed as though he knew his next words were a great shame. 'Forgive me, Cassian, you are right. I have just received news that my father has left his city. Not only that, but he was at the head of a substantial force.'

'Fuck! Where is he now?' Panic gripped at Cassian's insides.

'That we do not know. Our scouts were unaware that he had left the city, it was by mere chance that a trader sympathetic to our cause came into contact with my father's men.' Tigranes was struggling to hide his embarrassment.

'So he could be here, swelling the enemy ranks as we speak. We must inform Spartacus the enemy could be in far larger numbers than he had planned to engage.' Cassian's words were met with the distant sound of horns and their metallic call to arms. All present turned to look to the horizon knowing that the enemy were on the move.

'Too late, Cassian, the bastards are coming and we must follow our battle orders.' Cleomenes turned towards his men.

'Spartans, are you ready?' His words were received with a guttural cheer and the single thud from each man on his shield. 'Cassian, we have no choice, like it or not the enemy are upon us and no matter the number we must meet them.'

'Very well.' Cassian narrowed his eyes as he tried to make out the enemy in the distance. He wondered just how many would rage like a storm towards the bridge. He stepped to his front and turned so that his back now faced the enemy. 'Tigranes you need to retire and protect the families of the fighting men.' He then sent messengers to fetch the officers.

'What are you going to do?' asked Tigranes.

'We will do what Spartacus ordered, we will cross the bridge and kill every last one of those fucks.' It was bravado but Cassian knew now was not the time for timidity.

Cleomenes enjoyed Cassian's words. 'That is more like it, come on!' He screamed and held his mighty spear aloft.

Like some contagious disease, his battle fury spread along the line. Soon an entire army raged its anger at the oncoming enemy. Spittle, threats and insults flew from mouths as men built their wrath.

Cassian watched in awe, and was only torn from the sight when Balen approached on horseback. At his rear, the entire force of Parthians awaited his orders.

'The time has come, Cassian, what would you have us do?' asked Balen.

'Chase any cavalry they might have from the field of battle. However, take care not to give chase for too long. When you are clear to do so, split your force and attack both their flanks. Keep them away from Spartacus' position at all costs.'

'It will be done,' Balen replied, supremely confident in his men's abilities. The Parthian urged his mount forward and without ceremony, his men followed. Cassian saw the enthusiastic Tictus, the young warrior had disposed of his usual armour and had decided to wear the heavy tunic preferred by his Parthian friends. Cassian gave a silent prayer that Tictus would return safely to his mother.

The enemy moved forward but were not in battle line, they fully expected Cassian's troops to remain defending the bridge. The Parthian arrows began to land within their ranks; Cassian imagined the damage inflicted on an enemy, who in many cases did not have armour to protect themselves against the missiles. The enemy had now passed the hidden location of Spartacus and so Cassian raised his arm and gave the signal for the main force to cross the bridge. He knew that there was no turning back from this point. He looked to the enemy, wondering if the elder had force-marched his army and therefore defeat would come, no matter how brave his men fought.

***

Across the battlefield, Rubius and Democolese watched their enemy filter across the bridge.

'I though today would be difficult, as our men struggled to storm the bridge. It seems that our enemy leader is a fool and he has doomed his men,' announced Democolese. The agents of Crassus had informed Rubius that Spartacus himself would lead the enemy to battle. He found it hard to believe the famed gladiator would make such a mistake.

'Why would he make such a foolish move?' Rubius could not help but to ask the question aloud.

'Maybe he believes in his own legend and arrogance has blinded him to simple military common sense.'

'Perhaps.' Rubius was not convinced. He searched the battlefield looking for deception but the terrain offered no hiding place. Eventually, he concluded that the former gladiator hated by so many Romans had simply over estimated the qualities of his own men. After all, he no longer commanded the thousands of gladiators from the Roman Empire. Rubius switched his attention from the terrain back to the enemy and saw with shock that not only had they crossed the bridge but were advancing. Rubius quickly bellowed orders and the horns sounded once more calling for the main force to form a battle line.

***

Cassian heard the enemy's signal and watched them somewhat awkwardly begin to form a line ready to attack. Spartacus had been correct, these were no seasoned troops and the fact gave Cassian hope that the battle might just go their way. He watched as eventually the enemy formed and then began their advance, slowly at first but then with more pace. Cassian signalled for the horns to sound and his main force stopped and braced ready to receive a charge.

The enemy seeing this increased its speed sensing that victory was close at hand. They screamed their anger, determined to strike fear into their enemies' hearts. Cassian remained outwardly calm, despite his guts writhing with the agony of responsibility. He knew his timing must be perfect, the decisions he made in the next few moments could mean victory or disaster. He watched the front rank of the enemy closing on his men with only slaughter in their mind.

He had expected what happened but it still came as a shock. The entire front line of the enemy suddenly dropped into the earth. Spartacus' first deception had worked. A hastily dug trench stretching the width of the battlefield had gone unobserved by the enemy. The trench was not deep but when thousands of men hurtled towards it with no inclination that it even existed, it meant one thing. Men were sent sprawling, limbs snapped and men died from the weight of their comrades trampling them underfoot. The enemy had been too eager to match blade against blade and had paid a heavy price.

Cassian signalled again and his force moved forward until they stood only a few paces from the sprawling enemy. Then with cruel efficiency they let loose all manner of missiles. Spears and javelins were thrown into the air, and then fell amongst the enemy lines that succumbed to chaos. The Parthians, too, added their missiles to the enemy flanks and the result was butchery. The enemy were dying at an incredible rate but credit to the enemy's officers; they were managing to force their men onwards.

Tigranes had returned to stand at Cassian's shoulder and he watched as the enemy began once more to move on his small force. He looked at Cassian but the Roman did not react, he just waited. The enemy crashed into the shield wall and for a moment it seemed they would break.

'Cassian?' Tigranes was almost pleading.

'They must be fully engaged with no hope to turn and fight,' he answered. Finally, he raised his arm and the horns blew. For what seemed an age the battle remained the same with the enemy massing around Cassian's force. Then quite suddenly, Cassian could see men erupting from out of the ground. Spartacus had concealed his men well, upturned wagons leaving the terrain looking just like a normal rise in the ground. However, the rise in the ground now belched out men like Vesuvius discarded acrid smoke. Those men now careered with savage intent towards the rear of the enemy. Their charge had gone unnoticed for they had made no sound until within ten paces, which was when Spartacus screamed his war cry.

'Kill the bastards!'

His men obliged him, with eagerness and skill.

Spartacus led just a few hundred men into battle. It seemed such a pitiful amount of men but they attacked the enemy from the rear who were packed tightly together and unable to defend themselves. The result was disastrous for Rubius' men who were simply cut to pieces.

Spartacus took a man's arm off at the elbow and with the same blow cut deep into another man's thigh. He punched the man in the jaw before he could offer a retaliatory blow. One of Adrianicus' black armoured men finished the unfortunate warrior off with a sword thrust to the throat. Plinius hurled a javelin, which impaled another warrior, but before he could fall, Lathyrus lifted him up bodily and threw him into his fellow warriors. The plan worked with effortless ease. Many of the enemy were aware that they were under attack from an unseen foe but were unable to turn and fight in any great number. Suddenly, weapons were being cast away and men turned not to fight but to flee.

***

Rubius stared at the carnage that was taking place. Only moments earlier he had been confident of victory but in such a brief amount of time that confidence was gone.

'What is happening?' Rubius asked shaking his head in pure disbelief.

'We have lost the battle,' replied Democolese.

'Sound the retreat,' ordered Rubius.

'No point, they are running.' He pointed to an entire section of their army that had cast away their swords and were routing no interest in the fight. 'It will not be long before the entire army takes flight. Not even the gods will persuade them to take up arms.'

***

Tigranes across the battlefield slapped Cassian on the shoulder as he watched the vast amount of enemy warriors break from the fight. Hundreds lay dead but more importantly thousands were streaming away from the battle.

'You have beaten them. It is only a matter of time before the entire force runs.'

'Let the battle be won before we turn to celebration,' replied Cassian.

'The victory is earned they shall not stand,' Tigranes shouted with joy. It was as if the gods had heard the arrogance of Tigranes. They answered his over confidence with the sound of horn and the fluttering of fresh banners on the field of battle.

Cassian looked to the horizon and saw the fragility of victory smashed.

CHAPTER THIRTEEN

'Fuck!' Cassian knew that any hopes of victory were lost.

'How could he get here so fast?' Tigranes asked in disbelief.

'What does it matter, we have to warn Spartacus.' Cassian tried to think but the situation threatened to overwhelm his senses. It was at that precise moment that he spied Balen returning to the bridge to replenish his arrows. Cassian sent a messenger to bring the Parthian to his side.

Tigranes interrupted his thoughts. 'We have to sound the retreat.'

'If I sound the retreat, Spartacus will die,' Cassian responded.

'If we cannot get our troops back across this bridge then we will all die.' Tigranes may have been young in terms of warfare but he had summed up the situation perfectly.

Cassian stared at him and for a moment thought about ignoring the young ruler's words, but then with heavy heart knew it was the only course of action.

'Give the order for our force to break off and retreat back across the bridge.' As Cassian finished speaking Balen arrived, he was not pleased at being prevented from continuing the fight.

'I have a task to complete, Cassian,' he said, his tone severe.

'I have another task. Send word to Spartacus that we are retreating.'

'Retreat? But we are—'

'Look,' Cassian interrupted and pointed at the new army steaming towards the battle. 'You must warn Spartacus!'

Balen did not waste time on more words but immediately urged his mount forward and toward the last place he had seen Spartacus.

As Cassian's main force began to retreat in good order, which was mainly down to the skill of the Commagene warriors, more of the enemy turned to face Spartacus. With the pressure relieved at the front of their battle line, suddenly they found they had more freedom to alter direction and face the menace to their rear.

Spartacus was unaware of the peril that he and his men now faced. He was, however, aware of the amount of enemies that seemed able to turn and fight. Plinius prevented a warrior from gutting Melachus; firstly, he pulled his friend clear of a fatal blow and then slashed upwards with his blade, which removed the face from the attacker. The wounded man waved his weapon in the air as the agony and fear gripped him; Plinius ducked beneath the weapon and then rose quickly piercing the man through the gut. The man fell, his death throes lasting only a few moments. Suddenly, five attackers to Spartcus' left were sent sprawling as a great warhorse smashed through them. Spartacus dispatched one of the men who had been unfortunate enough to land closest to the gladiator.

'Balen, what are you doing here?'

'Get out now!' replied the Parthian as he swept his blade down splitting an enemy's skull.

'Why?' Spartacus called back.

'Another army has entered the field. Cassian has ordered the retreat.' Balen's mighty warhorse raised its mighty front legs and brought them crashing down on the chest of a fallen enemy, sending a red mist into the air.

'Fuck! Men, back to the bridge!' Spartacus glanced around. 'Run, you bastards!'

The only way out would be to fight their way along the side of the enemy, a direct route to the bridge would lead them into the centre of the enemy. Initially, they made good progress as many of the enemy were confused of what course of action to take. Some thought they should attack the bridge but many thought they should seek at the enemy that had attacked them from the rear. Nearly a third of the army did not care about the bridge or enemy; they had endured too much and streamed away from the battlefield, keen to reach safety.

As Balen raced away Spartacus heard a terrible cry, he turned to see Lathyrus clutching his shoulder. A spear had ripped through the mighty warrior and Spartacus knew that his friend would not be able to run any further with such a wound. If the enemy thought Lathyrus would be an easy kill, they were mistaken. The sailor ripped the spear from his body and used it as a club to fell at least three warriors. Spartacus rushed forward, eager to help Lathyrus but as he neared, he saw a blade erupt from the big man's chest. Spartacus screamed and threw one of his swords. The warrior who was just about to deliver a deathblow on Lathyrus, was thrown backwards as the blade hit.

'Plinius, help!' yelled Spartacus.

The young warrior on hearing Spartacus, glanced around to see Spartacus defending the fallen figure that he recognised as Lathyrus. Plinius made to go to Spartacus' aid but the lapse in concentration allowed an enemy to move in close unseen. Melachus called a warning too late as a blade raked down Plinius' thigh. The young warrior jumped backwards despite the agony and managed to parry his enemy's next blow. Melachus came to his aid and promptly dispatched the would-be slayer of Plinius. Melachus guarded Plinius as he moved towards the fallen sailor and when the two arrived, Spartacus shook his head at his friend's condition.

The gladiator looked around and saw that many of his men were either dead or wounded and so the choice to run was no longer an option. 'Form up, there is no point running.' He paused. 'If we must die, let's take as many of the bastards with us as possible.' As the remainder of his men carried out his order, Spartacus bent and held the old sailor's head.

'Bloody land, it's not fit for whores.'

Lathyrus' breathing was shallow and his friends knew he did not have long.

'Lathyrus…' Words failed Melachus and he could not hold back the tears.

'Steady, Melachus,' Spartacus whispered. 'It is good to die amongst friends.' He hesitated. 'Amongst family.'

The old sailor slipped quietly from this world in stark contrast to how he had lived. Spartacus knew that soon Lathyrus would have company on his final journey.

At the bridge, Cleomenes swore and threw a wine skin to the ground. 'Spartans! Do we crave glory which is our birthright?' He growled. His men snapped to attention ready to follow their leader to the gates of the underworld if ordered.

'Cleomenes, what are you doing?' asked Cassian.

'You have enough men to torch a fucking bridge. I go to Spartacus. Spartans, form up!'

The Spartans marched across the bridge, and upon reaching the other side instantly changed formation. The red-cloaked warriors now held a tight wedge and slowly the entire formation began to move. The Commagene troops opened and allowed the wedge to pass. Some of the enemy seeing the chance to force a breach in the defences, then charged, only to be trampled down by the Spartan formation. The enemy now were in confusion, without proper leadership they did not know which of Cassian's force to engage. The wedge broke them apart like a burning sword through unprotected flesh. Many more of the enemy decided that retreat was the better part of valour, some headed for Rubius to await further command but many turned and ran.

Cassian watched as the Spartan moved through the enemy lines, he stood both amazed at their brilliance and anxious at the slowness of their progress.

Spartacus was not aware of the Spartan warriors endeavour at a rescue. All he knew was that enemy pressed on all sides and now his pitiful defensive formation was falling apart. Men had been fighting shoulder to shoulder defending each other from the enemy but now those enemies were amongst them and his men were dying. He took the leg from one man and gutted another, which afforded him space to glance around at his men. The enemy engulfed Plinius and Melachus and he did not see them rise. Sikarbaal and Adrianicus now were his nearest allies and they fought like heroes, no matter of his personal feelings towards these men, he could not help admiring their qualities with a blade. He did not count the amount of men he sent to the next world but he felt the tiredness building in his body and knew that soon he would fall. A figure grasped at his leg causing him to stumble. He recovered just in time to block a sword thrust to his face. The blade raked along his cheek stinging the flesh. The attacker paid for the blow as Spartacus brought his blade upwards taking the man's balls. Another blade sliced at his upper arm sending crimson liquid in the air, he thrust with the last of his energy and felt the enemy's soft flesh and then bone beneath his blade. The blade stuck fast and his strength could not retrieve the weapon. He crouched low and plucked up an abandoned shield and deflected two blows. Then a strong hand grasped him from behind and pulled him backwards making him fall to the ground. He waited for the killing blow to land taking him from this world and from Cynna's embrace. The sword thrust did not come and he wiped blood and dirt from his eyes. A hand was offered, it was attached to a powerfully muscular arm and as Spartacus raised his gaze, a smiling Cleomenes came into view.

'There will be time to rest when we get back over that fucking bridge.'

'Cleomenes, Plinius is still out there,' replied Spartacus, his breath laboured.

'The gods have granted us precious few, Spartacus. If we stay then we will all die.'

The journey back to the bridge was a blur to Spartacus, his mind focussed on friends lost. The slow moving wedge was under constant attack, which intensified now Tigranes the Elder's troops had finally brought their blades to bear. Nonetheless, the formation helped along the way by the Parthians, kept up a relentless missile attack on the enemy.

When finally the last Spartan crossed the bridge, the flames began to rise into the sky. The enemy did not waste time trying to pursue their prey, they knew the crossing was doomed and so the two armies had fought all they could that day.

Cassian was the first to meet the survivors; he glanced around frantically for his friends. He spied Adrianicus, Sikarbaal and only a handful of black armoured warriors. Finally, he saw Spartacus sat on the ground.

For a moment Cassian did not speak; he had never seen Spartacus look so fragile.

'You are bleeding.' He finally broke the silence.

'It is nothing,' the gladiator replied solemnly. Spartacus noticed Cassian looking around in search of his friends. 'They are gone.'

'No.' Cassian refused to believe it. 'Maybe they are prisoners?'

'I held Lathyrus has he passed from this world and I saw Melachus overwhelmed by the enemy.'

Cassian did not want to say the name that clung to his lips. 'Plinius?'

'Gone.' Spartacus turned his head; he could not bear to see Cassian's grief while dealing with his own.

They sat in silence for some moments before Cassian attempted to lighten the mood.

'I see Adrianicus managed to survive.'

'He fought well, but he's still a bastard.'

A terrible scream smashed the solemn silence, which had settled on the army. Spartacus and Cassian both jumped to their feet to investigate the disturbance.

Chia was running towards the burning bridge, if it was not for the intervention of Sikarbaal she may well have fallen to her death. She struggled with her saviour beating her hands against his broad chest. Try as she might she could not break his hold and then quite suddenly she ceased to fight and hung limp in his arms. Cynna and Flora rushed to her side and started to walk the sobbing Chia back to the camp.

Cynna looked over her shoulder to Spartacus who merely nodded that she should continue in task. The gladiator then turned to the bridge. 'Get this fucking bridge to burn faster,' he said then paused, 'and best post a guard.'

'I will see that it's done,' replied Cassian.

As night fell the bridge turned into an inferno. Later when its rage had died, its darkened and broken timbers creaked with annoyance. Two armies had pulled back from the battle site, the smell of death lingering too long in their nostrils. The bodies of the dead remained where they fell and beasts would soon arrive to pick at their bones. Flesh would be torn away and the sun would bleach what remained into grotesque figurines holding their final desperate forms of men once of this world.

Two figures crawled slowly through the fallen men, knowing that the slightest noise may yet consign them to death upon the battlefield. The sun would be heralding a new day before they finally slipped beneath the upturned wagons hidden by Spartacus the previous day.

'Well, that was enjoyable.'

'Do you think Spartacus made it across the bridge?'

'Melachus, we only faced two armies this day, it would take three at least to see Spartacus fall.'

'How's the leg?' Melachus asked not wanting to think about Spartacus lying dead amongst so many other bodies.

'A scratch, that is all.'

'Plinius, you have been opened from hip to knee. If we do not find you a healer soon you may die of that scratch. Maybe we could give ourselves up?'

'They would cut our throats on sight. No, we will lay low for a day and when the time is right, we shall look to make our escape. Soon as those bastards move out, we will go in the opposite direction.'

Melachus did not know how they were supposed to do that with Plinius' wound but he did not press the matter. As it were, the upturned wagons still contained a few supplies and Melachus set about cleaning and dressing Plinius' thigh.

'Plinius, I wanted to thank you for saving my life, if you hadn't pulled those bodies over me and told me to stay still I would be dead.'

'If you don't pass me some more wine, I will kill you myself.'

'When I attempted to heal Lathyrus when he was wounded, all he wanted was wine. I shall miss him.'

'I will not miss his tales.' Plinius laughed quietly.

Melachus joined Plinius in the laughter and went in search of wine.

Chapter Fourteen

The second night after the battle, the warriors within the camp had been subdued. The leaders were called together and almost immediately, Spartacus offered to resign from his post as commander of the army.

Cleomenes was the first to react. 'My men risked a great deal to bring you to safely to this side of the river.'

'I know and I am grateful,' replied Spartacus.

'Gratitude is for old women. They do not want your gratitude. Pay them the respect their actions deserve. Resume your position at the head of our army. The blame for defeat does not lie at your feet.' Cleomenes shot a sideways glance at Tigranes as he finished speaking.

The action was not lost on the member of Armenian royalty, the young ruler blushed but stepped forward. 'Our subtle Spartan friend is correct, Spartacus. I miscalculated my father's intentions and the ability of his troops. My failure has led to the deaths of many good men. The information that I provided dictated your plans.'

Spartacus did not reply but stood in shock at a man born to royalty freely admitting to being wrong. That shock however, was nothing to what he felt when the next person spoke.

'I feel it achieves little to attribute blame. We have lost a battle but we are not yet defeated. Spartacus, I have fought at your side and although we rarely agree on matters, it is clear to me that you must lead these men.' Adrianicus gave a small cough to signal he had finished speaking.

'Was that difficult to say?' Cassian asked.

'Running naked through Hades would have been preferable,' replied Adrianicus. A ripple of laughter washed through the tent.

Spartacus waited for that laughter to die down and then his face a mask of seriousness. 'Then it is time to make plans. The enemy has lost a great deal of its warriors from its first army. Nonetheless, we can accept that we will be vastly outnumbered and I doubt that they will fall for our deceptions on the battlefield so easily. Therefore, we must be creative in reducing their numbers and then defeat them.'

'But how?' asked Balen.

'There is more than one way to destroy an army. We will expose them to their greatest fears and slice them apart a piece at a time. They will be a spent force when we meet on the battlefield, and no arriving army will save them from their fate this time.'

'Then let us drink.' Cleomenes held his wine aloft. 'To warriors that are dead and those that will die.'

All present raised their wine to the gods and each secretly asked for their favour.

***

An old man sat at the centre of an opulently furnished tent. Even when waging war, this man ensured he was surrounded by the trappings of his position. The two men to his front had not been asked to make themselves comfortable, or offered any refreshments. Tigranes the Elder eyed the men closely and made no attempt to keep the loathing from his face. 'Mithridates seems to have been mistaken in his choice of generals.' The men did not reply, it would have been a mistake to contradict a man such as Tigranes. 'Nonetheless, the choice has been made, tell me what do you intend to do next?'

Democolese remained silent believing the old ruler intended to assume command of both armies.

Rubius, however, saw an opportunity. 'If you would honour us by joining your forces with ours, then it would be a simple matter of chasing down what is left of the enemy.'

'A simple matter. Tell me, Rubius, do you hunt?'

Rubius sensed a trap and nervously nodded his head in reply.

'Then as a hunter, you should know following a wounded beast into its lair, is no simple matter. Besides, what makes you think I want to wage war on my son? He may be an ungrateful wretch but I have no wish to see him bleeding in the dirt.'

'Forgive me,' said Rubius, 'I thought as you had already bloodied your troops that you would—'

Tigranes cut across the remainder of Rubius' words. 'Win this war for you? I had hoped to end this rebellion in one stroke, capturing the bridge would have made that achievable. That, however, is not possible because of you two.' Tigranes paused and wrinkled his nose as though a repugnant odour had invaded his nostrils. 'Generals. I will not throw away my forces, I am afraid you will have to show a far greater skill at soldiering than you have shown so far.' The old man paused and for a moment studied the men before him as if weighing a problem within his mind. 'Nonetheless, I wish for my son's safe return and also wish to foster good relations with Mithridates. Therefore, I offer you military aid to the sum of three thousand men. This should enable you to bring my son's forces to heal quickly and therefore give him no alternative but to surrender. An adequate amount of men... even for your limited skills.'

'You are most generous.' Rubius bowed in gratitude, it was a false gesture. He would have liked nothing more than to take a step to his front and drive a blade through the old man's chest. He resented being spoken to like a naughty child by an old fool, but he needed the warriors and so he held his temper.

***

Two armies broke camp the following morning. Cassian and Spartacus watched the enemy march away over the horizon.

They remained in silence for some time before Cassian finally spoke. 'I spoke to Chia last night.' Cassian's tone was solemn. 'I made her a promise.'

'You promised to bring Plinius' body back,' Spartacus replied trying not to imagine the broken body of his friend, the loss still weighed heavily on his heart.

'How do you know?'

'Cynna asked me to do the same. She believes it will help Chia come to terms with Plinius' death.'

'So when do we leave?' Cassian asked knowing there was little Spartacus would refuse Cynna.

'We will give both armies time to get clear of this place. Then with rope we should be able to get down there.' Spartacus pointed into the ravine.

Cassian rather timidly approached the edge and looked down the severe drop; he blew out his cheeks. 'That will not be easy,' he announced.

'Far easier than climbing down that bastard of a rock, Vesuvius. It can be done,' Spartacus replied.

Cassian had heard the rumours of how Spartacus and his slaves had descended the side of the mighty volcano to catch the Roman legions off guard; he had discounted a lot of the myth surrounding Spartacus.

'Did that really happen?' Cassian asked struggling to keep the amazement out of his voice.

'It was not an act of bravery. We had little choice in the matter but the plan worked. Our enemies were thrown into complete confusion.'

Cassian remembered the waves of fear, which haunted the Roman citizens. The news that Roman legions had been wiped from this world by the slave army rocked Rome and many believed the great city may even fall. Normal life became one of suspicion, as each man of wealth looked to his slaves and wondered if they carried wine or a dagger. Some decided to treat their slaves with more care but it was a selfish act designed for self-preservation. Many, in those dark days, wore the mask of fear. Cassian could not help but think it may have been good for Rome and Romans to feel a little uneasy in their beds.

Spartacus and Cassian returned to the camp to inform Tigranes of their decision. The young leader was not overly enthusiastic that his army commander would be leaving the men behind but Spartacus held firm to his intentions.

The gladiator then surprised Cassian by placing Adrianicus in temporary command in his absence.

'Adrianicus, are you sure?' Cassian questioned.

'If our plan to retrieve Plinius' body goes wrong and we cannot return, who would you prefer to have leading our men? Tigranes is just a boy. Cleomenes will look to gain glory not victory and the two do not necessarily go together. The enemy are superior in numbers and to defeat them you will need deceit and intelligence and that bastard Adrianicus has both in abundance.'

With plans made and supplies collected, Cassian and Spartacus journeyed back to the destroyed bridge. Spartacus ensured the ropes were secured to one of the few remaining timbers.

Cassian peered into the deep ravine. 'Are you sure about this?' he asked.

'You seem to think I have knowledge of some great unexplained plan. I am sorry to disappoint, Cassian, but the fact is I blunder about in the hope that the gods will show me favour,' Spartacus replied, his enjoyment at Cassian's discomfort evident.

'Yes. All you had to say was, yes.'

Spartacus laughed. 'Surely you do not want to wither away until you are old and feeble? Weak in both body and mind and then simply sit and await death.'

'That is precisely my plan. Let others take glory, I have no need of heroism.' Cassian finished talking, took a deep breath and lowered himself over the edge of the ravine.

Spartacus watched his friend descend and then whispered to himself. 'We do not choose glory, my friend. It seeks us out and demands we act.' Then he too let the rope bear his weight.

***

The day marched on and it had been some time since Spartacus and Cassian had lowered themselves into the ravine on the first stage of their journey.

Across the river, two other men had decided it was time to move and try to rejoin their own forces. Melachus had cleaned the wound sustained by Plinius as best as his knowledge would allow, but he was still concerned how movement would affect the injury.

Plinius had guessed what concerned his friend. 'You worry too much, Melachus. The pain has all but gone, besides, Spartacus will need our skills in the coming days.'

Melachus was amazed that Plinius' only concern was that of carrying out his duty.

The two men managed with some difficulty to crawl free from the upturned wagons. It was with some relief that Plinius could stand tall once clear of the wagons, although the leg was still painful, it was bearable when the leg was allowed to be straightened. They picked their way across the battlefield, the limbs of the dead seemed to grasp at them seeking rescue far too late. Melachus was no warrior and the gruesome sight became too much and so he concentrated his vision on the horizon. It was because of this he did not see a thick pool of blood, which lay on the surface of a shield. Suddenly, he was falling and he released his hold on Plinius and the injured warrior was brought crashing to the ground. Plinius howled with pain as burning agony exploded in his thigh.

Melachus quickly got to his feet and offered Plinius his hand. 'I am sorry, Plinius.'

Plinius took a moment forcing back the pain with short sharp breaths. 'I think that you have some way to go if you wish to match our old friend Aegis in his healings skills,' he finally replied with a mixture of laughter and wincing.

Melachus did not reply but bent further forward to help Plinius to his feet. Suddenly, a shout erupted from his rear and he left Plinius lying where he had fallen. Melachus turned to see four men moving in his direction, he wondered if they had seen Plinius after all, they were still some distance away.

'Remain where you are, there are four men heading this way. I will head them off,' Melachus whispered even though it was unlikely they would hear his words at such a distance.

'Don't be a bloody fool, you cannot fight four men. Take flight. It is unlikely they will give chase.'

'And what about you?'

'They may not have seen me, I will just rest here a while.'

'Bravery is all well and good, Plinius, but you know if they stumble across your position then your wound will guarantee your destruction. No, I think it's best I speak to our guests.'

'Melachus!' Plinius tried in vain to prevent his friend walking towards danger.

Melachus was aware that his hand must stay away from his blade. One movement in that direction would alert the four men to possibly attack. Behind his back, however, his free hand clutched at a dagger. As he walked towards the men, he did not take a direct route. If they had seen Plinius then he wanted to make it as difficult as possible to find his friend in a sea of bodies.

One of the four called out a warning as Melachus neared. There was no plan, Melachus needed to get close if he had to fight then he would need the element of surprise. He raised a hand to his ear and gestured that he did not understand as one of the four once again gave a warning. Then another of the men held up his hand and rubbed his fingers together, the gesture was understood the world over. It meant if Melachus wanted to leave then he best have coin to pay for that luxury. He gave a smile and nodded his head, then took his coin purse and threw it to one of the men, who was now only a few paces away.

The warrior leaned forward to catch his prize and for a moment, his focus left the lone man to his front. Melachus dropped low bringing the dagger sweeping around and upwards. The blade hit its intended target in the groin. In the same move Melachus drew his sword and rose slashing at the next enemy. Perhaps, through luck rather than judgement, his blade ripped at flesh as another man fell clutching at his throat. The third warrior, however, simply side- stepped Melachus' attempt at claiming another victim. Then he darted forward, and drove his heavy spear towards the now exposed Melachus. His armour gave way to such a powerful blow and the spear smashed all aside as it ripped through his chest. The blow stopped Melachus dead; his sword lay limp in his hand. The victorious warrior knocked the weapon from Melachus' hand and then surprisingly just stepped back and watched. Melachus could feel the trickle of blood running from his mouth but the massive wound to his chest just felt like a heavy pressure. His legs faltered and he slipped to his knees and then toppled forward. The heavy spear dug into the dirt and so Melachus hung like a grotesque puppet to the delight of the two warriors who had survived Melachus' best efforts to send them to the next world. The two men then had a heated conversation and then walked away leaving Melachus to his last moments.

They all had seen Plinius fall; one of the warriors wanted simply to plunder the bodies, which littered the ground. The warrior who had so effectively dealt with Melachus, however, wanted to seek out the man they had seen fall. His reasoning had been that if a man had tried to hide his location and was willing to give up his life to do so; the fallen man may be of great importance and therefore carry substantial coin. His argument was strong enough to sway his comrades and they went in search of Plinius.

The injured Plinius had been listening to the unseen warriors move closer for some time. He had guessed that Melachus had fallen in his attempt to save his life and now he faced a very real possibility that he would never leave this place. He did not feel fear only anger at not being able to fight the men who had killed his friend and would prevent him from seeing his beloved Chia. He moved his hand and managed to clasp his dagger and then he prayed to the gods to grant him the opportunity to take at least one of the bastards with him. He could tell they were drawing nearer and he heard the movement of bodies as they searched for a man not yet dead. Suddenly, his fury at the thought of dying face down in the dirt forced him to stand. 'Come on you bastards!'

The two men smiled, they could see that the warrior before them was in no condition to match blade against blade.

The killer of Melachus lifted his hand and rubbed his fingers together.

Plinius laughed and then his face turned serious. 'You goat's cock! Come take it if you want it.'

The warrior did not understand the words that Plinius used but he understood their meaning and so his hand moved to his blade. Before a sword could be drawn, a terrible scream split the air, which made the warrior intent on killing Plinius turn. His comrade stood, eyes bulging with shock at the great blade protruding from his chest. The warrior slipped sideways to reveal his killer.

'Look, Cassian, the idle bastard was just having a rest.' Spartacus looked beyond the remaining warrior and smiled.

'Not sure we should even take him back,' replied a breathless Cassian.

'I swear in all my days, I have never met two men so full of shit.' Plinius tried to hide his relief to see Spartacus and Cassian.

Spartacus laughed and then looked at the remaining warrior who shifted uneasily knowing that he had just lost his advantage.

'I would have been inclined to let you walk free from this place.' Suddenly, Spartacus was moving and the warrior realised the fact to late, his hand did not succeed in drawing his blade before his neck felt the full force of Spartacus' blow. 'But Melachus was a brother to me, you bastard.'

Cassian and Spartacus helped Plinius to where Melachus hung for all to see, but no last words were possible because their friend saw with unseeing eyes and had already begun his final journey.

'Many good men have been lost but now is not the time to honour them. We must make it back across the river. With our help, do you think you can make it?' Spartacus asked.

'What choice do I have?' His eyes never left the fallen Melachus.

'None, so let's move.'

CHAPTER FIFTEEN

Rubius entered the healer's tent. He stared at the sleeping one-armed Victus. Despite the loss of a limb Victus seemed in better health. The spectral whiteness of the skin that had haunted him on Rubius' last visit had gone.

Rubius turned to leave not wanting to wake an injured man. Besides, he had little motivation to converse with Victus. Since their last visit, he had thought deeply on Victus' story and in truth, Rubius had nothing but misgivings surrounding the loss of Victus' men.

'Rubius,' a rasping voice sounded, 'is our army victorious?'

'They carried the field,' replied Rubius. He knew that his words did nothing to reveal the truth of the real events that occurred on the battlefield. He could see Victus wanted more information and so added, 'The battle was won but the bridge was lost.'

'So what now?' Victus asked.

'Now, you go back to Rome and heal at your leisure.'

'A few days and I will be able to resume my duties.' Victus had no wish to return to Rome. He knew if victory was nearby then so was wealth, a real fortune that would see him scale the social ladder within Rome.

'No, Victus, the campaign will be tasking to the fittest of warriors. You will suffer upon the road and become a burden to those around you when they have other tasks to complete.'

Victus bit his lip and waited just a moment for the rage to settle within his gut before he spoke. 'I have served you well,' he stated, the words aimed like a dagger at Rubius' sense of honour and loyalty.

'And you will be extremely well rewarded for that service. I will hear no more on the matter. I must place priority on completing this task above any friendship. Your transport will arrive shortly. I wish you all haste in both your journey and recovery.' Rubius turned to leave, he would be glad when Victus was carried away from this place, for any thought of friendship was rapidly vanishing.

'You just want me out of your way. What is it, Rubius, fearful that the men will soon know that I know how to win a war and you fall short? This is not a hunting trip where laughter and wine flow, you do what needs to be done and if that means you kill every bastard in sight then you had best have the balls to do it.'

Rubius turned quickly and raced to Victus' side, his face flushed with anger and he leaned in close so that the healers could not hear his words. 'Yes, I want you gone, you murderous fuck. You slaughtered women and children in those villages, people that were not even our enemy. I know you left your men to die and if I could prove it, you'd be missing your fucking head. Now I suggest you take my generous offer before I decide the last thing you will witness is the inside of this tent. Got anything else to say, you arrogant bastard?'

Victus remained silent knowing that his life was close to being cut short.

Rubius waited only a moment before turning and striding away.

***

It took two days for Spartacus, Cassian and Plinius to catch up with the army. Despite the young warrior's protestations

Plinius went straight to the healer's tent mainly due to the insistence of Cassian.

Spartacus and Cassian went in search of their families. As they wandered through the camp they noticed how the mood within it had lifted. Spartacus was pleased because if these men could put defeat behind them so readily then they were ready to taste victory. They spotted an area hidden from the remainder of the camp by tree cover. They could hear the unmistakeable sound of children's laughter. They manoeuvred around the natural obstacle and for a moment both stopped and just observed a world that existed away from war. Children played laughing so much that they fell about unable to control their lower limbs. Then both saw Sikarbaal as he allowed the children to climb on his back and treat him as a placid pony.

'I am not sure all within this camp will be so exultant to see Plinius' return from the other world.' As Cassian spoke, he looked at Spartacus and raised an eyebrow.

'You have noticed the way he looks upon her?'

'There is little doubt that our friend Sikarbaal is rather taken with Chia,' replied Cassian.

'She is a beautiful woman, a fact of which, she is well aware. Let us hope that this does not become a problem.' Spartacus was watching Sikarbaal; the man rarely took his eyes from Plinius' woman.

'Chia is devoted to Plinius, Spartacus. She may have faults, but disloyalty is not one of them.'

'Cassian, we both know her feelings for Plinius. Sikarbaal may need convincing that the object of his desires will always be out of reach.'

The conversation ended abruptly as Chia glanced up from her child. The forced laughter she held in place for her child's sake vanished. She rose and with a walk that suggested she held the woes of world within her breast, she moved towards the two men. Sikarbaal followed no more than a few paces to her rear.

'You found Plinius?' she asked. Her eyes showed the signs that many tears had had burst the banks of her fortitude. Her voice trembled, fearing the reply of those that stood to her front.

'He is in the healer's tent,' Spartacus replied with all the gentility he could muster. He found women vague creatures, especially in moments that required empathy. He would rather face the legions of Rome armed with nothing more than a smile, than encounter a woman with a tear in her eye.

Chia did not understand his reply. 'Why…?'

Cassian held up a hand preventing the completion of Chia's question. 'He will need plenty of care. The gods have seen fit to allow Plinius to remain part of this world.' He smiled at Chia.

She stood without movement as though her mind struggled to comprehend Cassian's words. Suddenly, she screamed and then kissed Sikarbaal on the cheek. She then kissed Cassian and launched herself at Spartacus, embracing the former gladiator. 'I know you have brought him back to me,' she whispered in his ear. She then kissed him, the coldness that had existed between the two of them since they'd travelled by sea, was forgotten. She raced away, leaving the three men in awkward silence.

Finally, Sikarbaal cleared his throat and spoke. 'Excellent news, I doubt she would have recovered from the loss of Plinius.'

'Plinius is a good man. They share a fondness for one another that is rarely seen, it would be a day of great sadness should that ever end.' Cassian had sent a guarded message that Sikarbaal should hide his feelings away and allow the love of Plinius and Chia to exist without interference. The message was received and the sorrowful figure of Sikarbaal nodded and then moved away without another word.

'Let us hope that will be an end to the matter,' Spartacus said as he watched Sikarbaal.

Cassian did not answer because deep down he doubted that the warrior whose eyes burned with such fire for the woman of another, could choose not to seek her out anymore than he could choose not to take a breath. Cassian knew that sometimes nature forced a hand, no matter the consequences.

***

The heavy timbered wagon that carried Victus moved along the track. Within, the former officer now relieved of his command and a limb plotted his way of gaining revenge. Crassus would hear of his bastard's failure to destroy the pitiful army, which defended Commagene. Firstly, however, he would take his case before Mithridates. After all, Victus reasoned, it was on Pontus' orders that he'd carried out the attacks on the villages with such savagery. If he could portray himself as the gallant warrior betrayed by his commander's foolish decision he may even find the entire army falling into his hands. Commagene was where the real wealth lay. Victus smiled, wealth and power were so close and he intended to grasp both. He lay back and cursed the pain that accompanied each movement; he consoled himself that an arm was a price paying for the rewards that lay ahead.

The wagon had been travelling for two days when it encountered its first village. The two guards entrusted with Victus' safety craved refreshment. They quickly dismounted and went in search of wine but were called back to the wagon by Victus. The Roman did not intend to leave the interior of the wagon and he pointed out that he should receive refreshment before they considered sampling the local swill, claimed to be wine.

The wagon driver spotted a woman and called out to her, the woman seemed nervous at approaching the men. A guard ordered her to find refreshment and threw a coin in her direction. The woman bent to retrieve the coin and then hurried away. One of the guards told the other what he would like to do with the woman and both gave way to salacious laughter. A voice sounded from within the wagon chastising them for their merriment. The guards scowled back but made no reply. Moments later the woman returned with two skins of wine and some bread. The guard grasped a wine skin and then smiled. Lifting one to his mouth he spat into the vessel and gave it a shake, the other guard laughed. He then handed the wine back to the woman. 'Give that to the arrogant bastard,' he whispered.

The woman nodded her agreement and walked towards the wagon. As she did, the guards and the wagon driver set about consuming the bread and the other skin of wine. She pulled back the curtain. The man inside was facing away from her and she tried to quietly place the wine by his side. Men of wealth often thought they had a right to claim all possessions that were near and that often included women of lower social standing. Suddenly, the man turned and for the first time, the woman saw his face. She jumped and then dropped the wine and raced from the wagon without uttering a word. Victus laughed at the fear shown by the woman; he had always enjoyed tormenting those he saw as beneath his breeding. The wine surprised him, its taste so pleasing that he had soon drained the skin of its contents. With a large guttural belch, he laid his head back down and was soon in a heavy sleep. It was from this sleep that he did not hear the raised voices of the villagers.

One of the guards turned to see a crowd forming. 'What do you suppose has got them so excited?'

'That bastard probably tried to get his one good hand between her legs,' replied the wagon driver. As he did so, he pointed to the woman who has delivered the wine to Victus. The guards and the wagon driver began to laugh but that laughter soon disappeared as they realised the crowd was heading in their direction. The crowd began to move with more purpose, anger issuing from every sinew. The guards realising the danger tried to draw their weapons but far too slowly. The crowd overwhelmed them, the men of the village did not carry sword or spear but in acts of violence club and cleaver are adequate replacements. The guards and wagon driver went down quickly, the make do weapons slicing and smashing bones with simple efficiency.

A man stepped forward and motioned the woman to join him at the wagon. He carefully opened the small door and pulled back the curtain. Victus was oblivious to the fate of his men and snored his contentment.

'Are you sure it is him?'

'It is the man. I would never forget the beast responsible for the death of my husband.'

If Victus had been awake, he may have felt the wagon lurch forward and begin its journey. He might even have sensed the difference in the track as it became a far more uncomfortable ride. When the wagon juddered to a halt once more, he still lazed in his ignorance. He briefly stirred when heavy thuds sounded outside but the wine held him too tightly and he closed his eyes. The thuds were the bodies of his men and heavy timbers placed onto the wagon, the doorway was blocked and then kindling placed strategically.

The crackling of recently set alight branches did not rouse the slumbering Roman. The bodies caught fire quickly; the hair retreated from the fire as it shrivelled in the face of ferocity and the flesh began to burn. Human fat dripped onto the burning timbers, it popped and gave off a pungent odour. The smell invaded the wagon's interior, wafting to the nostrils of the sleeping man.

He woke with a smile believing the guards had shown some initiative and cooked a decent meal. Gradually, however, his senses informed him something was wrong. Panic took over as he saw the smoke within the wagon. He called out for help but no reply was forthcoming. Fighting against the pain of his wound, he forced himself to sit up and push open the small wagon door. There was no movement in its timbers and so he turned as quickly as he could manage and placed his feet on those same timbers. He kicked out but the door remained stubborn to his attempts.

It was no use, his exit showed no signs of weakness. He screamed out, demanding to be released from the inferno. At first, he threatened those that may have been listening and then he pleaded offering great wealth to whoever should save his life. Small flames began to lick their way through the timbers; the small wisps of flames stung his exposed flesh. Now he was screaming, partly through pain but mostly through fear. He witnessed the flesh begin to peel from his body. His energy expended, he could do nothing more than await his fate. As the flames wrapped around his body there was a crack, as the heat of the fire had smashed the doors hinges. Suddenly, a blackened Victus could see the daylight but could make no move towards safety. He could see the face of a woman; she was smiling at his agony. The pain had stopped now and his last moments were consumed with a question. He did not know the woman, so why would she wish him harm?

The timbers of the wagon burned into the night and the self-proclaimed leader of men Victus Libirius Tumbris was nothing more than ash.

Chapter Sixteen

It would be many days before the enemy could bring its substantial army to bear against Spartacus' forces. The former gladiator knew that he would not be permitted to make the same mistakes for a second time. Preparation would be the key in concluding the war and see the army of Mithridates routed from these lands. The vast numbers of the enemy dictated that a direct confrontation should happen only after the enemy had endured many hardships.

Spartacus began to draw up his plans. Firstly, he ordered that a Parthian rider accompany each one of Tigranes' scouts. The reason was two-fold, the reports were more likely to be accurate and Spartacus did not completely trust Tigranes' men although he did not share those feeling with the young ruler. After all, those men had switched their allegiance from father to son, so was the switch genuine? Alternatively, would they be too willing to return to their former master now the first battle had been lost?

The next part of the preparation was to send Adrianicus and Cassian to plot every conceivable approach of the enemy and the terrain that it must encounter. He also sent Sikarbaal because the warrior had found it impossible to keep a healthy distance from Chia. Many in the camp were beginning to notice his attention to her, only Plinius seemed oblivious to Sikarbaal's sickness. Spartacus considered it a sickness; he had seen many a fine warrior and man brought to his knees because of a shapely breast. Spartacus knew Sikarbaal may well be lovesick but he was also a fine warrior and could well be a match for Plinius with a blade, especially as Plinius was presently wounded. Therefore, Spartacus gave the orders that would keep Sikarbaal from the camp and subsequently away from temptation.

Days passed with little news in terms of enemy movement. Scouts searched day and night trying to tie the opposing army down to a location. Without knowing their path it would be impossible to plot their downfall. When Spartacus had almost convinced himself that the enemy had simply vanished, excited scouts raced into the camp. After hearing the scouts' news, Spartacus decided to call a meeting of all his officers. He sent word that Cassian and Adrianicus should return, so they too could be present.

When all the officers had assembled, he gave orders that the scouts should repeat their news from earlier. It took time but the scouts had learned since the first battle not to leave any detail to chance.

'What of my father's forces?' Tigranes asked.

'The Armenian army has moved from the enemy's camp. Only a token force has been left, no more than four thousand men,' replied the scout.

'Where has he gone?' Spartacus could not understand why the old leader had split his forces.

Tigranes did not rush his reply. He feared making another mistake that would place the army at risk. 'As I have mentioned before, my father is reluctant to vacate his seat of power for any substantial length of time. I imagine he believes our army is no longer a threat. The men he has left behind is a diplomatic move, it shows his support for his ally, Mithridates.' Spartacus went to speak but Tigranes interrupted. 'I will send scouts to locate him and watch his every move.'

The response made Spartacus smile. 'You people will have a fine leader one day.' Tigranes nodded his gratitude at Spartacus' kind words.

'So, Thracian, do you think you can outwit this enemy?' Cleomenes was eager to know what Spartacus had planned for the enemy.

'Outwit? I intend to grind their army to dust.' It was bravado but Spartacus was aware that confidence flows down the ranks as a mountain stream races into the valleys. 'Every army, no matter how disciplined, is only as effective as its supply route. Take away the supplies and even the legions of Rome descend to chaos. The path that the enemy have taken will rely on water gathered from these villages. I wonder what will happen if we deny them that resource?'

'I will not destroy my people's water supply or put their crops at risk,' blurted Tigranes. The young leader flushed, indignant at the idea.

Spartacus held up a hand to placate Tigranes. 'I have no intention of destroying the well or placing your people in harm's way.'

'Then how do we prevent them falling into enemy hands?' Cassian asked.

'By making it look like the villages are deserted and the wells are poisoned. How many of you would drink when dead animals lay next to the only water source? Then imagine that you send for supplies and they arrived but the men never return. All this and you are blind because your scouts die in the night. All this and more, sporadic attacks which slow their progress making the lack of water have a devastating effect. When the final battle arrives they will be in no condition to fight, and hopefully, many will already have deserted. We have already seen that our enemy are not seasoned troops, placed under these trails I cannot see them willing to fight for long.'

'They are in a foreign land, they will desert,' Cassian added, reinforcing Spartacus' point.

'First we must achieve our plans. I will require your help, Cassian. It is, as you always say, the attention to detail which will bring victory.'

'I did not know you were listening,' Cassian replied with a smile.

'It is difficult to prevent you talking without the use of a blade.'

The group laughed and then they set about bringing destruction to their enemy.

***

With the enemy so far away, Spartacus allowed the troops to drink heavily that night. He recognised that all had fought with skill and valour in the battle and yet still tasted defeat. He knew men needed time to force the demons from their mind and prepare for another looming fight.

Cassian had disappeared; the former gladiator knew his friend would be focussed completely on the tasks that lay ahead. The Roman would take the plan apart, look for any potential problems and then set about solving any issue. Spartacus strolled away from the camp seeking solitude; he had recognised many years before that being in command was a lonely affair. Picking his way along a narrow track he passed the sentries, only spending the briefest of moments in idle conversation. He moved on, wanting nothing more than to be alone with his thoughts. For the first time since he had entered these lands, he noticed a cool breeze upon his skin. Closing his eyes, he allowed that breeze to wash over him, bathing in its purity. Then a cough dragged him from his moment of tranquillity. A form was seated on a large rock in the shadows. For a moment, Spartacus wondered if the figure was friend or foe.

'Forgive me, Spartacus, it seems I am not the only person who craves silence from time to time.'

'Cleomenes, I thought you would be drinking with your men. I shall leave you to your thoughts.' As he Spartacus finished speaking, he deftly removed his hand from the hilt of his blade.

'Please do not leave because of me. It is always good to have a friend nearby. The problem with a life as a warrior, you lose so many friends.'

Spartacus was shocked that Cleomenes so readily called him friend. They had spent little time together to form any kind of bond and the decision he made at the bridge to deny the Spartans the opportunity for glory had not been a popular one.

'You seem troubled, Cleomenes.' Spartacus felt the man's unease.

'The leadership of men is always a heavy burden. Few men could understand the extra weight I am forced to bear.' He paused as if deciding to continue. 'You are probably the only man who could possibly understand within this awful place.'

'What do you mean?'

'You have become legend in your own lifetime. Loved and feared in equal measure throughout the world. Your name will be written in the wind and will caress the ears of warriors for an eternity.'

'I am just a man, Cleomenes,' replied Spartacus. Talk of legends always made him feel awkward.

'That is my point, Spartacus. You are just a man but to those men in the camp you are far more. To my men I am Cleomenes, direct descended of Leonidas greatest of all Spartan men. It is not enough for us to be mere men.'

'You should concentrate on surviving this war, Cleomenes. Let others tell the tales of heroic actions.'

'Survive? I do not fear death, Spartacus. I fear the look of disappointment in the eyes of my men. I fear my people only being remembered for one act of glory. Leonidas cast a shadow across Sparta. He became a mountain that no other man could climb.'

'Then do not try, Cleomenes. If it were not for your actions I would be lying in the dirt. I do not show gratitude to the blood of Leonidas, but Cleomenes and the men he leads.' Spartacus' words seemed to soothe Cleomenes' restless spirit. 'Now, how would a mere mortal like to accompany a living legend on his walk of the camp?'

Cleomenes smiled and performed a bow. 'It would be an honour, oh, mighty Spartacus.' The two men laughed and then walked back to the camp.

The troops were in good spirits as the consumption of wine took its affect. Nonetheless, one section of the camp remained in sombre mood.

'They have far more to lose than the rest of us,' whispered Spartacus.

'We all risk our lives,' Cleomenes replied.

'That is true but if we fail those men,' he said, pointing towards the Commagian troops, 'they will forfeit more than just their final breath. What do you think will happen to their family and homes should Mithridates and his forces are successful?'

'I see your point. We had best make sure those whores from Pontus are beaten and sent running back to their land like whipped dogs,' Cleomenes replied.

Spartacus nodded his agreement and the two men left the troops of Commagene to their thoughts. As they continued their journey, they took the time to talk with the men and share a skin of wine. The remainder of the camp seemed in good humour; if they feared what the future held, it was hidden from the eyes of mortal men.

Spartacus was happy with what he had observed and was just about to tell Cleomenes that he would retire when a scream split the air. Spartacus and Cleomenes were running because the scream came from the section of camp where the families were housed. Spartacus' own family resided there and his pace reflected his concern. They reached the desired location only to find many warriors crowded around all looking in one direction. Spartacus pushed the men aside determined to see what lay ahead. Finally, as he cleared the crowd he saw what he feared. Sikarbaal and Plinius were circling one another and Spartacus could tell it would not be long before one or both were lying in the dirt. He leapt forward and held Plinius tight, preventing him from launching an attack. Cleomenes did likewise to Sikarbaal.

'What is happening here?' Spartacus demanded.

'He tried to kiss Chia. Bastard! I will kill you.' Plinius tried to push past Spartacus and get his hands on Sikarbaal.

Spartacus held his ground and refused to allow Plinius to close the distance between himself and Sikarbaal. Spartacus moved closer to Plinius and whispered into his ear. 'You are injured, if you insist on challenging this man then he will kill you. Tell me, Plinius who will stand at Chia's side when you are food for the carrion birds?' For a moment, Spartacus thought that Plinius did not hear his words because the young warrior struggled to free himself and set about killing Sikarbaal. However, the strength left Plinius and he dropped his arms offering no attempt at pursuing his wish to do battle. Then Plinius turned and without another word limped away, even Chia was left behind.

Spartacus rounded on Sikarbaal. 'What the fuck do you think you are doing?'

'I must have drunk too much wine.'

The explanation was feeble and so Spartacus answered it with a fist to the jaw.

Sikarbaal crashed to the ground but to Spartacus' surprise was on his feet again in moments. 'Be careful, Spartacus, I did not kill Plinius for Chia's sake. You do not have the same protection.'

Spartacus drew his sword within the blink of an eye. Sikarbaal however, matched the gladiator's speed with a weapon.

Chia screamed for them to stop. She approached Sikarbaal placing herself between the two blades. 'Sikarbaal, I have valued your friendship, when I thought Plinius was dead you brought great comfort in my most desperate moments. Nonetheless, you must realise I am and always will be Plinius'.'

She tried to raise a hand to his cheek but he caught her hand. 'Yes of course. Forgive me.' He turned to Spartacus refusing to look in Chia's direction. 'I will restrict my duties to those ordered by Adrianicus. Unless you wish to continue?' He nodded towards Spartacus' blade.

'I am sure Adrianicus has many tasks for a man of your skills,' Spartacus replied.

On hearing Spartacus' answer Sikarbaal strode away without meeting Chia's eye.

'A great shame, I was beginning to like the man,' Cleomenes announced.

'Yes.' Spartacus felt tired and so said his farewells. Then he sought out the warm embrace of Cynna.

CHAPTER SEVENTEEN

Two days later news arrived that the enemy had increased their pace, marching through most of the previous night.

'We will be hard pressed to complete our task in the first village if they continue at that pace,' announced Cassian.

'It will be close but I believe I can slow their progress. Balen, I am sure your men prefer not to be sitting around camp on their arses.' Spartacus addressed the Parthian knowing his men were growing restless.

'Too much rest is not good for an archer. It mists the eye and weakens the arm,' replied Balen.

'Tigranes, if you would carry out the tasks we have discussed. Adrianicus, you and your men are to assist Tigranes.' Both men nodded their compliance, Spartacus turned to Cassian. 'If you would prepare what is needed for the first village. I will send men to meet you there and they will bring you to my location. Then let the hunt begin and may the gods favour our audacity at least.'

Spartacus and the Parthian riders rode out immediately. Cassian's task was more complex, and would take time to prepare. Nonetheless, when the sun reached its pinnacle he raised his hand and gave the signal for the convoy to begin its journey. Spartacus knew that the convoy would arrive; his belief in Cassian's abilities was absolute. The gladiator urged his mount forward knowing that for Cassian to have time to perform his duties, the enemy now must be slowed.

They pressed on only stopping briefly to rest their horses. They raced through villages where inhabitants skulked in their homes, fearful the horsemen intended violence. Each night the riders did not stop until the lack of light became dangerous to their steeds. Food was taken and sleep rushed, for at first light they would once again ride. Each day mimicked the previous one until at last Spartacus called for the pace to slow.

Finally, Spartacus' forces left the track and sought out a suitable vantage point in the higher ground. All warriors knew that higher ground was a great advantage in war and Spartacus intended to use that advantage to the full. He gave orders that the men should rest, with only a few men sent to scout and determine when the enemy would arrive. When at last the news that the enemy force was in fact nearby, Spartacus called the men together and explained their mission. With Balen acting as interpreter, the Parthian troops began to understand their role and Spartacus could tell by the smiles that they were looking forward to some target practice. It seemed the enemy had once again slowed their advance, Spartacus guessed it was because many were not seasoned troops and could not maintain the pace.

As he was organising his first attack, Cassian arrived; the Roman was keen to be informed on the enemy's position. The gladiator explained that the enemy marched with their more experienced troops, in this case the Armenian warriors, to the front of the column. The last of the enemy force was the supply wagons and Spartacus saw an opportunity because the wagons were slow and cumbersome. In fact, they had become detached from the column and that made them vulnerable.

The advanced scouts of Rubius' army were slain in silence. Their bodies tied to their mounts and then those mounts held until the time was right. Spartacus and Cassian took most of the men and circled around the main enemy force. Balen took another group and dispatched any enemy scouts that rode on the flanks of the enemy.

Rubius was unaware but his entire army was blinded, his scouts were lost and an unknown danger neared. His blissful ignorance of that blindness was shattered as two frightened mounts raced towards his column. The warriors at the front of the column tried to calm the beasts and it took time to realise that the horses' former masters were also present. As the lifeless bodies were dragged from the excited beasts, shouts went up for officers to attend the scene. The shouts then turned to screams as arrows began to land within the ranks at the front of the column.

Spartacus lay on a huge rock that over-hung the winding track. He watched a fly struggling in an elaborate web. The harder it tried to pull itself free of the grasping sinews, the further it seemed to become entangled. The fly slowed in its attempt to free itself, the ferocity of its efforts sapping its precious energy. A spider rushed in to deliver the fatal blow, the pitiful insect had no fight to give and accepted its fate. The former gladiator became aware of screams in the distance and knew it was time for his men to go to war. He rose from the rock and leapt down onto the back of a passing wagon. His blade was out before his feet touched timber. Spartacus' sword swept down towards the wagon driver still unaware that his life was in mortal peril. Helmet, skull and brain material surrendered to the mighty blow and just for a moment, the world stood perfectly still. The other guards and wagon drivers looked with shock at the bloodied warrior who had slaughtered their comrade without ceremony. Then chaos descended as Spartacus' men emerged from the shadows intent on destruction. Cassian took the knees of a guard and then reversed the blade and punctured the eye and then skull of an onrushing enemy. Spartacus blocked a blade and then stepped inside his enemy's reach; he drove his fist into the man's throat. As the man died, Spartacus was afforded the opportunity to survey the small skirmish. The enemy were either dead or dying but Spartacus knew there was no time to stand and gloat; it was possible that reinforcement were already on their way.

'Destroy the supplies, leave them with nothing.' He bellowed the order and his men responded with simple efficiency. Goods were torn from the wagons and as they landed in the dirt they were smashed. The most precious of all, the water barrels were hacked apart, the cool liquid draining away to nothingness. Even the wagons were tipped onto their sides and the beasts that had pulled them cut free and driven off. Spartacus observed that the destruction was complete. He gave the order and the men who had emerged from the shadows returned to them leaving only slaughter behind.

Rubius and the other officers had dismounted fearing they provided too tempting a target for the unseen enemy archers. They knew the supply wagons were gone, the screams of dying men carried to their lines.

'We need to move.' As Democolese spoke, he heard the whoosh of an arrow pass close to his head.

'No, we must endure the falling arrows. We have no idea how many of the enemy swarm nearby,' replied Rubius.

'But our supplies are gone, we cannot simply remain here.'

'Come the dropping of the sun, their archers will have lost their easy targets. We will march and gain the supplies we need at a village up ahead. We can at least defend this position. Tell the men to seek what cover they can.'

Democolese nodded his agreement to Rubius' order. He turned to pass the order onto his aid only to see the man grasping at his throat. The man tried in vain to wrench the shaft from his flesh and moments later fell to the dirt. Democolese had liked the man but it was not the time for sentiment and so he set about completing Rubius' orders. Besides, he knew this day would bring death to many and it was foolish to dwell on the death of one man.

***

Adrianicus watched Tigranes talking to the village elder and shook his head. He wondered why Tigranes did not simply order the old fool to carry out his wishes. The village needed to be cleared and with all haste. Finally, the elder nodded his head and within moments the slumbering village burst into life. In truth, it was not a large settlement but it contained the lifeblood that all armies in the field craved, and that was water. Some of the greatest armies ever assembled had fallen to ruin because of the lack of the precious commodity.

The women and children were loaded onto wagons, the men of the village followed on foot. The village took on a spectral feel with only Tigranes and his men left behind and they were not part of this world. They did not fit and the village sensed the abnormality. Tigranes ordered that a wagon be brought forward, the stench it emitted had led the leader to have it left beyond the village border until the inhabitants had vacated. As it trundled along passing the black armoured warriors, they clasped a hand over their mouths and nostrils. One of the younger warriors gagged and then registered his disgust by covering a nearby wall with vomit. The wagon finally stopped and the driver stepped down, his face covered with cloth protecting his senses from the foul stench. He moved to the rear of the wagon and reached inside. He pulled a large packet the size of a small child from the wagon. Adrianicus approached the man, snatched the package and strode towards the well, which stood within the village. Adrianicus made it clear to all that were present that the task was far too important to be entrusted to a mere wagon driver.

Adrianicus bent and removed the wrappings; it revealed the body of a dog, which showed no outwardly signs of its manner of death. He positioned the unfortunate beast to give the best effect to the enemy as they marched into the village. Then he collected the substantial well bucket and tipped an unknown substance into it from a glass phial he had carried within his tunic.

'Sikarbaal, take that,' he said pointing to the wagon, 'to the far end of the village. Be creative with its contents.'

Sikarbaal nodded his agreement but struggled to hide his disgust at the task that lay ahead. Once more the wagon driver made the wagon lurch forward and Sikarbaal followed its path, trying his best not to inhale the stench which emanated from its cargo. The wagon trundled down the centre of the village and then left the view of Tigranes and the other warriors. At the very entrance of the village, Sikarbaal gave the signal for the wagon to halt and then the warrior climbed aboard. He tried in vain to move the object and in his anger, he ripped back the covers. His fury revealed a horse, which like the dog was lost to this world but showed no signs of what made it depart. The stench was overwhelming and he fought back the urge to vomit.

'You get back here and help,' he called to the driver.

The driver was no soldier and disliked being given orders, especially by a man not even of these lands. He was local and thought this man could show a little more respect, no matter how much coin they paid for the use of his wagon. For a moment, he thought of refusing, but the thought of displeasing the warrior outweighed the thought of handling the rancid beast. He climbed down from the wagon and moved to the rear of the wagon. He clasped at the beast's legs and pulled with all his might. At first, the horse refused to move; it had lost its life but retained the stubbornness that it had displayed before death. Both men were flushed with exertion as the horse shot backwards and flopped from the wagon. The startled wagon driver slipped as he tried to avoid the beast and went down beneath its considerable weight. The carcass smashed down heavily upon him causing him to scream out his agony. Sikarbaal jumped down from the wagon and rushed to the man's aid. He tried in vain to move the beast and only succeeded in causing the driver more pain.

'I will fetch men and a healer,' he told the man but as he turned to leave, a voice sounded.

'May I be of assistance?' The voice was instantly recognisable.

'Adrianicus, I think his legs are broken.'

'Well, I have some experience in such matter, shall I take a look?'

Sikarbaal had a strange sense of foreboding and placed a hand at Adrianicus' shoulder, preventing him from moving forward.

Adrianicus looked at the hand and smiled. 'Do not forget your position. Your infatuation with Plinius' whore has made you weak.' His words made fury race through Sikarbaal but the warrior managed to control his anger and reluctantly stepped aside.

Adrianicus moved forward and then crouched to the injured man's front. He raised a vessel to the man's lips. 'Something to ease the pain?'

The driver eagerly accepted what he believed to be an act of kindness.

Adrianicus rose and then turned. 'Bring the wagon, after all, a good wagon is so hard to find these days.' He then strode away without looking back.

Sikarbaal stared down at the driver.

The man looked back but he did not see.

***

Rubius gave the signal and the column lurched forward, he could feel the fear emanating from his men. His men had been sheltering from arrows most of the day and although those deadly shafts had ceased to fall, now his men faced a night march. His men had been able to consume very little in terms of food and water with the supplies being destroyed. This meant tired and frightened men looked anxiously towards the shadows as they picked their way slowly up the track. He had given the order that the injured would remain behind, promising to send supplies as soon as he reached the village. That decision now led to horror, because the column had not been marching long when it heard the unmistakeable screams of their men butchered by the enemy. Rubius was both horrified and filled with hatred for an unseen enemy. Rubius could not believe that warriors would slaughter injured men that offered no danger, he considered it a despicable act.

It was a view shared by Cassian who questioned Spartacus' decision to carry out such a task.

'It is not something I take pleasure in, Cassian. Nonetheless, we must break their spirit and hearing your comrades die in the night and wondering if you are next, saps a man's will to fight.'

Cassian knew what Spartacus said made perfect military sense but it still weighed heavily on his mind. 'What do we do next?'

'We torment them through the night and collect the arrows from the dead. Every step they make must be in dread. Stragglers will call out their slaughter and they will know that each shadow hides an enemy craving their destruction.' Spartacus knew that Cassian would struggle with this type of warfare and so in a kinder tone added, 'The harder we hurt them, the less of our own men will die when at last we enter battle.'

'I know.' Cassian paused. 'I have an idea.'

It is a fact that a few men can move with great deal more speed than a lumbering column of men. This afforded Spartacus the luxury of choosing when and where to strike at the enemy. It also ensured the success of Cassian's plan that would have such a devastating effect on the enemy.

The first that Rubius knew of Cassian's plan was when he spied flames rising in the distance, the tongues of fire flicking hungrily at the night sky. As the column neared, it was obvious that the fire had been lit upon the track. Rubius forced his men; he had little choice but understood the reluctance to head for what seemed to be an enemy trap. The nervousness turned to horror as he saw that the bodies of his men had been used for kindling. Then as the column moved past the flames and the stench of burning flesh, the arrows began to land in the ranks. The flames had provided the enemy with easy targets and his men either shrank away from the narrow passage highlighted by the fire or raced to be clear of the danger. Death was bad enough but the thought of being left in the darkness waiting for the enemy to swoop down upon them, gripped at his men's guts. Rubius could feel his men losing their courage and he could not blame a single man, for he had never felt so scared in his entire life. He would take the first opportunity to run, but these were his men and he knew he must stay and lead.

Chapter Eighteen

As the early morning sun broke, the village came into view. Rubius wiped the dust from his dry chapped lips. A sense of relief washed over his tired limbs as he imagined tasting the water within the village. He would have liked to climb aboard his mount but the beast was killed in the night and so any act of bravado in front of his men was lost. He urged his men forward, keen to access the supplies that lay within the village.

Hidden in the terrain hidden above the track, Spartacus watched and then gave the signal for his men to cease fire and pull back.

For the first time in what seemed an age the column below was not beset by the thud of arrows. The warriors within that column dared not to think that the enemy had failed and would trouble their march no longer.

'The men will need to rest.' Rubius had leaned forward to whisper the words to Democolese. 'I am not sure how long we could have kept up that march.'

'It was not a night I am keen to repeat.' Democolese stopped his nose wrinkled.' What the fuck is that smell?'

Rubius pointed to the body of a man and his mount. He sensed danger despite the absence of enemy attack. 'Do not let the men break ranks. We enter the village prepared for battle.'

Democolese nodded his agreement and issued the orders.

The column moved slowly into the village. Rubius half expected the enemy to burst from the homes of the villagers, his hand never wandered far from his blade. The object of his and the men's desire was sat proudly in the centre of the village. All would have liked nothing more than to break rank and taste the cooling liquid housed within the well. However, all but one man held their discipline; the sinewy warrior could not bear the thirst and was willing to accept the punishment for just one taste.

Democolese stepped forward to chastise the man, but Rubius held him tight and pointed to the dead dog out to his officer. The animal laid only a few paces from the well, its head pointing away from the water source as though it had already taken its fill. The warrior whooped with joy plunging his head into the well's bucket. The other men looked on enviously wishing that they too could feel the cooling elixir upon their lips. The warrior re-emerged a huge grin upon his face.

Rubius was about to order the first men in the column to move forward but his thoughts were interrupted by a guttural grunt. He turned to see the warrior's grin had disappeared and replaced with a contorted mask of agony. It was clear the man was trying to scream but the spasms racing through his body held his jaw locked open. Those closest to the man took an involuntary step backwards fearing a similar fate.

Rubius, however, moved forward, in a rapid movement drew his dagger and cut the man's throat, ending his tortured sufferings.

'Search the village, if you find any food or water; test it on the horses first. Move with all haste because we will be leaving at the earliest opportunity.' Rubius knew that remaining in the village would have afforded them at least some protection. Nonetheless, the fate of the single warrior and the deserted homes was having its affect; Rubius could tell this was a place that would erode the men's morale. Men, beasts and even the gods had left this place far behind and it seemed prudent to follow their example.

Rubius motioned for Democolese to join him as he strolled around the small village.

'We must change our fortunes and quickly, or this army will fall apart,' he whispered.

'I agree, but we have no idea how many enemy threaten our flanks. The men have not taken nourishment in nearly two days. What can we do without eyes? What is left of our scouts will not venture from the main force.'

'We must match the enemy in his deceit.'

'Do you believe the rumours that the Thracian leads their army?' asked Democolese.

'I have seen these tactics before. He attacks the minds of men long before he engages in battle. Few men understand how close he came to bringing an entire empire to its knees.' The concern and admiration showed clearly on Rubius' face.

'No son of a Thracian whore will send me to the next world,' Democolese announced.

'Do not under estimate Spartacus. He is a born killer, but that is not the sum of the man. He is intelligent and resourceful. Any man that still lives after the trials he has experienced deserves at the very least our respect. The man rebelled against Rome – how the fuck is he still alive?'

'So how do we defeat this man?' Democolese asked not completely joyful at the adoration Rubius seemed to hold for their enemy.

'We must think beyond the usual military tactics. It will not be enough to react to his methods. We must use all our strengths to defeat this man.'

'Then tell me how?'

'I want you to select five hundred men. Those men must be of the highest quality and above all else, trustworthy,' Rubius replied as if he was still thinking through his plan.

'I know the men we can trust.'

'Caution, Democolese, I expect our enemy watch our every move. Our main force will move from this place but the chosen men will remain behind. To our observers it will merely look as though we race to the next village in search of supplies. In truth, we will have to take what the Thracian throws at us and that will test our men. Nonetheless, it will give the five hundred men the time they need to obtain the supplies we need. I have found a way for them to return to us by a rarely used route.' He held up a scroll, which contained a map. 'I believe the enemy will be focussed on our movements. Once our army has the supplies it craves we will force the enemy to battle and the matter will be solved one way or another.'

'If we have an army left by that point.'

'We will lose men, but we have numbers on our side. Once fed and watered I am sure that our warriors will want a reckoning with the enemy.'

***

Spartacus and Cassian rode back to the location that they had pre-arranged with Tigranes. The young leader had left nothing to chance in terms of making sure his people were comfortable, every villager wanted for nothing. Tents gave shelter; there was wine and food in plentiful supply.

Cassian gave order to the next group of riders who would hound the steps of the enemy.

Spartacus watched as Cassian finished with the men and then he observed the warriors ride into the distance. The former gladiator fought the urge to take a mount and ride after them.

'They know their task and even I can tell that they are capable men, Spartacus.' Cassian's tone was one of understanding; he knew his friend preferred to be at danger's point. He could never be content safe in camp when men risked their lives on his orders.

'I know, my friend. Soon we will see if our endeavours bear fruit or are for nought.'

'If we keep up this pressure, I cannot see them holding together. They were breaking at the bridge and that shows that they already know how to turn their backs.'

'For a man who loathes all things military your judgement of warriors shows some expertise, Cassian,' Spartacus replied.

He spoke the truth; Cassian had learned the art of warfare, which was only made more surprising as he made no attempt of the fact that he despised war and all it involved.

'My father told me that to learn we must observe those that excel. I was no higher than your knee at the time. I wanted to carve a gift for my mother and had set my heart on a pony. My mother had been ill for some time and her only real pleasure was watching the ponies gallop around our grounds. I asked my father to show me how to carve but instead he had a slave teach me the craft. It wasn't that my father was too busy; he simply knew the slave was the master when it came to working with wood. Belachus was a wise men, his intelligence was not limited to just the carving of wood.'

'Belachus?'

'Yes, Spartacus, he was a Thracian. At the time, I was honoured to have known him and he genuinely seemed to like me. I thought he was content but I was too young to understand what the lack of freedom meant to a man. Sometimes, I would find him simply gazing towards the horizon but when I asked him what he was looking at he would simply say a distant memory. I never knew what he meant.'

Spartacus felt a twinge of anger deep within, did this Roman know what taking a man's freedom really did to him? He gritted his teeth and let the fury subside knowing that Cassian meant no insult. 'Your mother, did she like the pony?' he asked keen to change the direction of the conversation.

'I hope so,' replied Cassian.

'Hope so?' Spartacus felt confusion by his friend's answer.

'The morning I raced to her room to present the gift, I was stopped by my father. I had never seen him cry before, but on that day, his tears flowed like a river. I did not cry. I thought my mother was simply asleep. It was not until they laid her on the pyre that I realised she would never stroke my hair or laugh as I played. I placed the pony next to her heart and ran into our household, refusing to watch the ceremony. My father's household was consumed with sorrow, in many ways matching my own despair. I reminded my father of my mother and so despite his best efforts we grew distant. He saw her within my eyes and it tore at his heart.'

'And your brother?' Spartacus remembered that Cassian's brother had been killed by Crassus' agents.

'My father found comfort in the arms of another woman. She was a good woman but I never warmed to her or the resulting child. The fault was mine. I felt that my father somehow wronged my mother by loving another. It was not until much later that my father and I formed a better relationship. My brother was a good man but not cut out for life in Rome. He ran up huge debts and became the prey of dangerous men. That is when I took service with Pompey so I could offer my brother protection.'

'That is honourable.'

'No, Spartacus, it was to soothe my guilt. I was cruel to him as a child and if I had been a better brother, he may have grown into a stronger man. In the end it was all for nothing, Crassus saw to that.'

***

The search of the village had yielded only a few wine skins, a pitiful amount that would not quench the thirst of an army.

Rubius ordered that horses were to be slaughtered and the wines and meat be made into a cold stew. Each warrior received no more than a handful of the foul glutinous gloop but not one warrior refused to eat. It tasted no better than it looked but the enjoyment of a meal was not the intention. When the men had finished their nourishment, the order to march was given. Tired men forced aching limbs into action and the fears of what lay ahead weighed heavily in both heart and mind.

Those fears were justified because no sooner had the column left the safety of the village then the arrows began to fall and the screams answered their arrival. Rubius was finally forced to call halt to the march and order his men once more to take cover behind their shields. He would wait for nightfall before continuing and hoped the enemy had no further traps prepared to visit slaughter on his men.

As night fell, he ordered his men to march but many remained; the arrows had found flesh and they had breathed their last in a foreign land far from loved ones.

Five hundred men also moved through the night under the cover of darkness over the landscape. Rubius knew his march had been costly and hoped that cost had bought the five hundred men the chance to evade the eyes of the enemy.

CHAPTER NINETEEN

Nine days had passed since the unfortunate warrior had drunk from the well bucket. Each one of those days was filled with blood and terror for Rubius' army.

Spartacus had returned to the frontline. The gladiator turned general, was not disappointed in what his troops had achieved in his absence. He estimated the enemy losses to be in the hundreds but the real damage had been done to their morale. In all battles soldiers died; it was a fact of warfare. The men in the ranks accepted it as part of the life they had chosen. Nonetheless, no warriors, no matter their discipline, accepted the continued death of comrades without the opportunity to strike back at their aggressors. Furthermore, they were marching through the maelstrom of arrows without supplies. Even the least intelligent of men could imagine that to fight a battle at the end of this march exhausted and with no nourishment would mean only one thing, and that was destruction. Spartacus knew these men were close to breaking; it was perhaps only the thought of meeting their murderous enemy in the dark that prevented them from deserting.

'Cassian, we need a captive.'

'I thought we were showing no mercy?' the Roman replied, never too far away from his friend's side.

'Those,' Spartacus said pointing, 'are filled with dread. I believe if we show them a way to leave the horror behind they will be only too eager to take it.'

Cassian observed the enemy for a few moments and then nodded his agreement. 'I will see that it is done.'

Spartacus drank deeply from a wine skin. He then wiped the sweat from his brow as he watched the enemy. He imagined the exhaustion, the dry throats and cracked lips of those men. He spat on the ground as though his own plan turned the wine to bile. He had fought in many battles and despite the tales of old soldiers, rarely did honour flutter like Praetorian banners. In truth, it had little use in war; men lived by devising ways to kill other men as efficiently as possible. If it meant deceit and treachery then that was fine. Nonetheless, Spartacus had seen men thrown away for too long to like the pure futility and waste of human flesh. Whether it was on the battlefield or in the arena, the men that risked all rarely gained little more than a few coin, and their masters merely looked to the future and the inevitable death of countless others.

The darkness of night had thrown its shadow once more over the land before a terrified enemy warrior was thrown bodily at the feet of Spartacus.

'Please...' the man began to beg but his words were cut short.

'Did I say you could speak?' Spartacus needed to make the man hang on his every word. 'You are in great danger, how you respond could mean your survival or lead to you lying in the dirt breathing your last breath. You were caught leaving your comrades behind, turning your back on those I imagine you once called friend. Is that correct?'

'Yes,' the man replied but then quickly added, 'we have no food or water. How can we fight...?' Once again, he was not allowed to finish.

'But those who rely on you have stayed. They do their duty.'

'They want to run, but fear dying in the shadows.'

'You took that risk.'

'Better a quick death than waiting until the lack of water scrambles our minds and then face an enemy without the strength to wield a blade.' The enemy warrior had gritted his teeth forcing his fear from his heart.

Spartacus had noticed the change in the man and privately admitted to himself he was beginning to like the captive. It took a certain amount of bravery to walk towards unknown dangers.

'What of the duty you owe your master?'

'Master? Mithridates took my land, imprisoned my family and forced me to march under his banner. If I refused, my family would face slavery or worse. Would you honour such a master?' The warrior was angry with his misfortunate. 'If you wish to kill me, do it. It matters little, if it is in this place or on some shit stained battlefield. I will never see my family or home again.' The man slumped, his anger leaving him as he remembered his loved ones.

Spartacus took his time before speaking, observing the man at his feet. 'You require a bargain to be made?' asked Spartacus.

'Bargain?' the warrior asked confused by the words spoken by his captor.

'You wish to return home and find your family?'

'Yes.'

'Then I have a task for you, complete the task and you shall leave this place with enough coin to ensure you have the means to secure your family's release.' Spartacus could tell he had the man's full attention.

'What is it you would have me do?' The warrior's eyes narrowed wondering if he could place any trust in the man standing so proudly to his front.

'Return to your comrades, convince them to lay down the arms and leave the army of Mithridates. They will not be harmed if they desert from the service of my enemy.'

'They fear the shadows and the blades which dwell within them.'

'Speak to them,' Spartacus said pressing his point, 'if they come without weapons they have no need to fear my men.'

The warrior took his time before answering, as though weighing the options but in truth, there was no choice to be made. He must do as this man asked or die. Finally he nodded. 'I will do as you ask.'

'Be sure on your task. Safe passage will be granted to those that leave the enemy column without weapons and within the next two days. Those that stay longer will die, whether they desert or stay to fight.'

'I understand.'

Spartacus smiled and threw a wine skin to the warrior. 'Do not drink too heavily. Your friends out there still need to believe you suffer the same thirst. They will not think kindly of a comrade walking from the shadows, who suffers from the effects of wine.'

The warrior nodded and then savoured the cool acrid liquid as it was over his lips and down his dry dust-lined throat. He received further instructions from Spartacus and then with just another quick gulp of wine he walked back into the shadows.

As the man melted into the darkness, Cassian approached Spartacus. 'Do you think he will do as we demand?' he asked.

'Only the gods have that knowledge. He may simply seek refuge within the column or die when trying to convince the wrong man. War is a craving for hope and good fortune. It has always been so, since man first placed a hand on a blade. This war may be a matter of life and death to many here but the earth beneath our feet has witnessed it many times.'

***

The main camp of Spartacus' army had moved to a location chosen by the former gladiator days earlier. The camp in question was not a quiet affair. It was a place filled with chaotic movement, which impending battle required. The chaos was made worse with the constant movement of troops to and from the frontline, as the harassment of the enemy continued. As each weary warrior returned from their duty, they required nourishment to replenish their energy. Tigranes had also brought the inhabitants of the nearest village under the protection of his camp. All this added to the tasks of the already stretched personnel that would not be used in battle.

Cynna and the other wives were not content to watch the struggle, so they prepared meals and even enlisted the help of the children.

Plinius had grown weary of resting his wound and busied himself serving food to the warriors. He passed the time asking the warriors for news from the frontline.

'How goes it?' Plinius asked the next man in the line without looking up.

'The enemy must feel the gods have cursed each moment of their day,' came the reply.

Plinius recognised the voice and raised his head to see the face of the exhausted Sikarbaal. 'You had best be on your way and eat then,' he snapped.

Sikarbaal, however, did not rush away. 'I wish to apologise, Plinius.'

'What you wish is of no interest,' Plinius replied in rising anger, his face flushed in evidence.

'I allowed my feelings to dominate my judgement and my honour,' he persisted.

'So you have apologised, now move on.' Plinius looked to the next warrior awaiting food. He would not glance in Sikarbaal's direction.

The repentant warrior realised that his attempt at repairing the damage he had caused was futile and resigning himself to the fact, moved on.

Chia had heard the conversation and when Sikarbaal was out of sight, she approached Plinius. 'You should not be so hard on the man, Plinius.'

'Why do you defend him? Do you think when our blades meet he will be the better man?' Plinius' tone was accusatory.

'I do not doubt your prowess with a blade, my love. That is not the only quality the gods have bestowed upon you.'

'What?' Plinius asked confused by the response.

'You also have a kind heart.' She placed a hand on his chest. 'Sikarbaal is a good man, guilty of nothing more than confusing friendship with the possibility of love. Besides, he could hardly resist falling in love with me. I am quite beautiful.' As she finished speaking she gave a wry smile.

'Really? I hadn't noticed.'

Chia gave him a playful slap. 'What attracted you to me then?'

Plinius reached forward and placed a hand on each of her breasts. 'To be honest I never raised my sight above these.' Plinius ducked as he was forced to evade another blow. He restrained the flailing hands of his love and moved in close and kissed her passionately. Initially she resisted but soon matched Plinius' passion.

They broke apart and laughed before Chia dragged the conversation back to Sikarbaal.

'You should think about what I have said, after all, he is a good man.' She emphasised the word good.

'Very well, I will not seek out a fight with the man. Nonetheless, you should not expect that his actions will be forgotten and we will never be as brothers.'

Chia smiled at Plinius' change of heart. 'You are a good man. A better man.' She kissed him in such a way as to leave him in little doubt of her affection.

'You know there is a time and place for all things.' Flora had approached unnoticed by the two lovers and in mock disapproval, shook her head at their display.

'Sorry.' Chia blushed as she uttered her apology.

'And some of us would like to be fed,' added a warrior that was standing in line to receive nourishment.

Plinius and Chia laughed but quickly set about serving the battle weary soldiers.

***

Spartacus had ordered the attacks to be concentrated on the front of the enemy column. With the gathered information from scouts, and together with Spartacus' own observations decided that the best and most reliable troops should be gathered at the head of the enemy forces. The former gladiator hoped that his diversion of keeping those quality troops busy would give those enemy with thoughts of escape the chance to do just that and leave the employ of Mithridates. Cassian joined Spartacus and they heard the first screams that would accompany their heightened level of attacks at the front of the column.

The two men watched the rear of the column from a concealed vantage point and hoped that the plan would bear fruit. The shadows of the day began to lengthen and finally, Cassian's patience broke. 'They are not coming. He must have failed to convince them.'

'Maybe, but there is still time. It was a gamble and the man took a substantial risk. He may well have been caught spreading dissent or when returned within the column thought the danger too great.'

As he finished speaking two figures darted from the enemy column, their hands raised to show no weapons were concealed. Moments later another two and then more followed. Spartacus watched as a guard turned to see the fleeing men and for a moment he thought an alarm would be raised but then the sentry merely threw down his spear and rushed after his fellow deserters.

'Come, Cassian we will need to speak to these men.' They moved away, keeping the lengthening shadows and thick tree cover as an aid to hide their movements.

A good distance down the track to the rear of the main enemy force they stopped to observe approximately fifty enemy deserters seated by a wagon that Spartacus had ordered to be placed earlier. Parthian bowmen ensured that no man approached the wagon or attempted mischief of any kind.

Spartacus made to approach the men but Cassian placed a hand upon his shoulder. 'It could be a deception.'

'I have enough archers to cover any threat. Besides, I fear these men have neither the energy nor stomach to match a blade with me.' The gladiator moved forward, his emergence from the shadows sent ripples of fear through the enemy warriors. They seemed to physically shrink from Spartacus knowing that death could follow at any moment.

Spartacus walked past the men and climbed onto the wagon. He waited until the beaten men forced their gaze from the dirt to focus on him. 'You have chosen well. Remaining within your column would have meant only certain death. You can leave this place with your honour intact, because no warrior deserves to be led to war by such fools. You have kept your side of the bargain and I shall keep mine.

'Continue along this track until you reach more of my men. You will be given supplies that will aid you in your return to your lands. At the first village that you encounter you will be given further supplies and coin. The defeat of your masters is of no fault of yours and therefore you should receive some payment. However, before you leave this place be warned. Those that you encounter upon your journey will be treated with honour and respect. One incident of mistreatment will result in the death of each man. The bargain will be forgotten and my archers will seek you out on every step along the track.' Spartacus did not wait for a reply because the men knew that they must comply. Spartacus called one of his warriors and instructed the man to give the same message to every deserter and then Spartacus and Cassian slipped back into the shadows.

Chapter Twenty

That night and the one that followed saw the plans of Spartacus exceed even his expectations. Warriors deserted from the ranks of the enemy in their thousands. What started as a gentle mountain stream of those brave enough to make their bid for freedom, turned out to be an unstoppable torrent. The track from column to village was filled with an enemy no longer willing to fight. As they became more certain death would not swoop down upon them, they increased their pace, keen to put the memories of the ordeal they had faced far behind. The pressure by Spartacus' warriors to the front of the column ensured that by the time they realised that mass desertions had taken place their army had already lost over a third of its number. Even if Rubius and his fellow officers had of known of the desertions it would have been difficult to prevent such a mass exodus. By the end of the second day, Spartacus knew that what remained of the enemy would not run and were of a far greater quality. Nonetheless, he also knew that the damage caused to his foe had been substantial and although the two sides were still not equal in numbers they were far more evenly matched. Spartacus raised an arm and then issued the order that all his men should fall back to the main camp.

'But why not keep hitting them? Cassian asked.

'It will achieve little and I would rather our men rested. Tomorrow there will be a battle and our enemy is exhausted. They will not sleep this night, the fear still strikes at their hearts but our men will profit from a night's slumber. Besides, each of us deserves a night's rest before we begin the long journey to the next world.'

***

Rubius was not filled with the same satisfaction enjoyed by his enemy. His men were consumed with fear with a dread of what misfortune the gods would bestow upon their unfortunate force. Only hunger and thirst turned their thoughts from impending doom. Their leader knew that all his plans and hopes depended completely on the arrival of supplies. He had brought his bedraggled force to the arranged location in which he was to meet the five hundred men. Those men had been entrusted to deliver the supplies so desperately required to prevent his force descending into a mob, a mob which he had no doubt would want revenge on their officers.

This moment was as dangerous as any on the battlefield, whether he would live or die was very much in the balance. Rubius gave the order that the army should make camp and then allowed his eyes to search the countryside for another track. It was a relief when he eventually spotted a partially overgrown entrance to what looked little more than a footpath. He wondered to himself if the track had been too small to allow his supplies access. He glanced down at the map within his hand and thanked the gods that for once, a task had been completed with skill. He did not know the creator of the map but swore that should he ever survive these lands, he would seek out the man and present him with a gift to show his gratitude. The reason Rubius had chosen the small track was simple, it ran alongside the main track on which they travelled. Then it quite violently changed direction and quickly closed the distance until meeting at the very position that he now stood.

Democolese approached and he shook his head to show his discontent. 'This is madness. We cannot fight with only the breeze within our guts.'

'If the supplies—' Rubius attempted to respond but Democolese was in no mood for pleasantries.

'No, Rubius, I am taking what is left of my men and leaving this shit infested land.'

'Quiet!'

'I will not hold my tongue. You cannot continue, it is no better than murder.' Democolese flushed, his anger beginning to rise.

'No, listen.' Rubius had tilted his head to one side, resembling a bird as it heard the footsteps of an unwanted traveller.

Democolese remained silent but put no effort into understanding Rubius' need for the silence. Then as if the Roman was frightened to shout it aloud, in case it was a delicate illusion too easily shattered, he whispered, 'Wagons.' Then he was moving towards the small track.

Democolese watched the action and believed Rubius had lost his mind for he could hear no arrival of the much-needed supplies. Secretly, part of him wished an enemy archer took the opportunity to claim the prize of killing an officer. It would be deserved because Rubius had left the protection of the column knowing very well that danger lurked close by, and that danger had proved lethal with a bow. Democolese, along with those men nearest to him listened for the familiar sound of a bowstring twang, then the inevitable thud and scream, which would signal the end of Rubius. To their surprise, the woe filled cries of their officer never arrived but they did become aware of another sound. The wonderful rumble of heavy wheels upon a narrow track made

Democolese involuntarily move forward, he too forgetting the possibility of enemy archers.

Suddenly, Rubius emerged back onto the main track, his smile clear for all to see.

'Democolese, quickly send men to help secure the wagons and see them safely within our ranks.'

His second in command did not delay but bellowed the orders so all would know its importance and then he leant against a tree and forced himself to conceal the elation that he felt inside.

***

Cassian was the first to hear from the scouts that the enemy had managed to obtain supplies. The Roman was filled with fear that all their plans and hard work would be for nothing. He raced to find Spartacus hoping that the former gladiator would know how to remedy the possible disaster that their small force now faced. It took time for him to locate Spartacus who to his surprise was taking wine with Tigranes. He flushed crimson with his exertion and struggled to announce himself, but his deep gasps for air made Spartacus turn.

The former gladiator could not help but smile at Cassian's appearance. 'By the gods, Cassian, what is wrong?'

'The enemy.' He took another deep breath. 'Have managed to obtain supplies.'

'Is this a problem, Spartacus?' Tigranes asked, thankful that the error was not his or his men's responsibility.

'No.' Although the reply was brief, it showed confidence and a complete lack of alarm.

'No?' Cassian required an explanation because he could not see how this was anything but dire news.

Spartacus however, did not clarify his response, but instead asked a question of Cassian. 'If you were at the head of our enemy's army what would be your next move?'

After recovering from the confusion of Spartacus' response he thought for some moments and then replied, 'Rest the men and attempt to gather more supplies.'

'A sensible plan, however, your army has struggled to obtain supplies for many days. In that time they have endured much and the meagre amount of supplies you have secured will not last long. They have only two choices, retreat or attack. The supplies I have allowed them to obtain were to speed them to a decision either way.'

'You allowed?' asked Tigranes.

'Their army is battered but is not yet beaten. If they simply retreat the way they came then it is possible that in the not too distant future they may well wage war in these lands. The only way to secure our forces and the people they protect is to smash our enemy into so many pieces that they cannot possibly form a viable threat. Tomorrow they will advance on our position and battle will follow.'

'So how do you know they will attack and not simply retreat?'

'Would you like to return to Mithridates in defeat with just a shadow of the army that he placed in your care? The commander of that force will attempt to take advantage of the men's morale at receiving nourishment. He will spend the night building their rage at an unseen enemy.'

'They still have numbers on their side,' Tigranes added in a cautionary tone.

'That is true but one meal will not take away the pain of the previous march no matter how eager the warriors want revenge. Battle saps the energy of even rested troops but these men will suffer far more quickly, and it will be their undoing. When the darkness falls upon the battlefield our enemy shall be defeated.' Spartacus spoke without bravado but his confidence was evident.

Cassian looked over at the part of the camp that held their families. 'Let the gods grant it so.'

'If the gods wish to lend a hand, then all the better. Nonetheless, we should look to ourselves and rely upon our courage and blades. Let us beat these bastards and finish this war.' Spartacus raised his wine in salute of his comrades who returned the gesture. Each man thought of what the next day would bring but those thoughts remained private; secret fears that could only bring ill omens, should they be spoken aloud.

***

The morning came and with it, the reports that confirmed the enemy were advancing. Spartacus called for his officers and proceeded to relay his battle orders. The atmosphere was relaxed despite the impending battle. The men noticed the rock-like confidence emanating from Spartacus.

'Cleomenes, this is the time that the Spartans will shine and gain honour befitting their race.' Spartacus marked out his version of the battlefield in the dirt. 'It is a simple plan, but if we execute it correctly I have no doubt of its success. There is one important difference between this and the previous battle. Each officer will make the decision when to carry out his part of the plan and it is to each of you to ensure that those tasks are fulfilled.' Spartacus paused to glance at the faces about him and was pleased that none of his chosen officers looked overly concerned at the prospect at being responsible for the failure of the plan. Despite their confidence, he decided to explain his decision. 'There are two reasons why we must take more responsibility as individuals. Firstly, in the initial part of the battle their numbers may swamp our ability to communicate. Secondly, we will require every fighting man at our disposal and will not have a rear guard or a command post.'

Cassian suddenly realised that he would be taking his place within the ranks of warriors and be in the heat of battle. He could not help feel a nervousness rise in his gut for he had never experienced a true battle, he wondered if it differed from fighting in the arena.

Spartacus seemed to sense his friend's unease. 'Each of us will need to choose a trusted second in command that will fulfil our orders should we fall in battle. Cassian, I would be honoured if you would stand at my side?'

'Erm, of course, Spartacus,' he replied.

'Gratitude, Cassian. Tigranes I feel it would be unwise for you to enter the battle but if you and your guard could ensure the safety of the non-combatants?'

'No harm shall befall them,' Tigranes replied a little disappointed that he would not be required to test his blade.

'Then, fellow warriors, the talking is at an end and we must go to war. When the last cries of anger and pain stop and the final blow has fallen, let our enemies be bleeding in the dirt.'

The officers nodded their agreement and all raised wine in salute.

Spartacus had chosen his ground well. His forces stood ready to meet the onslaught at the end of a steady incline in the terrain. Cassian knew the reasons behind the former gladiator's reasoning. The enemy were tired, they would march in heavy armour and then charge up that incline and it would not be long before the fire would burn in their limbs and exhaustion swoop down swiftly on their bodies.

Both men watched the enemy advance keenly and hoped the opposing warriors were already beginning to feel the effects of the terrain.

'Today will be bloody.'

The voice made both men turn.

'What are you doing here?' asked Spartacus.

'I grow bored with woman's work.' Plinius smiled as he replied.

'You are not fully healed.'

'I am healed enough, besides, you two will only go and get yourselves killed if I am not here to protect you.'

'Yes, because you have such skill at emerging from battles unscathed,' Spartacus replied with sarcasm.

'It is a gift,' said Plinius laughing, 'so what is the plan?'

'We let the bastards come to us.'

'Have the poor wretches not walked enough?'

'After this day their journey will be at an end, at least in this world.'

'Let us hope not too many of us join them,' added Cassian.

'That is what I like about you, Cassian. You always look to the positives.' Plinius laughed again and slapped Cassian on the shoulder.

Spartacus smiled. He remembered a time when Plinius would not have met the eye of Cassian. The difference in social standing mattered little anymore to these men. They were brothers, a bond forged in blood and loss. That bond was about to be tested once more as the numerically superior enemy drew ever closer. Spartacus looked down the line of his men and could see Cleomenes out of the ranks whipping his men into a battle rage.

'Are you not going to say anything to the men, Spartacus?' asked Cassian.

'Not this time, Cassian. These are experienced warriors and know what must be done. A blade in the hand and an enemy to the front is all they need.'

At that moment, the mounted Parthian archers moved forward to cheers from the warriors within the ranks. The smell of sweating horseflesh reached the nostril of Spartacus; usually an unwanted and pungent smell but now he thanked the gods for both Parthian and beast. The enemy had no cavalry or foot archers in which to repel the Parthians, and so would pay a heavy cost for their lack of military planning. The composite bows carried by his allies were powerful enough to smash through some of the finest body armour in the known world and would have no trouble ripping the feeble protection that most of his enemy wore.

Before long the screams of agony erupted from the enemy as the shafts that had brought them so much misery on their long march, once again sought out flesh. The force that moved towards Spartacus seemed to slow; it was no longer a collection of warriors but resembled a single beast cowering from the deadly manmade hail. Spartacus had always loathed archers, mainly because he had precious few when he'd led the slave rebellion against Rome, and had seen many a fine warrior taken from this world before they could meet the enemy face to face.

Rubius shared the Thracian dislike especially when a shaft buried into his helmet. The gods had smiled upon him as the missile lodged between helm and flesh causing nothing more than a deep cut across his cheek. Nevertheless, his face burned with pain as he plucked the offending item from his helmet. Anger rising, he called out to his men that the gods had just shown which side they favour. Then the thuds of arrows slowed and finally stopped as the Parthians exhausted their missiles. The screams of the injured turned to whimpers and a strange calm settled over the battled. Rubius and his force had reached the place where the final opportunity to turn back from their intended violence could take place. That opportunity hung in the air like a shroud for all too a brief moment. Then Rubius screamed the order to charge as his entire army lurched forward intent of taking revenge for their past woes.

'Hold firm, do not yield!' cried Spartacus. An order repeated down his lines by the various officers.

On a nearby hillside the women of the camp ceased their duties, which included preparing dressings for the inevitable wounded which would stream into the camp. Each of them watched as the far larger enemy force crashed into the seemingly feeble line, which contained the men they loved. Flora raised a hand to her mouth to prevent a fearful scream, Chia remained silent but tears welled in her and eyes and Cynna stood rock-like with just a twitch in her jaw betraying the emotion within.

The enemy charge had not smashed the smaller army as many that observed from a distance believed. Instead the frail line of warriors strained under the pressure and then the real desperate fighting began as blades on both sides hacked against flesh. As time moved on the lines became blurred as the structure from both armies melted away.

Balen seized the opportunity and giving the order that his archers cast down their bows, led his mounted warriors into the battle. Their charge smashed into the enemy sending them sprawling and gave the Spartans the opportunity to carry out their part of the plan. Once more, they formed a wedge but they did not press forward but wheeled while still in formation and moved along the front of the battle line taking their enemies in the side.

Spartacus screamed his battle rage, his blade ripping those unfortunate enough to face him in combat to pieces.

Cassian's anxiety had disappeared the moment the enemy had crashed against his shield. The beast that he held caged deep within was released; it sprung into the chaos and tore his enemies apart.

Plinius had never needed rage in battle; he smiled his pleasure as he dispatched each enemy warrior. He thrust forward with his sword taking a warrior in the throat but as the man fell to his death, he ripped the blade from Plinius' hand. The young Roman simply caught the arm of another attacker punched the man on the bridge of the nose and took his weapon. The warrior was rewarded for giving up his blade so readily by being disembowelled by the same blade.

The enemy's numerical advantage was quickly disappearing as exhaustion and fighting far superior warriors was having a disastrous effect. Rubius looked around as he took the head from one of Adrianicus' black armoured warriors. Many of the troops provided by Mithridates were now reluctant to move forward and some were actually moving away from the battle. In that moment he knew that his first command would soon be at an end.

CHAPTER TWENTY-ONE

The once impressive army led by Rubius was a mere shadow of its former self. Many of its warriors were either dead, dying or running for their lives. If in the future, people spoke of this battle they would speak of its brevity.

Spartacus had been correct when he said that the enemy would be in no condition to fight, the encounter had been far too much for the bodies to gain anything other than destruction. The battle was never a true contest but Rubius and approximately one thousand men were yet to surrender. Those that stood by Rubius' side were the warriors given to him by the elder Tigranes. Despite their exhaustion and no love for their leader, they fought with honour and had refused to run.

The younger Tigranes now raced forward and with some difficulty reached the bloodied Spartacus. 'Pull the men back, cease the attack.' Tigranes struggled to make himself heard.

'What?' Spartacus asked dismayed that the battle should be stopped before total victory was achieved.

'Those men are sons of my land.' He pointed at the remains of the enemy. 'If I can prevent their death then I will.'

Spartacus looked at Tigranes and knew that the young ruler would not be dissuaded from his attempt. The Thracian screamed the order for his men to stop fighting and retire a few paces. Eventually, his men heard his orders and broke free of the engagement.

Tigranes urged his mount forwards and it was not long before the young ruler was placed at an equal distance between friend and foe. His bodyguard exchanged worried glances fearing their master would fall to a thrown spear. If Tigranes shared their fear, he did not allow the evidence of that anxiety show on his features.

'Men, you have fought well and have no need to sacrifice your lives.' His words for a moment were met with no reply but then an officer of the Armenian forces stepped forward.

'We serve your father and he gave us explicit orders.'

'I will wager that my father did not wish you to throw away your lives needlessly. I do not wish to pull my father from his throne and put myself in his place. I serve our empire as you do. I simply believe Mithridates, and members of the Roman senate have deceived my father. It is a deception that if allowed to continue will see our lands, our homes consumed in fire.'

The officer was a soldier and loathed the intricacies of politics; he turned to Rubius to see if the Roman had anything to add to the conversation. To his surprise, Rubius did not demand that he once more take up the blade.

'Your men have fought well. There is no need for you to die this day. Take your men and leave the field with honour.' As Rubius stopped speaking, Democolese clasped him by the arm, but before he could remonstrate, Rubius added, 'This battle is lost and our fate is sealed. We have failed enough men; let us not add yet more deaths to an already heavy burden that we must take to the next world.'

Democolese allowed his hand to fall and nodded his agreement and resignation to Rubius' decision. The Armenian officer did not waste the opportunity but passed the word that each man should discard his weapon and then he moved away from the battlefield and the remnants of his command followed.

Rubius and Democolese were suddenly alone amongst their dead; neither spoke or motioned for mercy.

Spartacus and Cassian moved forward quickly to be at Tigranes' shoulder as he approached the two men. The young ruler eyed his captives for some time before speaking. 'You visited my father's hall with Mithridates?' Tigranes pointed at Democolese who did not reply but gave the briefest of nods to signal that Tigranes had been correct. 'You have betrayed your allies, set brother against brother all in the service of that dog Mithridates. Your head will be sent to your master, and will serve as warning that my people are not so easily manipulated.'

Four of Tigranes' bodyguards stepped forward immediately and dragged the unfortunate Democolese away. Tigranes then turned his attention to the Roman who still stood proudly despite his total defeat. 'You, I do not know.'

'His name is Rubius, bastard blood of Crassus senator of Rome,' announced Cassian.

'It has been a long time, Cassian.' Rubius smiled not wanting to show the fear which raged within.

'You know this man?' Spartacus asked.

'Before Rubius was aware of his parentage, we were friends. More than friends, my father showed him great kindness. Nonetheless, this man before you attempted to gain favour with Crassus by trying to ruin both my father and my family.' Cassian spat the words from his mouth.

'It seems a son, even a bastard one, cannot escape his father's ways. I tire of this folly, pass judgement and let this day be at an end.' Rubius replied without fear.

Tigranes aware that he had lost control of the conversation stepped forward and puffed out his chest. 'Your crimes must mean your death, Rubius, but you allowed men of this land to survive your feeble attempts at victory, for that you can choose your own manner of execution.'

Cassian's eyes were not on the young ruler for they never left Rubius. He knew what the man would say long before his mouth uttered the words.

'Hand to hand combat. I will accept all challenges,' Rubius announced his jaw jutting out like a mountainous rock.

'Accepted, I will be your first opponent,' replied Cassian.

'Fuck, what are you doing?' Spartacus asked. He could not believe Cassian was being so rash in his judgement.

'Calm yourself, Spartacus. I will kill this man. An old debt must be settled.'

'Bollocks, I will just cut the little bastard's throat.'

The former gladiator moved forward his hand hovering over his blade.

'No, Spartacus, it is by my hand that his life will come to an end.'

Spartacus lowered his voice. 'You were friends, that means you have fought before. At very least you have sparred?'

'Many times,' replied Cassian.

'Did you ever win?'

'It was a long time ago, I have learned much since then.' As Cassian replied, he smiled knowing his answer would frustrate Spartacus.

'This is madness,' Spartacus announced and then stormed away and disappeared through the ranks of his own warriors.

***

As night fell, Tigranes ensured that the warriors that died were honoured and those that lived were supplied with only the best quality wine.

Those warriors cheered Spartacus as he stood to speak. 'I wish to salute the greatness of your victory. Each one of you played your part in a victory over an army with superior numbers.'

A voice from the crowd interrupted his speech. 'But not superior warriors.' The unknown soldier was cheered for his announcement.

'I could not agree more. I have fought many battles and have rarely seen your match in war.' Spartacus paused allowing the cheers to die down. 'I want to mention Cleomenes and his Spartans, for they fought like the very gods themselves and brought us a swift victory.'

Again, the crowd erupted; they chanted the name of Cleomenes. The Spartan leader stepped forward and bathed in the adoration. Then the words on the lips of the warriors changed and the name Spartacus reverberated around the camp.

Cleomenes smiled and leaned in close so only Spartacus could hear. 'I told you, Spartacus, you are a legend and I a mere man.'

Spartacus saluted the crowd and then turned to reply to Cleomenes but the Spartan had gone.

Tigranes spoke to the crowd and Spartacus missed much of what the young ruler said because he still scanned the crowd searching for Cleomenes. Finally, the former gladiator accepted that the Spartan had retired for the night and so reluctantly, he focussed on Tigranes.

'...now we must deal with those that led an army against us.' As Tigranes spoke two of his bodyguards walked towards him, one of which carried a large basket. The guard placed the basket at the feet of Tigranes and then retired a few paces. The ruler bent and pulled the severed head of Democolese from the container. He raised the grotesque body part and the warriors whooped with delight. 'Take the head of this foul creature to its former master and let him see our answer to his acts of treachery. Now we shall conclude this unpleasant matter.' Tigranes waved his hand and the prisoner Rubius was brought forward. At the same time, the basket that once again contained the head of the unfortunate Democolese was taken away. A tough looking warrior bodyguard barked an order that the men should form a circle and despite the heavy consumption of wine, the warriors obeyed instinctively. Rubius was placed in the centre of the circle and his bonds cut, then a blade was thrown at his feet. The Roman smiled and he retrieved the blade, ran his finger along its edge and then with a few sweeps, tested its balance.

The crowd hummed with excitement, they sensed blood and wondered how many men this enemy officer would face before he finally lay bleeding in the earth.

Then Cassian stepped into the circle, stripped to the waist but he somehow seemed more a warrior and less a Roman deal maker.

'It has been a long time since we crossed blades,' Rubius called out to Cassian. If he felt fear, it was hidden from all that were present.

'Those days were for children wanting to be gladiators. Today is not one for play,' Cassian replied his manner and jaw set like granite.

'How many times did you beat me?'

'Time changes all things, Rubius, except maybe your arrogance.'

The two traded their first tentative blows. The first success was scored by Cassian but not with the blade. His fist smashed into Rubius' face. The surrounding warriors cheered the success.

Rubius licked the cut on his lip tasting the crimson liquid, which ran freely from the small wound. 'I see you have learned new tactics.'

'Deceit is part of battle but it should never have a place between brothers. For we were like brothers were we not?'

The sound of blades rang out once more and did not falter until both men were tired and needed to pull back from the ferocious attack.

'For my part I was honoured to call you brother.' Rubius spoke through heavy intakes of breath.

'Then why play the part of traitor rather than beloved friend?' Cassian's anger surged again and he rained down blow after blow.

'You above all should know that choice is a luxury seldom granted in Rome.'

'There is no excuse for betrayal.' Cassian's anger was getting the better of him and just for a moment, he left himself vulnerable.

Rubius saw the opportunity, as did Spartacus who watched from the shadows. Spartacus gripped at his own sword knowing that Cassian would pay a costly price for his emotion but then he saw Rubius pull back from taking the chance to end the bout.

Cassian was unaware of his good fortune and again struck Rubius with a fist. 'Tell me why, Rubius?'

'The time is not right. We have business to conclude.'

'At which point you will be dead.' Cassian snarled.

'You forgot, Cassian, win or lose I am a dead man. It seems to me you are the only one with something to lose.'

'It is worth the risk.' Cassian attacked repeatedly, he yearned to slice at Rubius' flesh.

Rubius smiled at his former friend's effort but then as he defended a thrust his blade smashed apart, a shard flew upwards piercing his cheek.

Cassian seeing his enemy off balance rushed forwards and drove his blade towards the now exposed flesh.

Rubius could do nothing as the powerful thrust ripped through his stomach, his smile faded and he dropped the remains of his blade.

'I believe you have quenched your thirst for revenge.' Rubius slipped to the floor, the crowd cheered his defeat.

'Why, Rubius? I loved you, my father loved you.'

'Choices, Cassian... Crassus gave me a choice. Destroy your father's dealing or he would take a more drastic action.'

'He wished my father dead?'

'I could not allow that, better poor than dead. Therefore, I served Crassus not out of duty to a pitiful father but because I wished to save a man I would have gladly called father. Alas, your father died at the will of the gods but the damage had been done. I had already lost my brother. I am sorry, Cassian...'

Cassian dropped to his knees and called for Spartacus. The gladiator raced to be at his friend's side. 'Call for a healer.'

Spartacus looked with shock at Cassian's face, tears had replaced the mask of anger that his friend had so recently worn.

'It would serve no purpose,' Spartacus replied and placed a consoling arm upon his shoulder.

'Cassian...' Rubius whispered his strength failing him, 'no healer, my life is at an end. I leave this world with joy that before my final breath you know the truth.'

'Forgive me, Rubius, my friend. My brother.'

A bloodied hand rose slowly and touched Cassian's cheek. The smile on Rubius' face returned and then his eyes misted over seeing nought in this world. The hand dropped and Rubius, leader of the enemy army, left the world of man. The crowd did not cheer; even the most drunken of them knew that the entertainment was at an end.

They moved away in silence unsure of the night's happenings. Tigranes felt he was intruding on a private grief and so silently motioned to his men that it was time to retire. Spartacus signalled to Plinius and then whispered to him that he should fetch Flora. She would be the only person that could soothe Cassian's sorrow, just as she had done when Flabinus murdered Cassian's wife.

Spartacus shook his head, victory had been achieved, but the night still closed with sorrow.

Chapter Twenty-Two

Tigranes announced that the entire camp would march to Samosata the main city within the lands of Commagene. He made it clear that the people of the Commagene kingdom wished to honour the warriors that had delivered them from Mithridates.

Spartacus would have preferred to slip away quietly and avoid any ceremony. However, he knew that would not be an option. He would normally have discussed such matters with Cassian but since the death of Rubius, his Roman friend had rarely left the confines of his tent.

Three days passed and eventually the army lurched into action, and so the long journey to the city of Samosata had begun leaving for Rubius' final resting place. The small children were afforded places on the wagons but those of a certain age and the women folk trod the dusty track just as the warriors. The men who had failed to emerge from the battle unscathed took the majority of space on the wagons. This part of the army was a sorrowful section; the joy of victory did not grasp these poor creatures. Many would not reach the city of Samosata; their injuries would drag them from the world of men. It was with these wretches that Spartacus finally saw Cassian for the first time since the Roman had slain his childhood friend.

The former gladiator approached timidly unsure that his friend wanted his company. Thankfully, as he approached, Cassian turned and gave a welcoming smile.

Spartacus glanced at the wagons filled with so much woe. 'Glory seems so far away in the days after a battle.'

'This is one warrior who has no further need of battle honours.' Cassian straightened the warrior's tunic and signalled for men to remove the fallen warrior.

Spartacus raised his eyes from the dead man and fixed his stare on the skies. 'I thought darkness was going to descend and unleash a torrent.'

Cassian knew that Spartacus referred to his despair at the loss of Rubius. 'The day is bright and bathes in its warmth. Sometimes, I believe we must cast the darkness aside or be forever consigned to shadow.'

Spartacus was pleased to hear Cassian was not consumed with grief and patted his friend on the shoulder. 'I tire of eating with swine-like warriors. I believe our families should take our meal in isolation and enjoy our hopes for the future.'

'Agreed, I look forward to placing a hand on a cithara rather than blade.'

'You play?' Spartacus asked struggling to keep the grin from his face.

'Some say the instrument is for women, but it requires great skill and I enjoy its song,' Cassian replied a little too defensively.

'I cannot wait to hear you play.' Spartacus surrendered to the laughter.

'Fuck you,' Cassian replied, but his retort was in good humour. The two men tended to the wounded for some time before the wagons once again resumed upon its path.

***

As the day ended, it was with a heavy heart that Spartacus sort out the comfort of his family. Over fifty men had succumbed to their wounds and the following promised to bring further death amongst the warriors. He strolled towards the camp area, where those most dear to him awaited his arrival before taking nourishment. To his surprise not only his family and friends sat by the fire, Cleomenes was also present but did not take part in the small talk.

'Not with your men this night, Cleomenes?' asked Spartacus.

'No.' The answer was almost a whisper and the man himself seemed diminished. 'I have just bid farewell to two of my finest warriors.'

'Victory demands payment from us all.'

'The younger warrior's name was Bacchus. He was like a member of my own family. I was present at his birth. Even Spartans feel loss, Spartacus.'

'I never doubted that fact, Cleomenes. Let us hope that there will be far fewer farewells in the coming days.'

'Lathyrus and Melachus.' The words burst from Plinius and he did not feel the need to explain his outburst.

'Good friends and even better men,' Cassian added and then continued, 'they will be deeply missed, their parting equal to that of a father or brother.'

The group seemed to fall into despair. The small talk had stopped as each looked into the flames, their minds wondering into times passed.

After some time, Cassian suddenly began to laugh and immediately held up his hand to apologise. 'I am sorry, I have just recalled the very first time I met Lathyrus.'

'He was an enthusiastic beast of man.' Spartacus grinned as he spoke.

'For much of my younger years I thought he should take his place alongside Greek heroes such as Hercules and Perseus.'

'Really?' Plinius asked, struggling to keep the disbelief from his face.

'You have to understand, Plinius. I was just a boy, barely eight summers old when my father took me on my first trading mission. Lathyrus would tell me stories to prevent my heart yearning for home.'

'I remember my father telling my brothers and me such tales.' Spartacus paused. 'Tell us, Cassian.'

'Tell you what?'

'Tell us one of Lathyrus' tales,' replied Spartacus.

'I am not a storyteller, Spartacus.'

This time it was Plinius who burst into laughter.

'And what do you find humorous, Plinius?' Cassian asked with mock annoyance.

'You are the son of a trader and former agent of Pompey, your entire life has been telling tales.'

Cassian cast a slice of meat at him upon hearing his reply.

'Tell us, Cassian.' Spartacus spoke again his face suddenly becoming serious.

Cassian stared at Spartacus for some time and then realised that the former gladiator wanted to pay Lathyrus a proper respect. The old sailor was known for his stories and what better way could there be than to re-tell one of those tales.

'Very well, I was a young boy joining my father on a trading mission for the first time. Our ship encountered a terrible storm and we were forced to find safety on a small island. It had been truly terrifying but the skill of Lathyrus ensured that we all felt the beach beneath our feet. A fire was made and the men encouraged Lathyrus to tell one of his tales.' As Cassian spoke, the images from that magical night swam in and out of his mind. Then suddenly, he was looking at his younger self across the flames. The growling voice, which now flowed from his mouth, was that of his beloved fallen friend.

Lathyrus' Tale

'I was no more than a boy when I tipped the village elder into the well. Fearing punishment from the men of the village, I decided to run away and seek my fortune in distant lands. Before I left, my mother placed a few coin in my hand. She had raised me without the aid of a man and so the small bundle represented all the wealth she possessed. I told her what I planned and she shook her head, it was then that she told me I was a gift from Poseidon and I should look to the seas and not foreign lands for my fortune. She embraced me and like most boys, I felt awkward at the intimacy. If I had known it was to be the last time I would have seen my mother, then I would have remained with her and taken the punishment from the villagers.

'I travelled for many days by foot until I reached a small village on the coast. Despite the size of the village, there were plenty of boats only too willing to take on a willing pair of hands. My adventures as a sailor, master of the waves had begun, and to the old captain Crenna's surprise, I was a natural. Five summers later Crenna succumbed to the fever and with no heir, he left the craft to his newly appointed second in command. My youth had not been a concern to Crenna but many of the crew were not so forgiving of my age. I doubt if Crenna had even completed his journey to the other before the murmurings of mutiny began to sweep the ship.

'One night as we made one of our regular voyages the wine must have strengthened their resolve. I was plucked from my slumber and carried bodily towards the side of the ship. The mutinous crew intended to dispose of any evidence of their treachery. As I was hoisted high into the air Poseidon sent favour in the shape of a giant wave which crashed into the ship. The crew and I were sent sprawling to the deck but the god of the seas was angry and followed the great wave with a storm equal to its horror. That night was filled with fear and with the screams of men. Many of the mutineers were dragged from the craft and sent to their watery doom. I bellowed orders, trying against all possibility to save the craft. My skill was tested to its very limit but as morning broke a battered and broken ship limped for the nearest shore. The crew fared no better, over half had been washed from the deck and those that still lived carried numerous injuries and a terrible foreboding that they had angered the gods.

'The island upon first sight was a curious creation. Its coastline was devoid of any vegetation. Then as the island's terrain rose abruptly to a great height, a dense forest hid its upper half from any prying eyes. The craft was beached, and it was apparent that we would need a great deal of timber if we ever wished to leave. Nonetheless, I knew the men needed rest and gave the order that a fire should be lit and a meal prepared. The men did not dispute my command; they did not wish to anger the gods further.

'The following day we set out in search of the supplies, I ordered two men to stay behind and guard the vessel. Then seven men and I headed towards the precious timber that we craved. Initially the terrain was easy to traverse and the warmth of the sun seemed to ease the men's unsettled spirits. As the day wore on, however, the terrain steepened and the warmth of the sun became oppressive. As we entered the cover of the trees, it was with relief that we could take refuge in the coolness of the shadows created by intertwined branches. Progress was slow, as we were in constant battle with the undergrowth and the climb. Finally, I gave the order to make camp as the failing light was made worse by the *canopy of leaves making any sense of direction impossible. In vain, we tried to light a fire but for some reason, no flame would take hold despite the abundance of dry kindling. Each time a small spark seemed to gain purchase it was as though an invisible deity would place its lips together and send a gentle breeze to extinguish our chances of warmth and light.*

'The night was as cold as a scorned woman's stare and the darkness seemed to cast your heart into despair. We huddled close to one another partly for warmth and partly because of our fear. What creatures lay in the shadows just beyond the capabilities of our sight, only the gods knew.

'It was with some relief that I opened my eyes the next day as I felt the warmth of the early morning sun upon my flesh. Any joy at surviving that troubled night was short lived as my stare fell upon the branches just above our heads. My gasps of horror echoed those of my men for in the trees around us were the skeletal remains of what I guessed to be at least thirty men. The failing light of the previous night had prevented us from seeing the horror, but now each of us glanced about searching for possible danger. I was about to order the men to make the descent back down towards the beach but before the words would come a roar erupted in the distance. That demonic scream was followed by the sound of vegetation being torn apart and it was obvious something large and angry was heading in our direction. What made it more terrifying was the fact the unknown beast was between us and our path to the beach. I managed to force my fear to one side and ordered the men to run. Each of them set off in differing directions; I too ran fearing an encounter with the creature. I could not say how far I travelled before having to stop; the terrain sapped my energy, my chest heaved as I craved air. Then the first scream announced that the beast

had encountered one of my men. Whoever the victim was his fate had been sealed and his screams abruptly fell silent. I pressed on, hoping the creature had quenched its thirst for blood. My hopes had been futile; it became apparent that our foe was hunting each of us down. The terror I felt intensified as the screams of each of my men split the air and I knew that at some point the beast would get my scent. Nonetheless, the day pressed on and then darkness came and with it, silence. No longer could I hear the screams of man or the roar of the creature. For some time I cowered beneath a fallen tree until at last, I realised that the beast did not hunt at night. I took the opportunity, despite the darkness and pressed on using only the incline of the terrain as a guide. The branches tore at my skin but still I moved forward determined to place distance between the beast and myself. The whole night was one of exhaustion and pain, I fell numerous times and would be forced to pull myself upright and press on. I have no idea how far I managed to travel, the night blinded me to any sense of direction or distance. I raced to a point of safety of which I had no idea even existed. Then as the rays of the morning light began to invade the canopy, I knew that the beast would come. For a moment, I needed to rest, so I placed my back against a sturdy tree, and could not prevent my eyes from closing. The noise fifty paces away made me tense fearing to look, but gradually I forced myself to see the possible danger. One of my men stumbled into view. I was about to beckon him to me when the beast announced that the hunt had once more begun. I dragged my weary body on but almost immediately had to stop. The fear I felt urged me to go on, but my body refused. The smashing of trees announced that the beast was close and as I looked in the distance, I could make out a huge shape moving through the tress. I made myself take a step and then another, my pace quickened as the last of the men who'd ventured inland with me, met his fate. I knew that I was the only prey left for the savage and relentless hunter. I forced myself to look forwards, fearing to glance into the monsters eyes. Suddenly, my mind cleared enough to recognise a break in the trees. For a moment my heart soared believing that beyond the natural perimeter, safety may await. My body responded calling on reserves of strength that only moments before were not present.

'When only a few paces away from my perceived salvation my hope turned to despair as I felt a searing pain rip through my shoulder. The force of the blow threw me into the air and spun me around. As I fell backwards, I saw the beast in its true horror for the first time. Vaguely human in form the monstrosity snarled its anger, the mouth opened wide as if ready to devour my flesh. A serpentine tongue licked at the blood stained fangs and I closed my eyes hoping that when finally they re-opened, the beast would evaporate into mist as a child vanquishes an unwanted nightmare. I expected the fall to end and then be helpless upon the ground and be torn apart. The fall, however, did not end and in truth my body rushed away from the beast. The monster's one eye diminished into the distance and I threw out an arm hoping to break my fall. It was futile as I crashed through branch after branch and then one struck my head. Bright lights exploded before my eyes before darkness washed over me.

'When I awoke, I found myself lying on a bed of animal skins. My head throbbed and as I raised a hand to feel the wound, I realised that all my injuries had been dressed. Slowly I managed to sit and observe my surroundings. I had been placed near an inland lake, which I guessed was at the centre of the island. It was at this point I realised that the island must be a volcano. There were only a few trees within what I now know was the volcano's crater. To my rear, a small stone household stood and I could just make out the wisps of smoke, which suggested that somebody was preparing a meal. I suddenly felt ravenous; the trials of the previous days had worked up a mighty appetite. I walked towards the possibility of food and became aware that my clothing had been removed, clearly by whoever had cared for my injuries. I peered through the small doorway to the hut but it seemed deserted and then I became aware of singing. I left the building and followed one of the most beautiful sounds I had ever heard. There, bathing in the lake was a wondrous creature, hair red as the burning sunrise clinging to her breasts but not concealing their ample but perfect form. I was lost for a moment taking in the magnificence of her body, so much so that it was some time before I realised that she was now looking in my direction. I expected her to dive beneath the water and try to hide her nakedness. The figure, however, smiled and began to wade ashore. The smile was intoxicating and when the figure threw her head back making the hair leave her body revealing her form in all its glory, I nervously looked away but she laughed and for the first time spoke. She told me that it was only fair because she had spent some time looking at my body, as I lay injured. As I stood there feeling more than a little awkward, she clasped me by the hand and led me back to the hut. As she served the meal she told me that I had been expected; she was so warm and gentle I soon relaxed. It was not long that we conversed as though we had known each other all our lives. That night she took me to her bed and I confess from that point my heart was hers.

'For three days, the fate of my ship and the men left on the beach was driven from my mind. Every thought was of the woman I had now come to know as Selene. Nonetheless, on *the fourth day I rose early and as the woman who had already stolen my heart slept I walked down by the lake. I felt a sense of shame as I remembered the men I had abandoned. I watched the treeline high above the lake and wondered if I had the courage to test the speed of the beast. I was so lost in those thoughts that I was unaware of Selene's approach. She looked at my pained expression but before I could speak, she told me that my men had fallen and the ship lay smashed upon the rocks. Confused by her words I asked how she could possibly know what had taken place. She smiled and placed a comforting hand on my cheek. Then she told me that I already knew that this was no ordinary island and the usual laws of man did not hold firm in this place. Selene told of how she was both ruler and prisoner, how the beast, a Cyclops by the name of Strixus, slaughtered all who were unfortunate enough to find themselves marooned. Then with tears rolling down her cheeks she told me how she came to be imprisoned on the island. She was the daughter of Achelos the river god who had angered the far more powerful Goddess Demeter. Her three sisters were turned into the savage sirens, creatures that would lure sailors to their doom. Her father could not bear to see his youngest daughter face the same fate and hid her away on this island. Nonetheless, Demeter heard of Achelos' plan but could not break the powerful magic that kept her safe within the heart of the island. Therefore, she placed a spell on Strixus making him fall in love with her and so the Cyclops would prevent any male finding his way to Selene and maybe her heart. Selene sobbed but told me that she knew that one day I would come and that we would be lovers. I promised her that I would remain and be by her side. She placed a finger to my lips, told me I was a son of Poseidon and I craved the water.*

Nevertheless, when my travelling was at an end, and my tether to the mortal world was broken, then I would return. I placed my arm around her, led her back to the hut and promised that I would never leave. She stopped for a moment, gazed into my eyes and then nodded in acceptance of my words, but something deep within that stare told me that she already knew what the future held.

'*Days turned to years and Selene and I lived as man and wife in our own world. Nonetheless, as Selene had foretold, the call of open waters grew stronger in me every day. Then one morning I woke to see that Selene had prepared food, far more than we would usually consume. I asked her what she had planned, but she simply smiled and told me the day had arrived. Despite my questioning as to her meaning, she did not reply. She placed her hand gently in mine and led me to a cave, she lit a torch and as we walked, the track dropped sharply as if we were descending into the very heart of the volcano. Eventually, our path began to flatten and light could be seen up ahead. A few more steps and we were standing in brilliant sunlight. I anxiously glanced about as I realised that we had reached the coastline. Selene tightened her grip and told me that Strixus could not enter this part of the island and I should not to be alarmed. No more than a hundred paces to our front a small boat danced upon the gentle waves and I could not help but feel joy at its very appearance. Mesmerised, I walked quickly to the craft and climbed aboard. I dropped a hand over the side and felt the cool liquid run through my fingers. Before I knew what was happening a breeze caught the small sail and I was moving out to sea. I turned and searched the coastline for Selene, but she was nowhere to be seen. I called out her name but knew she would not answer. I slumped down into the craft having no interest in what path the gods had chosen. As darkness fell, a torch on the mast burst into flame but no fire's light could have shown me the way back to Selene as a thick mist settled around the craft. Sleep overcame me and at least in my dreams I could be with my love.'*

The torch on the mast faded to be replaced by the fire in the heart of an army camp. The voice of Lathyrus faded too and once again, it was Cassian speaking. 'Lathyrus told many tales, but that was the first that I heard and the one that remained within my mind.'

Spartacus raised his wine. 'Lathyrus son of Poseidon, may you find comfort in the embrace of Selene.' All present added their salute. As the families moved towards rest for the night, Spartacus called Tictus to his side.

'What is it, Spartacus?'

'I have a task, it will not be pleasant and you have every right to refuse.'

'Have I ever refused an order?'

'This is not an order, Tictus.' Spartacus paused. 'Lathyrus and Melachus they lay in the dirt of a foreign lands.'

'You want me to fetch bodies?'

'After such a long time it seems futile but they should be sent to the other world with more respect. They were men deserving of far better.'

'Consider it done, Spartacus.'

'Do not take a wagon. Use spare mounts and avoid any possible danger, do not place yourself in harm's way. I have spoken to Balen he will send thirty men with you.'

'I will leave at first light.'

Chapter Twenty-Three

It had been a number of days since Cassian had told the story of Lathyrus and Selene. The army now camped on the outskirts of a sprawling city. Tigranes had stopped the march before the troops entered the city; he knew that armed men and wine could turn a celebration into a disaster. He knew that the very essence of an army was the fact it was a collection of killers, and he was reluctant to release them on the populace of Samosata. He had agreed with Antiochus, ruler of Commagene and the city elders that the disarmed warriors would enter the city the following day. To keep the men from becoming restless and to allow them to dispel their more basic instincts he had the whores of the city ferried to the camp. He hoped that the women and vast quantities of wine would keep the men from straying.

Spartacus watched the men enjoy their entertainment and smiled.

'There will be sore heads in the morning,' came a voice.

Spartacus knew the words emanated from Cassian. 'Not only sore heads. Those whores will be earning coin until light breaks, men that have faced death are always keen to enjoy the following days with a little more vigour.'

Any reply that Cassian could have made was interrupted by the sound of marching men. The Spartans with Cleomenes at their front were leaving. Spartacus held up a hand to halt their progress.

'We have received orders from Sparta. Those we serve believe the political situation worsens and deem it prudent that we leave these lands with all haste,' Cleomenes announced.

'You will miss the celebration and your men deserve to be honoured,' replied Spartacus.

'That they do. Nonetheless, we are soldiers and journey where our orders dictate.' Cleomenes waved his men forward but the Spartan officer lingered at Spartacus' side. 'It has been an honour to wield a blade at your side.'

'The honour was mine, Cleomenes.'

'I will be glad to walk the soil of Sparta again, these lands shift with deception. It moves like a serpent and those men that see power here are its kin.' Spartacus nodded his agreement and held out an arm but Cleomenes grasped him bodily, pulled him close and whispered, 'Beware my friend, these lands breed treachery.'

The Spartan broke free, gave Cassian a hearty slap on the shoulder and strode after his men. Spartacus felt envious of Cleomenes. He, too, would like nothing more than to be free of these lands.

'One more day, Spartacus.' Cassian had guessed what troubled the gladiator's mind.

'Do you think men of war can ever settle in the stillness of peace?' Spartacus asked.

'When men have had their fill of deception and slaughter, I believe they would welcome the tedium.'

'Then let us pray the gods grant us that tedium.' Spartacus laughed.

***

The following day the army busied themselves trying to add splendour to battle weary armour. Even Spartacus showed signs of anxiety at the upcoming celebrations.

Cynna smiled at her lover's discomfort.

'I fail to see the humour,' Spartacus said, his irritation showing.

'The humour is plain to see,' replied Cynna unperturbed by Spartacus' frown. 'It is rare to see the great warrior as nervous as a small child.'

'This is not me.' The frown vanished. 'They expect me to enter that place without a blade.'

Cynna placed a gentle hand on his cheek; she knew it was not the lack of a weapon that her husband found disorientating. It was that so many wanted to honour him and Spartacus, in spite of his legendary status, never courted fame.

'They mean you no harm. All they want is to honour you and show gratitude,' she whispered. Cynna placed a gentle kiss upon his lips.

'Fine,' he replied grumpily.

Cynna laughed and sidestepped a playful slap the warrior aimed at her rear.

The sun was at its highest point before the column was ready to begin its procession into the city. Spartacus with Cassian and Plinius at his side took the lead. The noise of the masses could be heard in the distance. Cassian surveyed the city and was surprised by its splendour, it was not Rome, but still it boasted impressive buildings. Nonetheless, just like Rome it supported each level of society. Beggar and whore rubbed shoulders with nobility and each were visible in substantial numbers as the column meandered through the streets. He wondered how many of the wealthy citizens were having their purses plucked from their person as they watched the victorious army. On this day, all seemed oblivious to the danger, eager to witness the mighty Spartacus and his warriors. The glory of war was a fine thing to those who had not experienced the slaughter. Spartacus gazed into the delighted faces; he did not blame them for their excitement. Before he had experienced the dread of warfare, he too revelled in the stories of old soldiers hoping to gain coin for tales of their exploits. Given a choice, many would not have spoken of the horrors, but freedom to lie starving in a ditch was a poor freedom.

The army proceeded along the streets and as it did the crowds swelled, until the ranks were forced inward making its progress difficult. Just when Spartacus thought the column must halt the narrow street gave way and in its place, an enormous courtyard lay before the force. As they emerged into the courtyard, Spartacus could see Tigranes waving him forward. Next to Tigranes, a tall powerful man dressed in finery which somehow stood in contrast to his athletic build. Despite all the chaos within the courtyard Spartacus knew that the man was looking directly at him, whether in attempt at intimidation or some other reason, Spartacus purposely refused to meet the man's stare. His time for being intimidated by those of royal birth had long passed and he concentrated his efforts on ensuring all the warriors took their place in the courtyard. The crowd cheered and did not fall silent until the various dignitaries began to speak.

The speeches lacked imagination; they spoke of a great victory against the superior forces amassed against Commagene by the vile Mithridates. Tigranes the Elder's part was ignored, whether out of fear or respect for his son, Spartacus could not determine.

Quite abruptly, the speeches ended and as the crowd once again erupted in celebration, the warriors were once again encouraged to march. The army found itself navigating tight streets but the crowds had thinned dramatically leaving the men feeling a little underwhelmed.

'Are we ever going to stop this endless marching?' asked Cassian.

'It seems we are leaving the city,' replied Spartacus. That much was obvious, not only the crowds had thinned but also the buildings were now only small homesteads with all the more grandiose buildings left behind. As they broke free of the city it seemed their host had not yet finished showing his gratitude. To their front, covering the countryside lay another camp; entertainers plied their trade welcoming the victorious warriors.

Tigranes and the tall stranger approached on horseback, both smiled as they gave greeting. 'Spartacus, I have the honour to present Antiochus ruler of Commagene.'

Spartacus bowed his head, but refused to bend his knee; an action that did not go unnoticed by the ever-observant Antiochus.

'My people owe you a great debt, Spartacus.'

'Payment was agreed before the task began. I wish only that my family be allowed to live in peace and receive the freedom promised.'

'May the gods grant all that you ask and assure you that our part of the deal will be honoured. I have arranged entertainment and nourishment for you and your warriors. If you would permit, I would be honoured if you would join me at my household this night.'

'I am honoured but I would be reluctant to leave my family unprotected in an army camp, even one filled with allies,' Spartacus answered.

Antiochus laughed. 'Warriors can get a little enthusiastic. Of course my invitation includes your family. They will find my household more to their comfort.' Tigranes leaned in and whispered to Antiochus who nodded at the young ruler's words. 'Also Cassian and Plinius, I would be honoured if you and your families would attend, I have already heard of the great service you have performed for my people.'

'You are most kind,' replied Cassian.

'I will await your arrival.' Then both Antiochus and Tigranes urged their mounts forward, only halting briefly to speak with Adrianicus.

***

The remainder of the day was spent enjoying the entertainment. Plinius had agreed reluctantly to fight one of the wrestlers and lost pitifully. Chia, however, was a success as she danced with the many dancers on view. The warriors cheered at the way she moved and only the intervention of Plinius stopped a number of them becoming too boisterous. When finally the time came for Spartacus and the others to journey to the household of Antiochus, all were feeling the effects of wine and good entertainment. They found themselves to be in good humour, a rarity in recent weeks. Wagons had been sent for the journey but all refused, preferring to enjoy the night's beauty. They walked merrily through the streets of the city and even Spartacus joined in the laughter.

Eventually, they came upon the steps that led to the household of Antiochus. It was some shock when they realised the man himself stood at the highest step waiting to bid them greeting and welcome them to his home.

'I feared you would find it impossible to break away from the celebrations.' As Antiochus spoke, a wagon came to a halt and moments later Adrianicus and Sikarbaal stepped into view. 'Excellent, now we are all here, please come with me.'

Surprisingly, Antiochus himself showed them to their quarters and as the women and children made themselves comfortable the leader of Commagene suggested that the men should follow him. As they walked the corridors, Antiochus talked to each of the men as if he had known them a lifetime. He placed all present at ease; the fact that he was a member of a royal household was soon forgotten.

Then Antiochus stopped abruptly, two heavy wooden doors barred his path. 'For centuries my family have been entrusted with a precious blade. In defeating our enemy, you have made that task simpler. I believe that your actions have earned you the right to see that blade. Many have tried to obtain what lies within this room, most died in the attempt.'

Spartacus sensed that Antiochus was delivering a disguised warning. The ruler of Commagene pushed the heavy doors aside.

'No guards or even locks?' asked a surprised Cassian.

'If an enemy reaches this point then the city is lost. If the city is lost then the gods have already forsaken us and a mystical blade will be of little consequence to my people.' Antiochus moved further into the room and as he walked, his mood seemed to become more sullen.

Spartacus looked around the sizeable room, its walls were adorned with all manner of weaponry and the gladiator within could not help the urge to touch some of the blades.

'You approve of my collection, Spartacus?'

'Impressive. I thought I had done battle with most blades,' he replied.

'Many of these weapons were old before your father was born. They are all fine weapons but it is this that will be of most interest.' Antiochus had crossed to a table and lifted a small wooden box from its surface. He waited for Spartacus and the others to move closer and then lifted the lid to reveal the blade.

'It seems so plain,' Cassian announced.

'True, but sometimes the simple things in life are the most precious,' replied Antiochus.

Cassian noticed that when Antiochus replied he was not looking at the blade but at the men that observed it, as if judging their character.

'May we touch it?' Adrianicus asked, his eyes burned with excitement.

'Of course.' Antiochus placed the box back on the table and moved away to let the men examine the blade further. He then crossed the room to be at Spartacus' side who had already seen enough of the blade.

'You seem less than impressed?'

'The room is a delight, a fine collection,' replied Spartacus.

'I was referring to the dagger,' pressed Antiochus.

'I do not mean insult, but the dagger is just another weapon. It is the flesh that wields the blade, which is important. When battle rages you use the blade you test the man.'

'Thutmose had many victories with that blade.'

'Then honour the man and the warriors that risked all to secure those victories. I am sorry, Antiochus, you have been a most gracious host and…'

Antiochus held up a hand to prevent Spartacus from continuing. 'I do not take insult at your words, Spartacus. The opposite is true, it proves that the tales I have heard about you are true.'

'Is that a compliment?'

'The highest I can pay because I have seen with my own eyes that you value men above coin, power or even the gods.'

'The gods have their place, but are untrustworthy in battle.' Spartacus paused and looked towards Cassian and

Plinius. 'But give me good men and there is little that cannot be achieved.'

Antiochus smiled and gave Spartacus a gentle tap on the shoulder, pleased at the former gladiator's words.

'The day has been long and a good host should know when to allow his guests to rest.' The dagger was returned to its box, and the group made their way from the room. The conversation was pleasant but less enthusiastic as Antiochus seemed to be deep in thought.

They arrived at the quarters prepared for Adrianicus and Sikarbaal first and the ruler of Commagene tried his best to be jovial as he wished them a good rest. The rest moved on, eager to be with their families. Then suddenly Antiochus stopped and looked past the three men, as if wondering if they were being followed.

'The empire will soon erupt in blood and slaughter. This city may soon be engulfed in flame.'

Spartacus, Cassian and Plinius could not help but to look on in confusion.

'The Roman senate has finally lost patience with Mithridates and its legions are already on their way. Rome will wage war against our unwelcome ally. I feel that the elderly Tigranes will prove his loyalty to Mithridates and rally to his defence. Armenia will be lost and so I must do what I can to safeguard Commagene.'

'Declare your neutrality. For the love of your people, do not oppose Rome,' pleaded Cassian.

'I have no intention of fighting the legions of Rome. The younger Tigranes travels this very night to meet with a Roman delegation but even a fool can see my people are in a very precarious position. The presence of the dagger only adds to that peril.'

'What are you saying?' Spartacus asked although he guessed what Antiochus had in mind.

'Spartacus, I wish you to take the dagger.'

'No.' The answer was abrupt and left no room for negotiation.

'But why?' Antiochus asked dismayed at the answer.

'That dagger will bring danger to those I love. I will not knowingly place them in danger.'

Antiochus sighed knowing that Spartacus would not be moved from his position.

'Then I must destroy what we have dedicated our lives to protect.'

'I am sorry.' Spartacus felt pity for Antiochus. His family had protected the blade for centuries and he would be the one to fail.

Finally, Antiochus pulled himself from his thoughts and wished them good night.

Chapter Twenty-Four

As Antiochus and his guests slipped into an uneasy slumber, six figures dropped from the perimeter wall into the shadows of the outer courtyard. They moved with speed and stealth to a pre-arranged spot within the gardens. A sentry fell without a sound; his throat cut from ear to ear before he knew what danger lurked near.

The figures paused at the gardens similar to sinister beasts poised ready to strike at any unsuspecting traveller.

The beasts would have no traveller to feast upon, but two men were making their way towards their location.

The meeting took place in whispers. 'Adrianicus, are you sure this is the correct course of action?'

'Sikarbaal, you become more like an old woman each day. The dagger will bring us great fortune.'

'But the gods—' Sikarbaal was prevented from voicing his concerns.

'Enough, if you wish to take no part in the theft, then stay here and keep watch.' Adrianicus did not bother to hide his disgust and waved his other men forward.

***

Chia had nursed her child back to sleep. Plinius had taken too much wine to notice his beloved was restless; her attempts to wake him was met with a deep rumbling snore. She rose and decided to take a walk in the night air, hoping the exercise would soothe her spirit. Entering the corridor she was surprised to see Cynna.

'Are you struggling to sleep, too?'

'I suppose the excitement that Spartacus will not be thrust into harm's way. The opportunity of a proper home and the chance of peace is so close, I fear it's an illusion which will turn to mist.'

'Maybe that is what ails me.'

'Shall we walk together?'

Chia smiled and then nodded her agreement. As they meandered through the household and then outside they talked of what the future promised, both hoped that it would bring their families a lasting peace. It was not long before they wandered into the courtyard.

Cynna spied Sikarbaal sitting in the gardens, pointing out his location to Chia.

'He looks so solemn,' whispered Chia.

'I dare say that a few kind words from you would lift his morale.'

'Plinius would not look favourably to such an action.'

'Plinius does not need to know, besides, I shall wait just inside and should anyone pass by I shall give warning.'

'Why the concern for Sikarbaal?'

'You forget, Chia, that sorrowful creature saved my life. I would do what is necessary to repay that debt.'

Chia listened to Cynna's reasoning and then reluctantly nodded. She crossed the courtyard and entered the gardens.

Cynna smiled and walked back inside, she placed her back against a wall and slipped to the floor. She hoped Chia could bring some happiness to Sikarbaal and then she closed her eyes and awaited Chia's return.

Hearing footsteps Sikarbaal sprung to his feet. 'Chia what are you doing here?'

'I miss talking to a friend,' she replied gently.

'Not now. It is late and not fitting, you must go.' Sikarbaal tried to be stern.

'Talk to me, Sikarbaal.'

'Not now.'

'But why?'

'Chia, it is not safe you must—'

'I now know why your mind was not on the task,' came a voice to prevent Sikarbaal's pleadings.

A figure stepped from the shadows closely followed by a number of others.

'Adrianicus, she was just leaving.' The warrior knew that danger was near.

'Alas, that will not be possible.' Adrianicus sneered.

'What do you mean? Get out of my way.' Chia attempted to push past Adrianicus.

The blow was quick and left Chia with no opportunity to avoid the savagery. It succeeded in preventing Chia from making any further sound.

Sikarbaal watched as the form of Chia crumpled and then lay motionless on the ground. He rushed forward and pushed Adrianicus out of the way in his urgency to reach the unconscious Chia. The injury to the woman he had loved from afar allowed his usual heighten sense of danger to fade. He was not aware of the dagger that now moved towards him or the intent within its holder's eyes. A strong hand clasped over his mouth as the wickedly sharp blade sought out flesh. He attempted to struggle but almost immediately, the strength left his legs and he was powerless to stop himself falling to the ground alongside Chia.

'I believe your employ is at an end.' Adrianicus spat out the words, his distaste at what he saw as Sikarbaal's disloyalty in evidence. He struck down once more with the blade, feeling only contempt for the man he had once thought as a brother.

Sikarbaal did not feel pain as the second blow tore at his body. He lay there helpless expecting a third blow to end his life. Slowly he reached out his hand to try to comfort Chia but her form was lifted from his grasp. Silence fell like a shroud and the former warrior felt alone and vulnerable. If it had not been for the fate of Chia he would have gladly remained in that place, closed his eyes and waited for death. He tried to shout but blood rose in his throat and so using all the energy he could muster he dragged his lifeless body towards the main building.

✶✶✶

Cynna opened her eyes and for a moment, confusion at her location clouded her mind. Then she cursed her own stupidity as she remembered that she was supposed to act as sentry for Chia. Rubbing her eyes to chase the sleep away she realised light was pouring through the open door and she had slept far too long. She forced her tired body to stand and wondered if Chia had returned to her quarters. As she turned to return to her family, something caught her eye upon the ground just beyond the doorway. Then she realised it was a figure. Without a thought of her own safety she rushed forward. As she neared, she could see that the figure had obviously crawled to that position as a long blood trail traced the path it had taken. She bent down and turned the figure over. With horror she realised the ghostly white face belonged to Sikarbaal and wondered if Plinius had stumbled upon Chia's meeting with the unfortunate warrior.

She jumped as the eyes of what she thought to be a dead man flickered.She screamed for help and then placed a calming hand on Sikarbaal's cheek. 'Sikarbaal what happened?'

'Adrianicus.' He struggled for breath. 'Chia…'

'What about Chia?' Cynna asked, fearing that Chia lay bleeding in any part of the household.

'Adrianicus has taken her.'

Suddenly, the sound of footsteps could be heard in the corridor and in a matter of moments, people were swarming around the forlorn Sikarbaal.

Spartacus and Cassian pushed their way through the crowd to reach Cynna. Breaking through the chaos Spartacus dropped to his knees and placed a hand on Cynna's shoulder.

She looked at him tears rolling down her cheeks. 'Spartacus, Chia has been taken and Sikarbaal…' She could not utter the words that the warrior that had once saved her life was about to lose his own.

Spartacus reached down and wiped blood from Sikarbaal mouth.

'Spartacus…' Sikarbaal's words were no more than a wisp of smoke on the breeze. 'Find them quickly, Adrianicus can be cruel.'

'Which direction do they take?'

'I had lost his trust. He knew my allegiances were changing. Tell Plinius…' The warrior seemed to be drifting from this world. 'Tell Plinius I am sorry.'

'Hold on, Sikarbaal, a healer is on his way.'

'Tell Plinius…' repeated Sikarbaal. Then with one last exhale of breath, the chest lay still.

***

Antiochus sat dismayed at the treachery, his knuckles turned white with the strength at which he gripped the hilt of his sword.

'I wanted the dagger out of my lands but not in the hands of such a man.'

'Are you not going to try and catch the bastard?' Spartacus asked.

'How can I? My kingdom may be days away from war and I will need every available man ready to take up arms.' Antiochus paused and stared at Spartacus. 'I have no right to ask that you carry out this task, Spartacus.'

'We will need to leave immediately.' Spartacus had expected the request from the very moment that Sikarbaal had breathed his last and the fact that Chia had been taken had ensured that he would give chase.

'You have the gratitude of my people, Spartacus. I have already spoken to Balen and he has agreed to place himself and his men at your disposal. I have also instructed my stable to provide you with the very best of mounts that will not let you down.'

'If I recover the blade?'

'Dispose of it. I have no wish to know its destination only that a man such as Adrianicus will never profit from its power.'

Spartacus nodded his agreement and immediately left the troubled Antiochus to his thoughts.

Spartacus gave the Parthians their orders, which they obeyed without hesitation. They would split into groups, with thirty riders to each group. They would fan out from the city taking every possible route that the treacherous Adrianicus may have chosen for his escape. Spartacus did not doubt the quality of the Parthian horsemen, but still gave the order that the enemy was not to be engaged. The safety of Chia was of the utmost importance and did not want a rash attack to lead to her death. The reason behind such large units selected was that on finding the enemy, any group could leave men to track Adrianicus and still send men to each of the other groups. This would enable Spartacus to have numbers on his side when finally he came face to face with Adrianicus. As Spartacus climbed onto his mount he looked across at Plinius.

'She is alive, Spartacus. I would know if she was dead.'

'Then we will bring her home, Plinius, no matter how long it takes.'

'We are with you, Plinius,' added Cassian. He reached across to place a comforting hand on Plinius' shoulder.

'Thank you,' replied Plinius. He urged his mount forward keen to track Adrianicus.

Spartacus watched him go and pitied Adrianicus when Plinius found him upon the battlefield.

***

Four days had passed since their departure and no word had been received on the whereabouts of Adrianicus. Spartacus could only assume that the devious Roman had chosen to ignore the usually well-travelled routes and took to going across country. He raised his hands to halt his men, deciding it was time for the men and mounts to rest. As he made to dismount the rains came with such force it stung the flesh. Initially, they took refuge beneath some trees but lightning struck no more than two hundred paces away. Spartacus decided that retreat was the better part of valour and looked for a more suitable shelter. Then he remembered a cave he had spotted, and with the rains becoming even more ferocious, he signalled for his men to follow. The distance they had to cover was not great but with darkness descending and the rain hampering progress, by the time they'd reached the cave all were soaked to the very bone.

A fire was made although it took far longer than all had hoped before the warmth of the flames could be felt. Both armour and tunic were discarded as semi naked men huddled close to the fire. They cursed the gods for sending them such misfortune, but cheered as Balen roasted cuts of meat on the fire.

'Balen what is your home like?' asked Plinius.

Cassian guessed that the young warrior was determined to drive the thought of Chia's suffering from his mind.

'Beautiful, my friend. You can ride for days without encountering another person. The women are spirited and their quality only matched by our mounts.'

'Is the land good for crops?' asked Cassian.

'My lands are fertile and will grow almost any crop, but you experience this for yourself, as your lands are some of the finest in Parthia.'

'How do you know this?' Spartacus asked his interest suddenly awakened.

'Because they used to be mine.'

'We have taken your land?' Cassian was horrified at the possibility.

Balen laughed at the Roman's response. 'Calm yourself, Cassian, I gave the land freely. I offered land and my services to prevent war between Rome and Parthia. If that war were to take place, my lands would be the first at risk. Besides, it is such a pitiful amount of land, I will not lose sleep.'

'Are you a man of great wealth?' Cassian asked.

'Wealth can be measured in many ways, Cassian.'

'Such as?'

'How much coin would you trade for a smile from one of your sons? I have gold and land but they are just possessions.

How much wealth has Adrianicus? All the coin in the world cannot replace his lost honour.'

Cassian nodded his agreement and Spartacus raised his wine in salute of Balen's words. Lightning forked across the skies.

Spartacus looked out. 'Even the gods are angered by his very name.'

Chapter Twenty-Five

The morning heat did not waste time in drying the previous night's deluge. Spartacus stepped from the cave and took in a deep breath, revelling in the freshness of a new day. He was about to return to the cave when an image caught his eye. In the distance two riders were heading in his direction. He called out to his men and quickly made his way down to the track.

Upon seeing Spartacus, the riders increased their speed, the gladiator hoped they brought the news they all craved. They moved across the ground quickly, before long they were calling for their heavily sweated mounts to halt.

'Spartacus, we have found them.'

'Where?'

'No more than a day's ride, they camp on a river bank.' The Parthian stroked the neck of his beast as he spoke.

'Did they see you?'

'No, but Spartacus, they are not hiding. I believe they make camp while they await another party.'

Cassian and Plinius arrived breathing heavily from the run.

'Maybe Adrianicus regrets his actions and seeks to make amends.' Cassian still hoped that Adrianicus would show remorse and turn away from his path of treachery.

'The only thing that will make amends is my blade ripping through his guts.' Plinius snarled.

Spartacus looked to his men. 'The reasons why Adrianicus holds his ground cannot be determined. All that matters is that we close the distance quickly and ensure that Chia is returned safely. Gather your things, we move out immediately.'

***

The black clad warrior approached Adrianicus.

'Can we trust them,' he asked.

'While I have the blade any ruler in the known world would gladly bend over and take my cock. The powerful seek only one thing, and that is more power.'

The warrior nervously laughed at Adrianicus' words but wondered what stopped the approaching troops from simply taking the blade.

They both watched the oncoming column with interest. Then the order went up for the warriors to halt and the leader stepped forward and with a simple nod made it clear he was ready to strike a deal. It was at that point that Chia screamed her defiance. The guard showed no regard for her gender and slapped her with ferocity. The leader of the newly arrived column crossed to Chia and helped her to her feet.

'Cleomenes,' she said through the agony, which burned in her jaw.

'Touch this woman again and I shall tear your fucking eyes from your head.' Cleomenes spat out his anger.

'I command here and that is my hostage.' Adrianicus was annoyed that Cleomenes dared to give chastise one of his men. 'Hit the whore again.'

The guard raised a hand but before it could strike at Chia, Cleomenes struck the man in the throat. The dark armoured guard clasped at his throat and fell to his knees but his agony was not over. Cleomenes stepped forward and reached out his powerful hands, thumbs met eyes and a scream filled the air. Moments later the ground welcomed another dead man to its bosom. The remaining black warriors drew their swords.

The entire column, all of which drew their weapons in perfect unison, answered the action.

'You stupid fuck. The blade is of no importance to Spartacus but take the girl and he is sure to follow.'

'I do as I please and do not need permission from a Spartan.' Adrianicus now flushed with anger.

Cleomenes glanced around looking for the one man who would not have allowed this madness. 'Where is Sikarbaal?'

'Sikarbaal was a disloyal fool. He paid the price for his disobedience.'

'You killed Sikarbaal? I curse the gods for ever allowing you to whisper poisoned honey within my ear.'

'But you *did* listen to my words and if you want the blade, you had best take your orders like a good little soldier.'

Cleomenes blade was drawn in a moment, it swept through the air narrowly missing Adrianicus' throat.

The Roman took a step back and slowly pulled his weapon as if he did not have a care in the world. 'I will enjoy this.'

'Doubtful, I am no fat trader to be killed from the shadows. I am Spartan trained from birth to kill without ceremony, but this day I shall take my time. Today Adrianicus, you will die slowly.'

The two men traded a few blows and suddenly the smile was gone from Adrianicus' face. He had never faced such raw power from an opponent. Deceit and speed had always been his strength but each faint and disguised attack was swatted away with ease. Adrianicus begin to feel a strange sensation, one of panic. Fear raced through his mind clouding his judgement and so it was only a matter of time before pain coursed through his body. He jumped backwards fearful of another blow, hearing the Spartans grunt as one in recognition of a successful strike.

Adrianicus looked down at his arm, below the elbow was now only torn flesh and sinew. He called for help but only one of his warriors moved forward, the rest shrank back fearing the wrath of the mighty Spartan leader.

Cleomenes spun on the spot and at the same time brought his mighty blade down onto the warrior keen to help his master. The blade split helmet and then skull, the warrior made no sound. Death came to him before his brain could register his fate.

'I told you, Adrianicus, a piece at a time.' Cleomenes moved forward sweeping his blade before him. When at last he stepped back far more blood had covered the ground.

Adrianicus stood like a grotesque statue; both arms had been cleaved from his body. The Roman did not scream or sob, the shock of his experience had robbed him of his senses.

'You have taken my honour, I cannot repay that crime. I shall have to content myself with taking your limbs.' Cleomenes screamed his anger by placing all his rage into one monstrous blow.

Adrianicus fell, his legs ripped from his body. Head and torso now lay face down in the dirt.

Cleomenes looked to the distance and could see riders approaching, sighing he flipped Adrianicus onto his back. 'I wish I could enjoy your death but it seems I shall have to kill a friend or die by his blade. The one comfort is that your head will sit atop my spear. At its base your limbs will provide nourishment for any scavenging beasts.' Cleomenes took out his dagger and took his time pressing its blade through the delicate flesh of the neck.

Adrianicus' eyes bulged for a moment and then the head rolled free of the torso.

Cleomenes stood and called for his spear, he drove the base of the weapon deep into the earth and then retrieved the severed head of Adrianicus. 'A fitting end for such a man.' He adorned the spear tip with the head and then turned to the remaining black clad warriors. 'Do you wish to live?' They nodded but each was careful not to make contact with the imposing Spartan. 'Then collect the parts of your former master and place them at the base of the spear. I have no wish to dirty my hands by touching shit any longer. When that is done you may run, and to be sure to run with all haste for I may change my mind and forget to be merciful.'

***

Spartacus ordered the Parthians to form an attack formation, even though he did not intend to commit his men into a suicidal frontal attack. It was just a show of force, designed to impress on the men to his front that he intended to get both blade and Chia back. When he and the other riders had closed within one hundred paces, he called the halt. He, Cassian, Plinius and Balen then urged their mounts forward.

Cleomenes stepped from behind his men supporting the battered and bruised Chia.

'This was not my doing, I return her to you.'

'Where is Adrianicus?' Plinius barked out the question.

Spartacus knew the young warrior was close to losing his control. 'Fetch Chia,' he whispered to Plinius in a gentle tone. Then turning his attention back to Cleomenes, he said, 'His question still stands.'

Cleomenes waved his hand and his men parted to reveal the fate of Adrianicus.

Cassian felt bile rise in his throat. He had come to despise the man Adrianicus had grown into, but it was still a shock to see him as no more than lumps of flesh.

'It was a mistake for him to treat Chia with such cruelty. It will not be a mistake he shall repeat.'

'Gratitude, Cleomenes.' Spartacus paused; it was the moment he had been reluctant to reach. 'And the blade?'

'The dagger leaves with me, Spartacus.' His tone deepened, he wanted it known he did not intend to hand over the dagger of Seker.

'You know I cannot allow that, Cleomenes.'

'Allow? You are not my commander any longer, Spartacus. Do not presume to give me orders.'

'Then I shall ask as a friend, return the blade.' Spartacus kept his voice free of any malice; he wanted nothing more than Cleomenes to give up the blade freely.

'I am sorry, Spartacus I cannot, turn your men around. The dagger means nothing to you so leave in peace.'

'Men died for that blade, our friends died for it. That bastard...' Spartacus pointed to the slain Adrianicus.'...knew the importance of it as a symbol.'

'So do I, Spartacus. If you want the blade come and take it. I will wager Spartan against Parthian.' As Cleomenes finished speaking his men answered his words by rapping blade against shield.

'Have you learned nothing? You are many days march from Spartan soil. These bows will kill your men long before you ever reach it.'

'Then we have a problem, Spartacus. If we do battle here, your men will die. If I march then my men will die, it seems there is only one answer.'

'Cleomenes, turn back from this folly,' pleaded Spartacus.

'I have lost my honour. I will have this blade.'

Spartacus sighed and with a heavy heart, he nodded. 'Then let us get it over with.'

'What the fuck are they talking about?' Plinius asked unable to get meaning from their words.

'Friend will kill friend for a symbol. A piece of metal that only has power to sway the mob.' Cassian shook his head as he answered Plinius.

For the second time that day, Cleomenes took out his curved blade and prepared to face an enemy in single combat. The Spartan commander took a piece of cloth and wiped the already blood stained blade. 'All men will obey our wishes. The man who stands victorious will leave with the spoils, no other man is to interfere and no other bloodshed will take place this day. Is that clear, Spartans?'

They acknowledged their leader's orders with the customary rap on the shield.

Cassian moved to Spartacus' shoulder. 'Spartacus, let him take the cursed blade.'

'Hold your argument, Cassian. This must be done for those that died. Besides, what do you think will happen to Sparta, should word spread that the blade is within its lands? It will be torn apart for the sake of one man's quest for glory. I have no wish to kill Cleomenes but this is a task that must be seen through to the end.'

Cassian retreated and Spartacus and Cleomenes began the bout, both circled, neither wanting to be the first to strike.

'In the arena did you ever fight a Spartan?'

'I've never had that honour,' replied Spartacus.

'Then you are in for an experience. I have to admit a number of Thracians have fallen to this blade.'

'Cleomenes, have you not heard? I am no longer Thracian, I am legend.'

The two men moved towards one another and the sound of sword against sword rang out. Time and time again beautifully executed moves were countered by exquisite defensive strokes. Both men were masters with a blade and those that witnessed the titanic battle could only look on in awe. Time stretched out with neither of the men giving ground, this was no ordinary bout, it was an epic struggle. Powerful strokes, however, sap the energy of even the greatest warriors and exhaustion causes mistakes. Cleomenes was the first to take advantage of his opponent's fatigue. His blade sliced into the upper arm of Spartacus but before his men could celebrate the strike, the former gladiator cut deep into the Spartan's thigh. The two broke from one another, both tried to force air into their lungs.

'It will be a shame to kill you, my friend.'

'Then turn back from your intention. Leave the dagger and return to Sparta.'

'My people will rise to past glories with the blade in their possession. I will not rob them of their rightful place in this world.'

'All empires dream of such things, Cleomenes. They are false hopes, no matter how strong the will. All empires have precious little time to bathe in the adoration of the gods. That blade will bring destruction to Sparta.'

'Enough talk.' Irritated, Cleomenes attacked with a burning fury. The ferocity and power was too much for Spartacus to defend against and Cleomenes' blade cut against his front armour. The blow smashed apart the feeble armour and cut deep into Spartacus' stomach, making the gladiator turn in agony.

Cassian and Plinius closed their eyes expecting Cleomenes' next blow to end the life of their friend.

Cleomenes sensed victory and raced forward, as he did he aimed his blade at a vulnerable foe. Then confusion spread across the Spartan's face because Spartacus was suddenly gone. Cleomenes tried to slow his forward momentum and withdraw his weapon but it was too late. Spartacus had dropped to the ground to avoid the onrushing Cleomenes; in one move he had rolled towards the Spartan and brought his blade up into his friend's flesh.

The Spartan stopped and looked down at the blade, which now protruded from his lower chest. His own blade slipped from his grasp as he dropped to his knees. Spartacus could not prevent Cleomenes from falling to the ground as his own wound sapped his energy.

The gladiator struggled to his feet; sadness etched upon his face. There was no joy in this victory only a dying friend in the dirt.

'My sword, Spartacus,' he asked in no more than a whisper.

'You bloody fool, Cleomenes.' Spartacus placed the Spartan's sword in his hand.

'Do not let them take me home, build the pyre here.'

'It will be done.' Moments later Spartacus raised his head as his friend lay dead at his feet. 'Build a pyre. Let it be known that this did not happen. Cleomenes died in battle, fighting against Mithridates. He died a hero of Sparta.'

The Spartans saluted the gladiator's words and set about building a pyre for their beloved leader.

As night fell, the flames which would speed Cleomenes to the next world, flicked at the night air. The Spartans saluted their commander for the last time and marched into the night. Spartacus and the Parthians, however, remained and made camp.

Cassian did what he could to tend Spartacus' wounds. 'Your concern is unfounded, the cut is not deep.'

Plinius leaned over Cassian's should to look at the wound. 'Had worse shaving,' Plinius announced and then laughed.

'That's because you are so bloody awful with a blade,' replied Spartacus. For the first time that day the gladiator had managed a smile.

Chapter Twenty-Six

Spartacus had not yet disposed of the famed dagger. On the journey back to the city of Samosata, he was afforded a number of opportunities. Caves, wells and deep ravines all presented themselves; but he chose not to hide the blade in any. Spartacus had been sent to retrieve the blade by Antiochus, only the gods knew how many men knew of those plans. If Spartacus returned to the city without the weapon then surely those that craved it would set out in the hope of possessing the blade. If he had seen those possible hiding places, then so would the seekers. He wondered if he was over thinking the problem when the army camp on the outskirts of the city came into view. The camp had grown in size, which surprised the former gladiator.

'Something has happened,' remarked Cassian.

'Looks like they are preparing for war,' Plinius replied.

'It is not our concern.' Spartacus had no intention of remaining and fighting another war; especially if that war was against the legions of Rome.

'Agreed.' Cassian nodded. 'We are owed payment for a task completed. May I suggest that we move on as soon that it is possible?'

'My Parthians will join you. Besides, I wish to be present when you all encounter your lands for the first time.' Balen smiled.

'It is an experience we are all keen to have and will only be delayed by the troubles in this land.'

A voice called to Spartacus, the gladiator was surprised to see Antiochus striding towards him and seemingly in high spirits. Spartacus and the others quickly dismounted, Spartacus was a free man, but to sit aloft a mount looking down on Antiochus would be seen as a great insult by his people.

'Gratitude to the gods for ensuring your safe return.'

'Thank you, my lord, you seem in joyous mood.'

Antiochus leaned in close to Spartacus so his words could not be overheard. 'War could engulf these lands in a matter of days. If possible, I would spare my people that anxiety. They will need a strong leader. I pray the gods grant me the fortitude in both mind and body.'

'Your people have no concerns in that regard.'

'Your praise honours me, Spartacus. I expect you will be leaving for your new lands shortly. I have prepared coin and supplies for the task. Your man Tictus returned with the bodies of your comrades. I have placed them over there.' Antiochus pointed to a tent that sat away from the other tents. 'They have been well cared for.'

'Gratitude.' Spartacus was suddenly, gripped with an idea. 'May I ask for one further favour?'

'Both my people and I owe you a great debt, Spartacus, ask and if it is within my power it will be done.'

'My fallen comrades were of the sea. I would have them return to its bosom. Have you men spare that would carry out such a task?'

'I have just the man. Tigranes has requested I attend a gathering with the Roman general Lucullus. It will take place at the coast. Go honour your friends and I will ensure they reach a suitable resting place.'

Spartacus and the other offered their gratitude but as Antiochus turned to leave Spartacus said, 'You have not asked me about the blade or Adrianicus.'

'Chia is at your side, which means that Adrianicus no longer walks in the realm of men. As for the blade, we have discussed the matter and I have confidence in its fate. I am interested in whether our former ally had any conspirators.'

'No,' Spartacus lied. 'I believe he hoped to sell the blade to the highest bidder.'

Antiochus stared at Spartacus for a moment and then smiled. 'Then the matter is closed. I hope the gods grant you a future of peace and good fortune in your new lands. Now forgive me, but I have a pressing matter which I must be attended.' Antiochus moved away quickly leaving Spartacus and the others wondering if the ruler knew that Cleomenes had turned traitor.

Spartacus turned and began to walk towards the tent that held the bodies of Lathyrus and Melachus.

'I must get Chia to a healer, I will return to you as soon as I am able,' said Plinius.

'Plinius, do not race, my friend. Chia requires your attention far more than Lathyrus. He would be appalled that you would leave a beautiful woman on his account,' Spartacus assured.

Cassian smiled remembering the old sailor's many tales of his exploits with women.

'Spartacus, Cassian.' Chia spoke quietly, the blow to her jaw had made speaking difficult and she did not always seem aware of her surroundings. 'Thank you.'

'Cynna would never have forgiven if I had allowed harm to befall you,' replied Spartacus.

'Where is Sikarbaal? He tried to stop Adrianicus from taking me.'

Plinius held her tightly and looked into to her eyes. 'Sikarbaal is dead. Before he died, he brought news of your abduction.' Plinius paused. 'He was a brave man who loved you.'

Chia wept and slowly Plinius took her by the hand and went in search of a healer.

Spartacus and Cassian walked to the tent, which held Lathyrus and Melachus. Both men paused at the entrance. Neither had a wish to see their comrades so many days after death but both knew it was a task, which must be done. Finally, they entered and as they did an attendant bowed to them and then continued with his duties. The tent had lamps set about it, which gave off the smell of strong aroma's masking the stench of death. In the centre of the tent two forms lay, they were wrapped from head to toe in dressings. Cassian and Spartacus were grateful for they wished to remember the two as they were when alive and not in a butchered state.

'Leave us, we wish to honour our friends in private. Stand guard at the entrance and allow entrance to nobody.'

The attendant made to leave but Spartacus caught him by the arm. 'These men were as brothers and we would have suitable time to reflect upon their passing.' He placed coin in the man's hand who nodded to testify a deal had been made.

'Spartacus?' Cassian asked, unsure why the gladiator needed access to the tent be denied to all.

'We haven't much time, help me, Cassian.'

Spartacus moved over to the larger of the two bodies, which was obviously that of Lathyrus. Once there, he began to unwrap the dressing on the torso.

'What have you in mind, Spartacus?'

'If Lathyrus was truly from the loins of Poseidon, then he will return to the mysterious island and the embrace of Serene. He cannot go empty handed and will require a gift worthy of the daughter of a river god.' He pulled the dressings aside to reveal the pale marbled skin below. Just below the chest a large wound was present, clearly the work of a large bladed weapon such as a spear. Spartacus took his own dagger and enlarged the wound. Then reaching inside his own tunic, he retrieved the dagger of Seker. Spartacus worked the famed blade through the wound until it disappeared completely from view. Then with Cassian's help he replaced the dressings leaving no trace that they had ever been removed.

'It will make a fine gift.'

'And serve to keep those that seek only power from the blade,' responded Spartacus.

Cassian called the attendant and instructed him to have two caskets made for the bodies. When the attendant looked confused, Cassian told him the bodies were to make one last long journey and he would have them arrive in one piece.

'Antiochus himself will be transporting the bodies. He will be displeased if our friends are not ready for when he departs.'

'It will be done,' the man replied.

Cassian handed over yet more coin, which brought a smile to the man's face despite his surroundings. The Roman then indicated that the man should get started on his tasks, the attendant rushed from the tent.

'It is time we prepared for own journey, Spartacus.'

***

The city of Samosata fell into the distance, as did the lands of Commagene. As the group travelled along the many differing tracks, Balen talked of his people, land and customs. He told of the many gods worshipped and of the rulers that governed a huge empire.

Cynna and Flora were never far from Chia's side and an anxious Plinius watched her as closely as a falcon watches its prey.

'She will recover, Plinius, time will heal all,' Cassian said, trying to put the young warrior at ease.

'Sikarbaal's death seems to have plunged her into despair. It's as though she does not have the fight to heal her wounds,' Plinius replied.

'Of course his death has hurt her deeply, he was a good friend.'

'What if it was more than that?'

'Plinius, Chia loves one man. I am at a loss to understand why, but she has always loved you. Is it not obvious to you why she feels such despair? She feels guilt not the loss of a lover.'

'Guilt?'

'Sikarbaal was a man who loved her and fell because of that love. She believes that in some way she is responsible for his death.'

'But Adrianicus killed Sikarbaal because he was a treacherous bastard.'

'No, Adrianicus killed Sikarbaal because he chose the love of Chia over loyalty to him. In Adrianicus' mind, Sikarbaal was the traitor. Chia knows this and she feels the weight of guilt. She is not a warrior, Plinius, when we ride into battle or stand in the arena we know that the brothers at our side may die to protect us, just as we will die to protect them. We have grown used to comrades making sacrifice; it is a new and unwanted experience for Chia.'

'How long will she be like this?'

Spartacus answered. 'Only the gods know, but she will return to her old ways. Our new life can only speed the process.'

Balen stopped and held up his hand to call the small convoy to a halt.

'What is it Balen?' asked Spartacus.

'We are about to enter Parthian lands. The majority of my men will now return to their homes, from here we travel alone.'

'Is that wise?'

'We have a small guard, besides I am well known in these lands. You families are perfectly safe.'

'Are there no brigand or cutthroats that patrol these tracks?'

Balen laughed. 'We have plenty of the murderous bastards, but I am a bigger bastard than any of them and far more skilled in the art of murder. They would not dare raise a blade to me, they have learnt that from past experience.' Balen did not elaborate but merely waved his hand and the small convoy lurched forward.

As the day wore on, Parthian warriors exchanged their farewells and left the column, eager to see families of their own. Many days were remaining of the journey; most nights were spent in temporary built camps. Occasionally, Balen would lead the convoy to the lands of a friend and Spartacus and the others were afforded comfort and fine foods. Nonetheless, the journey was becoming both demanding and tedious; even Tictus, so fond of being on a mount, wished the journey was at an end.

On the sixth day, the convoy rounded a sharp bend in the track and revealed a beautiful valley. Balen stopped and dismounted stretching upwards towards the sky; the action was answered with the bones cracking in complaint after the long ride.

Cynna moved forward and called for Spartacus. 'Look, Spartacus, is it not the most beautiful thing you have ever seen?'

Spartacus nodded smiling at her delight; he sometimes forgot all the hardships that she had faced.

'Do you really like it?' asked Balen.

'Oh, yes,' she replied.

'That is good.' He put an arm around her and pointed in the distance. 'Down there where the trees meet the river, do you see?'

'Yes.'

'On the other side of the trees there is a place my father built. It has been used as a hunting lodge since I was a boy. That is your new home.'

Cynna screamed with joy and smothered Balen with kisses. 'Thank you ... Thank you.' She kissed him again.

Spartacus could not believe it; he had not felt joy like this since he was a child. He pulled the Parthian into an embrace. 'Thank you, my friend.'

Balen laughed at their joy. 'Come then, let us take a closer look. Cassian, Plinius your home are less than a day's ride in the same valley. I promise you will not be disappointed.'

The convoy moved on but the tedium was gone and the exhaustion had left the tired muscles. The distance from track to home was covered quickly and it was more than Spartacus could have hoped.

'Spartacus you have workers here, but they are paid a wage. I doubted you would want slaves. Your crops have been planted and the people here have the knowledge to run the estate. You will want for nothing.' Balen smiled at Spartacus.

Spartacus looked around his new land and the place he would call home. He reached down and removed scabbard and sword and then he hung them on the wall next to the main door.

'I will have no need of this.'

His friends cheered as a man of war had finally found peace.

Cynna embraced him and they walked into their home as the diminished convoy moved on.

CHAPTER TWENTY-SEVEN

For fifteen years, a sword hung upon a wall. It was not drawn in anger or sliced the flesh of any unfortunate creature, man or beast.

Spartacus walked from his home to see riders approaching from the direction of Cassian's lands. As they neared, Spartacus could recognise Cassian, Plinius and Balen but the fourth rider was unknown to him. He raised his hand in greeting and beckoned they should enter his home. They dismounted and followed the former gladiator inside.

'Spartacus, this is Surena commander of the Parthian army,' Balen announced.

'You are welcome in my home, Surena, but I must warn you I am no longer a warrior.'

'Spartacus,' Cassian interrupted, 'Roman legions have crossed the Mesopotamian deserts and intend invasion.'

'This is an empire, Cassian. The Parthian army can surely deal with legions that have faced the trails of the desert.'

'Most of the Parthian army are engaged against our Armenian enemies.' Surena spoke for the first time. 'I have limited numbers at my disposal and your knowledge of the legions could prove vital.'

'No, I just want to be left in peace.' Spartacus shook his head refusing to contemplate the thought of returning to his former life.

'Spartacus, Crassus leads the Roman force.' Cassian had spoken slowly and deliberately, knowing his words would have an impact.

All present saw that Spartacus was taken aback by the news.

Surena took his opportunity. 'I do not require your blade, I want your knowledge. You shall have any reward.'

'Spartacus.' The voice was that of Cynna. 'This is our home. Do not let Rome take this from us, they have already taken too much.'

'Very well but I shall require payment.'

'Name it and it shall be yours.'

Spartacus looked at Cassian and knew what his friend wanted. 'If we are victorious and Crassus falls into our hands, then this man,' Spartacus said pointing to Cassian, 'shall choose his fate, no matter what deals may be achieved in his release.'

***

The Roman legions had conquered many lands; the use of the legion had never failed. Nonetheless, the battle had not started well for Crassus. The Parthian bows had struck fear into his men, their shafts rained down on his troops. When the legion formed a testudo, or square, to protect against the deadly hail, the heavy Parthian cataphracts charged in and caused death and mayhem. When the legions broke apart to do battle, the cavalry simply retreated and allowed their bows to do the killing.

Crassus needed to act; he had to drive the Parthian archers away from his lines. He'd called for his son Publius and ordered him to force the enemy to retreat.

For a moment Publius remained stationary, it was obvious that the young commander who had experience in warfare as a junior officer in Gaul was not sure the order from his father was the right course of action. He chose obedience rather than embarrass his father in front of the other officers.

At a safe distance, the command post of the Parthian army watched the movement in the Roman lines. A powerfully built warrior who carried no weapon smiled at what he saw.

'What amuses you, Spartacus?' Surena asked.

'Crassus is nothing but predictable. I expect in business dealings that can be a positive trait but in battle it is a terrible flaw.'

'What do you mean?'

'Crassus does not act with certainty. He does not use bold moves designed to throw the enemy into chaos, instead he uses the legions to lean on the enemy hoping they will break apart. Look there, he splits his forces and intends to drive our cavalry from the field.'

'It seems like a bold move to me.' Cassian could not see Crassus' error.

'He will chase away the cavalry but his main force I wager will remain perfectly still. Surena, allow the Roman force the illusion of success. Pull your cavalry back until the smaller Roman force is too far from their main force to receive aid.'

'Spartacus, may I go with him, I cannot abide sitting on my arse when there is a battle to be won.' Plinius turned to his leader, waiting for an answer.

'You are a free man, Plinius do as you wish, but I do not expect to have to tell Chia you have fallen.'

Cassian was astounded to see the battle play out exactly as Spartacus had described. The Roman army split apart and a substantial force gave chase to the Parthian cavalry. Both enemy and ally disappeared from view, but the main Roman force pinned itself to its defensive position. Neither Crassus nor Spartacus could see the desperate battle that took place between the forces commanded by Surena and Publius. In truth, only one side felt the desperation as the Parthian cavalry turned its horses around and fell upon the Roman forces.

Arrows fell amongst Publius' men and soon their ranks faltered and broke apart.

A promising Roman officer watched as his men were butchered all around. The battle for him and his men was over and he slumped to the ground, pulled a dagger and opened a vein. The shame of being taken captive was too much for the son of Crassus.

The day was nearly at an end before Crassus learned of the fate of his son. Deeply affected by the loss, he ordered the retreat to a minor village called Carrhae. This was no organised retreat as the Parthian cavalry hunted many within the Roman ranks. It was not until they'd reached the safety of the town that they could form a purposeful defensive line. Within the village, Crassus was a beaten man, devoid of interest in the battle. He thought only of his personal loss, many of his officers lay dead on the field of battle. The Roman forces were without leadership.

Surena took the opportunity to offer peace talks. Crassus rode out with what was left of his command and met with Surena. However, the talks descended into chaos with blades drawn and the battle re-commenced. Crassus was struck and fell from his mount. The legions believed him dead and panic spread through the ranks. At Carrhae, the Roman legions fell apart and were obliterated. Gaius Cassius Longinus managed to lead ten thousand men out of the slaughter but the rest lay bleeding in the dirt or were taken prisoner.

Spartacus and the others rode into the village of Carrhae. The population cheered Surena and those that rode with him. The gladiator was glad that the threat of Roman invasion was at an end but only one man interested him. The slave rebellion had been crushed, Cassian's wife killed, many good men sent to the next world all for this man's lust for power.

Spartacus wanted to see the beast that had stalked his life. Surena, however, had other plans and called for a celebration, the prisoner would wait until the next morning.

Wine and food were consumed in vast quantities, but Cassian did not raise wine to his lips. He walked away from the celebrations to the centre of the village, there a figure lay chained to a well.

'He placed wine in the man's hand but did not speak.'

'Thank you.' Crassus eagerly drank the wine. 'You do not come from these lands.'

'My home is here,' replied Cassian.

'Who is your master?'

'I have no master, I am a free man.'

'Fortunate indeed, many who consider themselves free are governed by other forces.'

'One man has tried to govern my life but I think his interference is at an end.'

'Who is this man?' Crassus asked, as he took yet more wine.

'Do you not recognise the man before you, Crassus? You have tried for so long to end my life I would have thought you would at least know my face when you gazed upon it.'

'Who are you?' snapped Crassus.

'Me, I am nobody. Tomorrow you will face your captors and answer for your crimes. Tell me, Crassus as you sit chained to that well, what use is your wealth or hunger for power?'

'When a new day arrives I will be ransomed back to Rome. The senate will yelp like the feeble dogs and soon this disaster will be forgotten or at least not talked about.'

'Oh, perhaps you are correct, after all, who would refuse the vast amount of gold just to see your death. It would be pure madness.'

'Who are you?' Crassus felt an unease as this man looked at him.

Suddenly, Cassian rushed forward and grasped Crassus by the throat. As he spoke spittle shot from his mouth hitting Crassus in the face. 'Who am I? I am Cassian Antonius and tomorrow, Crassus, your life will be in my hands.' Cassian was tempted to squeeze the life from the man but he forced himself to let go of the flesh beneath his hands.

'But you are Roman.'

'I was Roman, Crassus, but you destroyed my home and are responsible for the deaths of my wife and many of my friends.' Cassian smiled before he spoke again. 'Think on that as you sleep this night, because I assure you I will be thinking of all the wrongs you have perpetrated against me. Tomorrow we will discuss them at length.' Cassian walked away without another word.

'I am a senator of Rome,' Crassus called after him, but he received no reply.

***

The morning sun warmed all that it touched. Crassus had not slept well and now the rays of the same sun breached the lids to his eyes. For a moment, his mind could not comprehend his location but then the nightmare of the previous day's battle and the loss of his son rushed into his mind. A guard approached and gave him water and then unceremoniously lifted him to his feet. He was led through the streets of the village and then brought to a sudden stop beside a blacksmith. Before him all manner of devices, all of which could inflict a wide range of injuries, lay before him.

'I am Crassus senator of Rome if any harm befalls me, then these lands will burn.'

The crowd jeered, although, many would not have understood the Roman's tongue his tone would given them the general idea.

Two men stepped from the crowd the shorter applauded Crassus' threat.

'Alas, Crassus, I believe they do not fear the legions. So tell me, Crassus, now your threats have fallen short of the desired intention, what have you left to offer these people?' Cassian asked.

'I have wealth. The senate will pay a vast ransom.' Crassus looked to the side where a pot bubbled with ferocity.

'I believe you know my friend, Spartacus, you were responsible for the death of many of his friends.'

'It was a rebellion, I did my duty.'

'They were slaves, backs cut to shreds by the lash. They only wanted freedom and you butchered men, women and children. You did not serve Rome, you have never served Rome. You have only ever sought glory for Crassus and Rome and its people were there to serve you. Tell me, Crassus, what crime had my wife committed?'

'I have had enough of your questions. I will not be interrogated by the likes of you.' Crassus spat out his anger. He knew these men could not kill him and he would not play along so they could impress the crowd.

'I feel you are still under the illusion that your position protects you from our wrath.' Crassus did not answer refusing to even look at Cassian. 'Spartacus, would you assist me?'

The gladiator nodded and clasped Crassus' head in his hands.

Cassian took up a pair of blacksmith tongues and forced them into the senator's mouth. When he pulled them out, they held Crassus' tongue in a tight embrace. 'This item has offended many people, ordered the deaths of many more, maybe I should simply cut out the rancid flesh.'

Crassus looked defiantly at Cassian not believing for one minute he would carry out the threat.

'You are brave, Crassus, far braver than I thought you were capable. No its not bravery is it? It is pure arrogance.'

The blade was brought up quickly and Crassus screamed. Blood poured from the senator's mouth as he made to look at his own tongue freshly cut from his body.

Cassian stooped to look at Crassus and whispered, 'Do I have your attention now?' Cassian looked at the implements on show and considered using a number of them on the unfortunate Crassus. He wanted to hurt the man, but something within held him back. For some time he just looked at the man then decided that the world just needed a man like Crassus dead. 'I have dreamed of the things I would do to you since the day my wife died. I have imagined all manner of horrors that I could inflict upon your person. Nonetheless, a real man should not gain pleasure from the death of a beast, even a wild beast such as you. So I will make this quick and give those you have sent to the next world vengeance. Spartacus, hold his head.' Cassian crossed to the bubbling pot and with a ladle withdrew some of the boiling liquid. 'You have performed unspeakable acts of depravity to obtain gold, Crassus. It seems fitting that you should leave this world with some of your wealth. We took this gold from your personal baggage and we are not thieves, so I shall return it to you.' Cassian approached and the senator tried to struggle but Spartacus was far too strong. His mouth was forced open and the ladle tipped. The smell of burning flesh filled Spartacus' nostrils but he did not relinquish his hold.

The senator screamed but the liquid gold soon blocked his throat and mouth. His body jerked as it struggled against the agony and then the body stopped all movement.

Spartacus allowed Crassus to fall to the ground, the senator was already dead.

Cassian drew his sword and hacked off the head.

Surena walked towards the remains of Crassus and playfully tapped the head with his foot. 'I am not sure he will be able to answer many questions now.' He called for a messenger and instructed him to deliver the senator's head to the nearest Roman forces. The messenger asked if any message should be passed to the Romans. 'I think that will suffice.'

THE END

HISTORICAL NOTE

Within this book, I have tried to stay true to historical events, however, I have moved timelines around slightly to allow the story to flow and enable the heroes of the book to be placed within the Armenian Empire. In regards to actual events, Mithridates was a constant thorn in the side of the Roman Empire. He raised many armies against them and secured some impressive victories. Alas, for Mithridates it all ended in crushing defeat and death. The state of Commagene did in fact side with Rome in the latter conflict and preserved its independence when disaster raged all around.

The elder Tigranes was allowed to keep his seat of power, but the younger Tigranes was not so fortunate. His father, angered at his betrayal, sent him to Rome as captive. The Roman general Lucullus did indeed attack Mithridates though I have altered the timeline within the book.

Crassus and his son met their end at the battle of Carrhae, and Publius a military commander with far more skill than his father did commit suicide as his men died around him.

As for Crassus there are differing accounts of his demise, many believe he was killed as the Parthian general Surena attempted to secure a peaceful end to the hostilities. Whether the head was filled with gold or not, it is uncertain, but it would certainly be a fitting end to a man so driven by coin. The battle was one the worst defeats for the Roman legions; it is believed that as many as twenty thousand men perished with a further ten thousand being taken prisoner.

The casualties on the Parthian side has been stated as little as a hundred men.

The Romans may not have become intimidated of the Parthian forces, but in the future, they would definitely be more wary of their skills. That is not to say that the legions did not score impressive victories in future conflicts.

I have tried to make the story both interesting and believable, although, any work of fiction would struggle to match the political intrigue that occurred in the region.

This is my final Spartacus adventure. I hope that you have enjoyed the series.

It would have been so easy to kill the legendary figure but sometimes a good man should be allowed the reward he most craves.

Thank you for your time.

Authors Books

<u>The Spartacus Chronicles</u>
Spartacus: Talons of an Empire
Spartacus: The Gods Demand Sacrifice
Spartacus: The Pharaoh's Blade

<u>Stand Alone</u>

Wrath of the Furies

<u>The Ripper Legacies</u>
The Reaper's Breath (A Jack the Ripper Tale)
The Reaper's Touch
Coming Soon
The Reaper's Kiss

Author

If you wish to contact me please do not hesitate.
Email robius1@sky.com
robertsouth-author.com

Printed in Great Britain
by Amazon